9/01 LAD 7/16/01 26 cur FEB 1999

Strawberry Sunday

A JOHN MARSHALL TANNER NOVEL

Stephen Greenleaf

SCRIBNER

GREENLEAF
STEPHEN

SCRIBNER
1230 Avenue of the Americas
New York, NY 10020

SCRIBNER and design are trademarks of Simon & Schuster Inc.

Designed by Colin Joh

Set in Aldus

Manufactured in the United States of America

10 9 8 7 6 5 4 3 2 1

Library of Congress Cataloging-in-Publication Data

Greenleaf, Stephen.
Strawberry sunday: a John Marshall Tanner novel/Stephen Greenleaf.
p.   cm.
I. Title.
PS3557.R3957S75   1999
813'.54—dc21   98-40955
CIP

ISBN 0-684-84954-2

To Esther Newberg

Strawberry Sunday

CHAPTER ONE

They call it exsanguination.

That's when you lose so much blood that your body stops functioning—the brain ceases to process, the heart arrests, the lungs quit pumping, and at some point they pronounce you dead. By the time they got me to the hospital, exsanguination was a distinct possibility—I'd lost nine pints of blood, almost half the allotment for a man my size. Another point or two down on the dipstick and I'd be in a coffin down in Colma. They told me later that if I'd been Roman Catholic they would have administered Last Rites.

As it was, they tried to save me with some slightly less exalted emissaries who go by the name of surgeons. I was alive because I'd had the good fortune to be shot on the side of Potrero Hill just opposite San Francisco General Hospital, which is where the ambulance took me, which put me in the hands of one of the great trauma teams in the country. They would never claim that they were the only ones in the world who could have saved me that night, but that was probably close to the truth.

The reason I was bleeding was a gunshot. The bullet had taken out a chunk of my spleen and kidney and had nicked the renal artery on its way through as well. All of them are gorged with blood and all of them leak like a sieve when you cut them. Hence exsanguination.

Most of my blood lay puddled on the ground in a scruffy vacant lot on Twentieth Street east of Illinois Street down by the bay. The lot was next to an abandoned powerhouse that served as the de facto headquarters for a group of rogue cops who called themselves the Triad. There was a lot of Triad blood in that lot as well, but the cops who died that night didn't bleed to death, they died far more expeditiously, courtesy of a bullet in the back of the head.

The person who shot the cops and also shot me was a man named Charley Sleet, who'd spent most of his life as a detective lieutenant in the San Francisco Police Department. Charley didn't shoot me because he wanted to kill me, he shot me because he wanted me to kill him. The reason I didn't want to kill him was that Charley was my best friend. As it turned out, I shot him anyway, partly accidentally and partly on purpose, but not before Charley shot the two ringleaders of the Triad in cold blood. The bottom line was, I survived but Charley didn't. That was the way Charley had wanted to end it, for reasons having to do with courage and honor and friendship and essential things like that, but for me it was the beginning of what would surely be a lifelong nightmare.

Charley was dead because I'd shot him in the heart, not because I was a great marksman, but because his heart was such a big target. Impossible to miss, really, because Charley Sleet was the best man I'd ever known, the bravest and kindest, the most energetic and altruistic person on the planet or at least the portion of it that was familiar to me. It's certain I will never know his equal and will never find solace for the fact that I'd killed him, even though he wanted me to, even though he was already dying from a disease that would have felled him eventually anyway. The best I can hope for is to find a way to live with it. Which was what I'd been doing for the past six weeks, when I wasn't busy trying to stay alive.

I'd been in surgery for nine hours, in Intensive Care for ten days, and was into my seventh week of recovery in a semiprivate room on the third floor of the west wing of the giant hospital. There'd been the initial wound and then there had been complications—some sepsis and some staph—so I was laced with a variety of medications, plenty of everything except for the pain. The pain filled me like water fills balloons, occupied me, expanded me, and warped me to the point that it was all I could think of, all I could remember or project, all that I prayed to be delivered from—I went from being afraid I would die to praying I would die quickly to being terrified that I would have to live with such towering waves of pain forever. I made so many bargains with a God whose existence I seldom admit to in normal times that my conversations with Him sounded like a shopping trip to the Casbah, haggling over a hand-loomed rug.

A bargain had finally been struck, on terms that would presumably not be fully known till Judgment Day—the pain had subsided and the sepsis and staph had vanished as inexplicably as when they first appeared. Now for the first time I was going to be allowed visitors. I had on clean jammies; an aide had trimmed my hair and shaved me and helped me take a shower, then changed my limp sheets. Such as I was, I was prepared to receive my public.

The first person to come calling was Ruthie Spring, one of my oldest friends, widow of the detective who'd first schooled me in the trade almost twenty years ago. Ruthie is a former combat nurse and sheriff's deputy who is now a private investigator herself as the heiress to her husband's agency. As usual, she arrived in a hail of curses.

"Damn it all, Marsh, I thought those white-coated faggots'd never let me in here. They act like you're a frigging rock star coming off a smack habit and I'm in hire to the *Enquirer*."

I laughed at Ruthie's outfit as much as at her outrage. She was dripping with a variety of silver jewelry in the shape of stirrups and lassos and horseshoes and such and was wearing a suede suit cut like a barrel racer's. After her first husband, Harry, was murdered, Ruthie had married money in the form of a guy named Conrad. Conrad thinks Ruthie likes horses. Ruthie can't seem to get it through his head that she regards horses the way she regards telemarketers.

"The only thing I've got in common with rock stars is I'm pierced in too many places," I said.

She regarded my IV and my oxygen tube and nodded. "Heard it was bad. Which figures, given it was Sleet who drilled you. Looks like you been rode hard and put up wet."

"Thanks a lot."

Ruthie reddened at the possibility that she'd insulted me. "But you look real good, Sugar Bear. Losing a pound or two won't hurt you a bit. Going to come through this just fine, long as he didn't shoot off your pecker."

"Still intact in that department."

Ruthie swooped toward a chair, dragged it to the bedside, and sat down and crossed her legs. Her boots were made out of some species that was probably endangered; her suede pants were flared at the bottom the way mine had been in the seventies. Ruthie was one of a kind.

She glanced at the door to make sure it was all the way shut, then thrust a hand into the depths of her massive handbag of hand-tooled pink leather. "Got some twenty-year-old unblended in here, Sugar Bear. How about I pour you a stiff shot?"

"Too early for that, I'm afraid."

"Hell, it's almost three o'clock. Most of Texas has been drunk for two hours."

"I meant in my recovery. Some of my holes are still holes—wouldn't want it to leak all over the floor."

Ruthie shrugged and walked to the closet. "It'll be in here when you need it."

"Thanks."

She fished in her bag again. "How about some Oreos?"

Ruthie had come armed with my primary nutritional passions. "I think I'd better stick to hospital food awhile longer."

She looked at me as though I'd gone mad. "Must not be as bad as they say."

"The food? It's worse."

Ruthie regarded me with skepticism. "You're going to be back to normal at the end of this, aren't you, Sugar Bear?"

"Pretty much."

"No permanent damage?"

"Not that they know of."

"So you'll get back whatever it was Sleet took out of you."

I resisted the temptation to ask what Ruthie thought that was. "So they say."

Something in my face must have told her I was running down in terms of social voltage. "Well, I'll be toddling off. Just wanted to let you know me and Conrad are thinking of you."

"Appreciate it, Ruthie. You guys are still good, right?"

"Hell, yeah. Take more than a frisky husband to bring me down. Long as they keep making lubricants, I'll be the best little wife in Pacific Heights."

I laughed. "How old are you anyway, Ruthie?"

"Sixty-three come next month."

"That's hard to believe."

"Tempus seems to fucking fugit whether you give it permission or not."

I looked around my cheerless room. "I sure as hell hope so," I said.

Ruthie walked to the window and looked out. "Going to miss that chunky bastard."

"Me, too."

"Sometimes it seemed like the only one in the world who made sense was Sleet."

"Lots of times," I agreed.

"He didn't buy into the nonsense, know what I mean? Cut straight to the chase. Ever damn time."

"That he did."

"Remember once I asked if he'd seen some big-assed Hollywood movie and he said, 'Why would I want to pay good money to watch people slaughter each other?' " Ruthie turned to face me. "The sumbitch went out with a bang, though, didn't he?"

I tried to grin. "Tell me about it."

"Papers are full of crapola about the cops he took down. Public servants risking their lives for the city—usual bleeding heart bull-shit. From what I hear, they stole everything in town that wasn't nailed down."

I nodded. "They were pretty bad apples according to Charley."

She cocked her head. "You're not in any trouble yourself, are you? For capping Sleet, I mean?"

"Don't know yet, Ruthie. Someone from the D.A.'s office is coming by later. Been trying to see me for three weeks."

"Maybe you better have Hattie on hand when they get here."

The reference was to the best criminal lawyer in the city, a friend of mine for a lot of years, a man even the D.A. himself held in awe. I couldn't afford a tenth of Jake Hattie's normal rate, but since I'd done him some favors, usually I didn't have to. "I'll think about it," I said.

Ruthie waved toward the trappings of the room, the ungodly gadgets that were going to keep me alive come hell or high water or any inclinations to the contrary should they arise, provided I could pay the tab. "You're insured for this shit, right, Marsh? It ain't coming out of your hide?"

"I'm covered for most of it, I think. Deductible and co-payments will add up to something, I imagine; I'm not sure how much."

"Let me know when you find out."

I smiled. "I can handle it, Ruthie."

"I know you can. But Conrad has more money than anyone but that goofy Gates boy and all he's doing with it is buying a bunch of expensive toys."

I laughed. "What's the most expensive thing he's got?"

She raised her arms in a model's preen. "Why that would be me, Sugar Bear. Sayonara, or whatever it is the dagoes say."

"I think that's *ciao*."

"Speaking of which, think I'll go get me a double bacon cheeseburger, seeing as how Conrad ain't around to hassle me about cholesterol. Last thing I want to do is live forever, know what I'm saying, Sugar Bear?"

After I told her I knew what she meant, Ruthie flounced out of the room as dramatically as she'd entered it, leaving behind several eddies of air and the strong scent of lavender and a warm spot at the precise coordinates of my heart.

An hour later, the poker gang arrived en masse. Clay Oerter, the stockbroker, was in the lead, followed by Al Goldsberry, the pathologist, and Tommy Milano, the restaurateur. Clay was dressed for the office, which meant a three-piece suit cut and sewn in London. Al was dressed for the office as well, which was in the basement of a different hospital than the one I was lying in, which meant chinos and polo shirt and Nikes. Tommy was dressed like Tommy, which was an eclectic blend of longshoreman and litigator—the shoes on his feet were straight from Milan and the shirt on his back was from Indonesia by way of Kmart.

"Hey, Marsh," Clay began as the others fidgeted nervously behind him. "You look great, man."

"I do not."

"Yeah, but you will. Right? Hundred percent in a few more weeks."

"On the outside, at least. Hi, Al. Hi, Tommy."

"Good to see you, Marsh," said Al.

"Me, too," said Tommy. "I brought some of that bread you like, I don't know if you want it or nothing, but I thought . . ." He reached under his coat and hauled out a two-foot baguette.

I felt like the godfather accepting tribute from the neighborhood. "Put it in the closet next to the scotch," I said. "And thanks."

"I didn't bring anything," Al said sheepishly.

"You didn't have to."

And suddenly there was a silence that encompassed all of us, because the fifth member of the poker group had been Charley and our thoughts traveled toward him like metal toward a magnet.

"I miss the dumb galoot," Clay said finally, getting it out on the table where it belonged. "Even his stinking cigars."

"Me, too," Tommy said.

"Me, too," I said.

"We know there was nothing you could do, Marsh," Al said. "We know he forced your hand."

"Yeah," said Clay.

"Yeah," said Tommy.

"So don't go feeling guilty. Okay?"

When I shrugged, it hurt from my groin to my Adam's apple. "Easier said than done."

"Look at it this way," Al advised. "If Charley didn't want it done, it wouldn't have gotten done. What I mean is, you're good, but you're not Charley."

"I'm not Charley," I agreed.

"Charley wasn't Charley, either," Clay said. "He killed all those people, I guess—the cops; the guy in the courtroom. But that wasn't him. That was the tumor."

"Yeah," said Tommy. "That was the fucking brain tumor."

Then, involuntarily and unconsciously, they all looked at me as if I suffered from some of the same, a growth in my skull that had made me a monster, loosed demons no one knew I had, made me a man to beware. I must have looked like shit.

"Any of you guys go to the funeral?" I asked.

"Yeah," they all said.

"It was nice."

"Yeah."

"Nice music."

"And lots of flowers."

"Lots of cops, too, I imagine," I said.

They looked at each other and fidgeted. "Not all that many," Clay muttered.

"Not enough," Al added.

"Some guys in plain clothes. A few uniforms. But no cycles and no white gloves."

"So nothing official," I said.

Clay nodded. "Nothing official."

"Assholes."

"He killed those two cops," Tommy offered in explanation, ever the mediator.

"Three," Clay corrected. "The one before, then the two the night he died. According to the papers, the inquiry's still open. They must have figured they couldn't honor him since he might be a cop killer."

"Is that bureaucratic bullshit or what?" Al said angrily. "Charley wouldn't have killed those guys unless they were scum."

"Yeah," Tommy said. "Scum."

"They talk to you yet?" Al asked. "The cops?"

"Docs wouldn't let them in. But some assistant D.A.'s been trying to get in to see me."

"You'll tell them how it was."

"Yeah. Tell them Charley was just doing what had to be done."

The silence returned. I didn't know how to break it without starting to cry.

"I looked at your chart at the desk," Al said finally. "You're doing great. In case you don't believe what they're telling you."

"Thanks, Al."

"So when you getting out?" Tommy asked.

"End of the week, if nothing goes wrong."

"That's great," Clay said. "Maybe we'll stop by over the weekend. Deal a few hands of stud if you're up to it."

Clay was always ready for a game. "That'd be great," I said, then inadvertently glanced at the clock.

Clay took the hint even though I wasn't sure it was one. "Well, we better hit the road. Good to see you, Marsh."

"Yeah."

"Yeah."

"Don't be a hero," Al said. "Take it easy till you're back all the way."

"Yeah."

"Yeah."

"You did what you had to do. No reason to get down about it."

"No."

"Hell, no."

"So take care."

"Yeah."

"Yeah."

"You guys, too," I said.

"We will," Clay said. "And maybe we'll catch you on Sunday."

They filed out of the room, friends who would do anything they could do for me as I would have for them, but nonetheless as relieved as I would have been to have done their duty by their fallen comrade and be on their way to less unnerving environments.

After they were gone, my day nurse peeked in. Her name was Gertie. She was tall and gruff, as stiff and as pointed as jackstraw. "How you holding up?"

"Fine."

"Want me to call off the parade?"

I shook my head.

"That district attorney said she'd be here at four unless someone told her she couldn't. Said it was important," Gertie added, then looked at me more closely. "I can head her off if you want me to."

I shook my head. "If they're going to try to lock me up, I might as well know it now."

CHAPTER TWO

In the meantime, they wanted me to walk, so I walked. Four times a day if I could; less if I was too worn out to keep to that schedule. I was supposed to be walking for therapy, to tone my muscles and to head off complications like adhesions and pneumonia. But the real reason I was walking was Rita.

Rita Lombardi was her name. She was twenty-five years old, of Italian descent, and hailed from a town I'd never heard of named Haciendas, somewhere between Watsonville and Salinas. Her hair and eyes were soft brown, her nose and chin were as pointed as awls, her skin was the color of sole, and her spirits were as rampant as wind. She was engaged to be married to a man named Carlos Reyna and she was the most delightful young woman I'd ever met with the exception of my daughter Eleanor. Although I'd had major surgery, and was taking half a dozen potent pharmaceuticals a day, Rita Lombardi was by far my best therapy.

We'd encountered each other for the first time two weeks earlier, in the corridor outside my room. We were each walking with help, supported by nurse's aides and by the transparent juices dripping out of the IVs we towed in our wakes. We'd smiled as we passed each other in the hall, one day and then the next, walking in opposite directions, wishing we were anywhere but where we were. On the third day we'd met yet again, this time navigating on our own with the aid only of our walkers and our determination. Rita stopped to talk the usual hospital talk about the food and the nurses and the smells, but her manic energy and her oddly genuine interest in my welfare made the usual somehow remarkable. Her eyes pierced the shields that shutter my soul, laying bare my inner secrets, making it impossible to be other than candid with her. The third day we walked together, I told her about Charley and me and how he'd died, told her more than I'd told anyone else before or since.

After that, we got together twice a day, at ten and two sharp, and walked in tandem for a full hour each time, an hour that seemed more like a minute. I don't know what Rita imagined during these moments, but my own private fantasy was that we were on board a ship to the Caribbean, taking a turn on deck before we retired for the evening, elegant and aristocratic and in love with ourselves and our lives and each other. That's what medication can do to you, I guess—I'd never had that sort of silk stocking fantasy in the previous forty years.

Rita was in the hospital because of two birth defects that, now that her body had fully matured, could finally be surgically remedied. Her legs were the main problem—she'd been club-footed at birth, in both limbs, to the point that she couldn't walk any distance without the aid of crutches. Her face needed attention as well. She'd had a large birthmark on her right cheek that made her look, in her words, like she'd slid into third base on her face. She'd had several plastic surgeries to remedy the facial flaw and now they'd taken care of the feet, and her new look and new alignment had made her ecstatic—from time to time I was certain she would start flying around the ward like a wren. Regarding her now, with her complexion free of blemish and her feet straight and true in their flexible soft casts, it was hard to imagine she had ever been other than perfect.

I took a quick nap, then strolled into the hall. It still hurt in the gut when I walked, and my legs still moved as if someone other than me was the puppeteer, but it was lots better than the first time I tried it, when I was certain with every step that I was going to split wide open and spill my viscera over the floor, an embarrassment to myself and to the doctor who concluded I was ready to promenade, and a nuisance to the aides who would have to mop up after me. But now I was a veritable sprite, tripping through the tulips or at least the vinyl tile, feeling like jumping for joy when I saw Rita Lombardi shuffling toward me with a smile on her narrow face that made Meg Ryan seem like a grump.

She wore powder blue pajamas with daisies blooming all over them and carried a little brown bear. The bear looked more in need of medical attention than either of us—Rita told me his name was Brownie and he had been given to her by her father when she turned two. Her father had died shortly afterward, so the bear had become both sentimental and symbolic; even now she refused to sleep a single night without it. I have some things in my life that serve the same function and given what happened to Charley, I expect to have a few more.

"Good afternoon, John Marshall Tanner."

"Hi, Rita Maria Lombardi."

"You look like a man who's ready to travel."

"Friday morning, they say."

She wriggled like a rabbit. "That's so *cool.* I'm really happy for you."

"How about you?" I asked, with an odd tic of trepidation at the thought of life in the ward without her.

She sobered. "This afternoon, I think."

My stomach knotted and my voice took on an artificial echo. "Really? That's wonderful. But I thought they wanted to wait till next week."

"I guess I'm coming along better than they thought I would." She touched her cheek where the birthmark had been replaced by a slice of fresh flesh. The graft had come from her hip. She'd made a bawdy joke the first time she told me about it.

Rita put her cane in her left hand and gripped my arm with her right. "You remember your promise, I hope."

"What promise was that?"

She squeezed. "You promised to visit Haciendas as soon as you get back to normal. Four fourteen Fremont Street. I wrote our address and phone number on your pad two days ago."

"I know; I've got it in my wallet."

"So that means you'll come, right?"

For some reason, it was important to Rita that I see her in her home environment, maybe to prove to both of us that she was fully healed in the eyes of the world and not just the hospital, so I said what I had to say: "I'll be there."

"By the end of the month?"

"If I can."

She nodded as though my promise had been etched in stone, as I guess it was. "Shall we stroll, Mr. Tanner?" she asked.

"We shall, Ms. Lombardi."

We walked the halls as though we were flanked by the trees and bistros of the Champs-Élysées rather than the recovery rooms of sick people. Rita told me about the book she'd been reading—Julia Alvarez, whom she loved. I told her some stories about Ruthie Spring and the boys in the poker group. Then I asked what she was going to do the first thing when she got home.

Her voice soared and her hand tightened on my forearm. "I'm going to go dancing. At a bar called the Cantina. I'm going to play every record on the jukebox and dance with Carlos till they make us go home. It'll be the first time I've danced in my life."

"That sounds like fun."

"You can come, too, when you visit. In fact, I know just the woman to fix you up with. Sal Delder. She works as a receptionist at the police station."

I tried to stem my shudder. "That's nice, but I'm not much of a dancer."

Rita elbowed me in the ribs, which sent a spur of pain scraping down my torso as though someone were chiseling a notch in my spine.

"You never say anything good about yourself, do you know that?" Rita chided as I tried not to convulse from the pain.

"No, I didn't know that."

"I want you to say something good about yourself. Right now. Just one thing. What's the best thing to know about the man named Marsh Tanner?"

I smiled at her homegrown psychotherapy. "The best thing about me is I have friends like you."

"That means you must be a good person, right?"

The therapy was going in the wrong direction. Before I could say anything to reverse it, Rita poked my ribs once again. "You're doing it again, aren't you?"

"What?"

"Blaming yourself for what happened."

"Maybe a little."

She tugged me to a stop and turned me so I faced her. "I get so *mad* when you do that. *He* did it; not you."

"But I helped."

"How?"

"I didn't stop him."

"He had a gun. He'd already shot two men. How were you supposed to stop him?"

"I wasn't supposed to stop him," I said. "I was just supposed to try."

Rita shook her head with elaborate exasperation, as if I were an obstreperous school kid. "You were no more responsible for what happened to Mr. Sleet than I was for what happened to my legs and my face."

"Your legs and your face are lovely."

She abandoned her burlesque of the angry schoolmarm and looked at something down the hall, then told me what she had probably needed to tell me ever since we met. "You didn't see me

23

before, so you don't know," she said softly, as though uttering a furtive confession. "My feet were twisted like someone had ripped them off and glued them back on sideways. Even with crutches, the only way I could keep my balance was to shuffle along all hunched over so it was impossible to look at anything but the ground in front of me. Hermie, is what they called me. For hermit crab. I was forever bumping into things. Things and people. They acted like they'd touched a toad when I bumped them. Some of them. Most of them, in fact."

The echo of her lifelong torment drifted down the hall, to meld with other sad stories being told at the foot of sickbeds. "But now look at you," I said with as much cheer as I could muster. "You're the belle of the ball."

"Yes I am." She laughed like a child, then stuck out a foot and did a slow pirouette on her walking cast. "Look at me. I can stand up straight and look people right in the eye."

That's not always a good idea, I almost said, thinking of the last time I'd ridden the Number 3 bus, but I held my tongue.

She clutched my hand to her chest. "I'm so glad we met, aren't you? It would have been *creepy* in this place without you. The noises; the smells; Nurse Gertie. Yuck."

"Double yuck," I said. We chuckled and resumed our stroll. "Is Carlos coming to get you?"

"If he can get away. But it's the height of the season now; he's busy in the fields. I might have to take the bus to Salinas."

"Tell me some more about strawberries," I said, partly because I was interested and partly because Rita loved to talk about them, almost to the point of obsession. Rita worked as a bookkeeper for her boyfriend, Carlos, who had something to do with growing the berries. In our previous conversations, she had made the business seem both enchanting and sinister and Carlos a mix of clergyman and mobster.

"You don't really want to hear any more about strawberries," Rita said. "I've bored you to death already."

"No. Really. I love strawberries. I just wish they didn't have that green thing on top, so you could pop them straight in your mouth."

"That's called the cap."

"So is there money in strawberries or what?"

Rita sobered. "If you really want to know, the only crop more profitable than strawberries is marijuana."

"You're kidding."

"Nope. In a good year you can make up to twenty thousand dollars an acre. Of course there aren't all that many good years."

"Why not?"

"Weather, mostly."

"Even so, it sounds like you and Carlos are going to be rich."

I'd expected a smile, but she laughed rather mordantly. "I'm saying just the opposite. The landowners and marketing companies are getting rich. Everyone else is barely surviving, and survival comes at a very high price. Do you know what they call strawberries in Mexico?"

"What?"

"The Fruit of the Devil."

"Why?"

"Because it takes so much suffering to grow them. And there's more suffering now than ever in the fields. The life expectancy of a strawberry worker is less than fifty years."

I was surprised and said so. "I thought Cesar Chavez and Jerry Brown took care of the problems with farmworkers."

"They tried, and it helped for a while, but most of the protections have been cut back by the politicians who came along later. And even the laws that haven't been repealed, like the minimum wage, are mostly ignored in the fields. The average income of a *campesino* is only five thousand dollars for twenty-five weeks' work with the fruit. That's half of what they were making when Chavez was leading the union."

"That's it? Five thousand a year?"

"For many of them. Especially the ones without families."

"Then why do they do it?"

Her voice became grave and her eyes became spectral. "Because in Mexico they earn five dollars a day and they're starving."

"All of the landowners are white, I assume."

"Most, but not all. In the Pajaro, many are Japanese. And in north county, many are Mexican."

"How did that happen?"

"They worked hard, saved money, and got financing from some of the big marketing companies. They farm tiny plots, of course; ten acres on average. And they pay the lowest wages in the industry."

"Why doesn't the union make them shape up?"

"Because the union is Mexican, too."

"Most of the strawberry workers are Mexican?"

"Ninety percent."

"Are you talking about illegal immigrants?"

"At the peak picking season there are lots of illegals—friends and relatives of regular workers or crews hired from labor contractors, who use mostly illegals."

"I thought the Border Patrol was cracking down these days."

Rita laughed. "Immigration sweeps through after the crop is harvested and sends the illegals back where they came from. Then, the next season, Immigration closes its eyes and lets them come back and pick fruit. But more and more workers are permanent residents now, with homes and families and kids in the schools. There may be two or three families sharing those homes, or living all year in a labor camp, but at least they're real homes, not cars or caves or holes in the ground."

"The working poor."

Rita nodded. "An imported peasantry, is what it amounts to. Ever since the Franciscans started growing strawberries in this country in 1770, the problem has been who would pick the crop. The first pickers were mostly Chinese, then the Japanese took most of the jobs until the Second World War, but after the war it's been almost entirely Mexicans."

"Why haven't conditions gotten better for them?"

Rita sniffed and rubbed her eyes. "Because the union is weak and the workers have no power. UFW membership is less than ten thousand now; it used to be more than fifty. Plus there's no one around with the strength and charisma of Chavez."

"Who runs the union now?"

"Chavez's son-in-law, Arturo Rodriguez. He's a good man and he works hard and has had some success, especially with the public corporations that own the land or market the fruit, but . . ." She shrugged. "Without a strong union and a magnetic leader, the workers have to take what they can get, which is still next to nothing."

I poked her. "Maybe you should be that leader."

I expected her to laugh but she didn't. "Don't think I haven't thought about it. But I'm not Hispanic. And I'm not a man. Farm work is still very much a macho culture."

"What about Carlos? Or is he a landowner, too?"

She straightened with pride. "Carlos is an independent grower."

"How many acres does he own?"

"None, yet. That will come later."

"So how is he involved?"

"The landowners hire men like Carlos to tend the plants and harvest the crop. Carlos farms thirty acres for Gelbride Berry Farms. Then he and the Gelbrides split the profits."

"Sounds like sharecropping."

"It is sharecropping. Only worse."

"How?"

When she answered, her words were rasping and urgent, the invocation become a testimonial. "Carlos is a good farmer. He's smart, energetic, a hard worker. Plus he knows the pomology and he's liked by his workers."

"So he must be doing well."

Rita paused for effect. "Carlos owes Gelbride Berry Farms more than sixty thousand dollars."

"Wow. How did that happen?"

"Because last year it rained at the wrong time because of El Niño. And because he signed an evil contract."

"Why did he sign the contract?"

Rita muttered a curse. "Because he had no choice. If he wanted to work in the business, he had to make the deal."

"Why?"

"Sharefarming is the way the owners avoid the farm labor regulations by passing the responsibility on to men like Carlos, who can't afford to obey them. Workman's comp, unemployment insurance, health care—Carlos can't afford that. Not even the owners can afford that, or so they claim."

Rita's voice rose to a pitch that caused two patients and one nurse to look our way in wonder. "What I don't understand is why they never get enough," she said in what amounted to an invocation.

"Who?"

"The owners. They make more and more money, and live better and better lives, but they never say, 'That's all I need, I'm happy, let the workers have more of the profits, let them live decently as well.' I don't see how they can live the way they do and call themselves Christian, when the people who work their fields live with such hardship and disease."

Tears came then, tears of frustration and confusion, of anger and accusation. I waited for her to wipe them away on the sleeve of her jammies, then tried to buck her up. "I'm sure things will get better in time. People like you—"

"They're going to get better right away," she said stiffly. "The minute I get back to Haciendas and get in touch with the Gelbrides."

I started to ask Rita how she was going to manage that, but we were interrupted by her nurse, who wanted her back on the ward for her final exam before heading home.

"Well, this is it, I guess," she said, her eyes still misting over, her voice quaking just a tad.

I tried to keep my own voice on a level pitch but I'm not sure I succeeded. "I guess it is."

"Would you mind very much if I kissed you, Mr. Tanner?"

"It would be my distinct pleasure, Ms. Lombardi."

She leaned over and pecked my cheek, gave me a brisk hug and a wave, then shuffled off toward her room with her nurse, her newly repaired legs not quite up to full speed, but almost. Both my cheek and my heart stayed moist and tingly until I was visited by an assistant D.A.

Her name was Jill Coppelia. She was in her early forties or so, with big blue eyes, light brown hair, a gently expressive face, and long legs and long arms and a long look that made me uncomfortable.

"We meet at last," she began.

"Sorry I was tied up."

"How are you feeling?"

"Fine."

"You don't look fine."

"I never did."

Her smile was warm and soothing; she would have been good at getting confessions and earning promotions. "If you're not ready for this, I can come back."

"Let's get it over with."

She smiled wider this time, companionably and attractively, putting me more at ease than I wanted to be. She was the friendliest D.A. I'd ever met, which wasn't saying much. She was also the first woman in more than a year who had made my libido perk up, which was saying even less.

"I'm in charge of the Sleet investigation," she began.

"I didn't know there was a Sleet investigation."

"There always is when an officer goes down."

"That may be, but this case is open and shut."

She raised a brow and crossed her arms. "Is that so?"

"If you're good at your job, you already know it."

She colored and shifted position and looked for a place to sit down. There was a chair in the corner and she spotted it, but when I didn't invite her to sit, she stayed standing.

"We've gotten statements from the other officers who were out there that night," she went on, "and we'd like to get one from you."

I shook my head and gave the answer I'd already decided to give her. "Sorry. No can do."

She blinked and frowned. "What do you mean?"

"I mean that whatever Charley did or didn't do that night, you're not going to get it from me."

"Why not?"

"I don't rat on my friends."

"Your friend is dead."

I smiled. "All the more reason."

"But all we want is the truth."

"In my experience, what goes in one end of your office in the form of truth often looks ugly and warped when it comes out the other end in the form of an indictment. Some sort of legal indigestion, I guess."

"I'm not that kind of lawyer," Ms. Coppelia said primly.

"I'm glad to hear it, but the answer's still no. Why don't you have a seat?"

She went to the chair and sat down. When she crossed her legs, I paid attention. Apparently the source of the sex drive isn't close to the spleen.

"The survivors say Sleet killed Gary Hilton and Milt Mandarich—"

I interrupted her. "He's the big guy?"

"Right. The survivors say Sleet killed Hilton and Mandarich because they were going to file a complaint against Sleet with Internal Affairs."

"Then the survivors are lying assholes."

"Can you prove it?"

I ignored her question. "Complaint about what?"

"That Sleet was shaking down several business establishments in the Tenderloin and North Beach. Offering protection for money."

"Extortion."

She nodded. "That's where they were headed."

I shook my head to show my disgust. "Did you know Charley?"

"A little."

"Does that sound like something he'd do?"

"No. Not really."

"Then maybe you should find out the *real* reason he took Hilton and Mandarich out."

She recrossed her legs. I wondered if the show of thigh was deliberate. If it was, I wondered what she hoped it would get her. Then I wondered whether I'd give it to her.

"I'm betting you could help me do that," she was saying. Jill Coppelia was at ease and self-controlled, attempting to manipulate me according to a preconceived plan, going with the flow but channeling it in a direction she felt was productive. I began to admire her a little and lust for her a little more.

"Charley's dead," I said. "That terminated any and all of my obligations to the SFPD."

"You're still a citizen, Mr. Tanner."

"I was a citizen when Milt Mandarich broke my finger to get me to tell him how to get to Charley."

That one tilted her off center by at least a degree. "I didn't know about that."

"You don't know a lot of things, it sounds like."

She pouted. "So why don't you help us find out?"

I shook my head.

The pout became close to a sneer. "We could impanel a Grand Jury and subpoena you."

"And I could hire Jake Hattie to head you off."

"Jake couldn't keep us from offering you immunity and putting you in jail for contempt if you don't talk."

"Why would I need immunity?"

"You shot a cop, for one thing."

"And for another thing, I saved two more cops from dying the way Hilton and Mandarich died."

"The proof of that is only anecdotal."

"The word of the survivors, you mean."

She shrugged.

A twitch in my gut curled me up. When I finally straightened out, Jill Coppelia was by the bed. "Do you need the nurse?"

"No."

"Water? Medication? Anything?"

"I'm fine."

She patted my hand. I waited till she sat back down. "Look," I said stiffly, "Charley Sleet was my best friend. Plus he had a brain tumor. So why would I murder him, even if I wanted to? Why wouldn't I wait till the cancer took its toll?"

She shrugged. "Motive isn't an essential element of a criminal conviction."

"Then how do you expect to prove malice and intent, which the last time I looked *were* essential elements?"

She shrugged. "Why do you think we haven't put you in the prison ward in this place? Even though there are lots of guys on the force who think that's where you ought to be."

I thought it over while I looked her over. What I saw was enough to soften me up. "Okay. You gave me a break, so I'll give you one. Does the name Triad mean anything to you?"

"You mean the Chinese family organizations?"

I shook my head. "This is something else, and you need to find out what it means. But put your own guys on it, not the SFPD."

"You're saying this Triad has something to do with the department?"

I kept my mouth shut and smiled.

"That's it? That's all you're giving up?"

"That's it."

"It doesn't seem nearly enough." She stood up and smoothed her skirt and came to the bed and looked down. "We could go at this another way," she said, with something more ardent in her voice than a threat.

"How?"

"We could hire you to help us as a special investigator."

"Not for a while, you can't."

"Why not?"

"As soon as they let me out of here, I'm going out of town."

"Not far, I hope."

"Not in terms of geography."

She handed me her card after scribbling a number on the back. "Call me when you get back. By then I'll have come up with new reasons why you should cooperate with us."

"Those reasons became irrelevant when the Honor Guard didn't show up for Charley's funeral," I said.

CHAPTER THREE

Without Rita's charm to speed it along, the week crawled by like a slug, obese and repellent and interminable. But the healing progressed, the pain diminished, the strength returned, and suddenly it was Friday morning. I was dressed and packed and waiting when he got there.

"Well, Mr. Tanner."

"Well, Dr. Stratton."

"How are we feeling today?"

"We're feeling tip-top, shipshape, A-okay, and then some."

He smiled. "I'll be the judge of that. Let me give a listen."

He slid his stethoscope off his neck and pressed it to my body in several places, most of them ticklish. I don't know what they hear in there, maybe a little voice that gives them medical updates on the hour, sort of like a miniature NPR. Or maybe it's just for show.

"Pulse is steady; lungs are clear; the gut is gurgling away, doing its work. I think we've done all we can do for you here."

"That must mean my insurance is running out."

His laugh was slightly forced. "It's more that we need the space. Gunshots are as fashionable as tattoos this season—we're starting to take reservations. Although I must say yours was one of the sexiest we've seen in a while. And it wasn't the first bullet to pass through the vicinity, was it?"

I thought of a night in an alley near Broadway almost twenty years back, in the first weeks of my career as a detective, when I'd been gut-shot by an assailant who was unknown to me then and now. "I'll try not to develop a taste for it."

"Good. Because if you'd had this wound back then, you'd be dead. In a way, you owe your life to the street gangs."

"How so?"

"They've given us lots of practice. Our techniques are much better than they used to be."

"I'll drop them a thank-you note."

The doctor grinned and stuck out his hand. "Go on, get out of here. Take your pills and call me if you turn for the worse. I've made an appointment for the end of next week, just to be sure you're on schedule."

"Don't I get wheeled to the door?"

"We don't have the manpower anymore."

I waited until he looked me in the eye. "I appreciate what you did for me, Doctor."

"It's my job."

"I'm glad you're good at it."

He reddened and looked away. "Speaking of jobs, if I were you I'd consider a new line of work."

"When they start paying wages for watching the Giants, I'll hand in my license and bury my gun. Which is where, by the way?"

"The police took it the night you came in. Evidence of something or other, they said."

I picked up my bag containing my jammies and the unopened bottle of scotch—the Oreos were already history. "If you're ever in need of detective work, I owe you a big favor."

"The only thing I need to find is some spare time."

"I'll lend you some. I'm one of the few people I know who's got plenty."

"Out," was all he said.

Half an hour later I was home, inhaling the musty air of my apartment, flushing the brown water out of the taps, tossing out the bad food in the fridge, hauling the sheets and towels down to the laundry room—I was so manic and efficient I worried that my stay in the hospital had made me a neat freak.

While it was good to be home, and while even sour and mildewed air was preferable to the medicinal musk of the surgical ward, by the time I finished cleaning up I was both exhausted and depressed. Exhausted because despite the adrenaline rush of the morning, my body wasn't nearly back to normal—my lungs were laboring and my heart seemed close to fibrillation. And depressed because nearly everything I came across, from the poker chips on the shelf to the beer bottles in the fridge, reminded me somehow of Charley. He was gone and would never be back and I would be lonely forever because of it. It hadn't hit me fully in the hospital, I guess, because now it hit me like a Tyson right hand, or at least a Tyson bicuspid.

Usually what I do in such circumstances is drink. I don't recommend it, I don't even claim that it helps, but that's what I do when I'm sad. Thanks to Ruthie Spring, I had some quality scotch in my duffel bag that was beckoning me as seductively as an episode of Robbie Coltrane's *Cracker*. But I was still taking four different medications a day, none of which called for alcohol as a chaser; in fact, I'd been explicitly warned to lay off. So I made do with the second best tranquilizer I know of—I ate.

A trip to the store produced Oreos, Red Vines, burnt peanuts, a bag of tortilla chips and a jar of salsa, and a pièce de résistance in the form of a chocolate cake frozen and packaged by Pepperidge Farms. The clerk at the cash register couldn't stop giggling at the subtext to my purchases and I was already halfway into an anticipated sugar high as I climbed the hill toward my home, but what the hell? I'd had a tough time, I'd lost thirteen pounds, my best friend was dead, so I deserved a fucking treat.

But one man's treat is another man's folly. I ate so much preprocessed bilge I got sick, involuntarily purging into the dingy porce-lain stool in my bathroom, finally falling into a slumber that didn't lift till ten the next morning. Eleven hours of sleep not even courtesy of a hangover. Maybe that part of the regimen would become a habit.

Thankfully, the quality of my menu picked up. The woman across the hall brought vegetable soup in a vat the size of a hogshead. The triple divorcée from Guido's bar brought a casserole dish full of her patented tuna and noodles. And the widow of one of my former clients sent over a five-course meal catered by one of the city's best restaurants. So I was feeling fairly fat and sassy when someone brought me something far better than food, far better than booze, far better than anything any doctor had ever prescribed. On Sunday evening at six, Millicent Colbert brought me my daughter.

My daughter's name is Eleanor. She was born to a surrogate mother and turned over to Millicent Colbert and her husband Stuart pursuant to the contract they had made with the surrogate, a contract drafted by the lawyer who had hired me to verify the surrogate's suitability for the role. I got to know the surrogate a little too well, as it happened. That it was my sperm and not Stu-art's that fertilized the surrogate's egg is unknown to both of the Colberts—I hope it will always be thus. That my sperm was able to find purchase in the surrogate's ovum was a surprise to me as well, since I thought the birth control method I'd employed had made such a union impossible. Not so, as it turned out, although concep-tion was by the surrogate's design rather than by accident. In any event, I've been a proud papa for more than two years, although the papa part of it I kept under wraps even from Charley Sleet.

Millicent greeted me with a kiss and a grin. She wore a form-fitting blue jump suit that was cinched by a silver conch belt and snow white tennies that looked fresh out of the box. It was what she always wore when I saw her, maybe because she looked great in it and I always told her so. Her blond hair was drawn back in a bun; her eyes were made even bluer by some form of mascara. Somehow Mil-licent made tending a child seem as casual as minding a goldfish.

Eleanor greeted me with a hug around my kneecaps. That she was already walking and talking and had taken on a distinct personality was a continual wonder to me. That she and her mother included me in a large portion of their lives is the blessing I'm most thankful for. That something vile and violent might happen to Eleanor one day, that the world that provides me my living might lash out and scar her for life, is the stuff of most of my nightmares.

They filed into my apartment and took seats side by side on the couch. They bounced till they were comfortable, then crossed their hands in their laps in a precision as deft as a drill team's. I thought for a minute it was some kind of burlesque, then decided it was only good breeding.

"Hi, Mush," Eleanor said suddenly.

Millicent rolled her eyes. "That's her new name for you. Mush."

"Hi, Mush; hi, Mush."

"I like it," I said, then placed my hand over my surgically repaired interior. "Fitting, too."

After a couple of minutes of baby talk, I hauled out the box of toys I'd bought for when Eleanor paid me a visit—dolls, balls, rattles, and blocks—and dumped them on the floor for her pleasure. After receiving permission from Mom, Eleanor slid off the couch and began to rummage. I watched with as much pleasure as I'd had in two months.

With her daughter fully engaged with the toys, Millicent inspected me closely. "You're hurting still, aren't you, Marsh?"

"A little."

"And you've lost weight."

I glanced at the half-empty bag of burnt peanuts. "Not for long."

"Do you need anything at all? Can I bring Juanita over to clean house for you some afternoon?"

I shook my head. "I'm fine, Millicent."

"I'm doing it anyway. And you need food, surely. Come to dinner on Tuesday."

I hesitated, then opted for truth. "I make Stuart nervous."

"No, you don't."

"Yes, I do."

She smiled. "Well, maybe a little."

"Why don't we skip dinner? I'll drop by some afternoon for a snack."

"Juanita's off on Wednesdays. Come then; I'll make that coconut cake you like."

"Perfect."

Eleanor threw a ball at my head. I caught it just before it bounced off my chin and rolled it back to her. When it ran through her legs she sat down with a thump. "E three," I said.

"What was that?" Millicent asked.

"Baseball talk. How's she been doing, anyhow?"

"She's been doing great. I would have brought her to see you in the hospital but they said it was against the rules."

"It's good you didn't. Lots of germs floating around those places. You'd think they'd do something about it."

Millicent's smile was disappointingly perfunctory. "You won't go back to work for a while yet, will you?"

"Probably not."

"I don't like to think this could happen again."

"Odds are good that it won't," I said. Though not as good as she thought they were, given the night in the alley off Broadway.

"Stuart said he would be happy to put you on the security staff at the store. You could work any shift you wanted to."

I shook my head. "I don't think so. But thank him for me."

"It would be safer than what you do now."

"Among other things."

Millicent's aspect turned grave, her eyes shaded by her brow, her forehead rippling with concern. "It would be horrible for Eleanor if anything happened to you, Marsh. Horrible for both of us," she added firmly.

I was tempted to slide to her side and give her a kiss, but I made do with a pat on the hand. Our attraction is such that someday

Millicent and I will probably have an affair. I hope we'll be smart enough to keep it short and secret.

"I'll watch my step," I said. "Don't worry." I looked toward the girl with the toys. "Would Eleanor like to play horsey?"

"Horsey! Horsey!"

"Do you really think you should—"

"I'm fine," I interrupted.

It was a lie, and the next ten minutes almost killed me, but I did it nevertheless. Horsey on the living room floor, Eleanor screaming with joy and kicking uncomfortably close to my incisions, me gritting my teeth and enduring the pain, a dumb idea but an essential one, at least so it seemed at the time.

Thankfully, Millicent called a halt before something gave way. She helped me put the toys back in the box and made me promise to come to her house at mid-week. They left after kisses all around and I was feeling so good and so gregarious that I fished in my wallet for the paper that had Rita Lombardi's phone number written on it.

The phone rang for a long time. The person who picked up was male and under stress, his voice leaden and lugubrious and lightly accented. "Lombardi residence. What is it?"

"May I speak to Rita, please?"

He paused. "Who is this?"

"A friend from San Francisco."

"Rita doesn't have any friends in San Francisco."

"I met her in the hospital up here. We were both patients. We used to take walks together for therapy."

"Yeah, well, that was a waste of time."

"Why?"

His voice broke like a stick. "Rita's dead. What therapy is going to fix that? Huh? You tell me. What therapy is there that's going to bring Rita back to life?"

CHAPTER FOUR

I was so dumbfounded I almost dropped the phone as I replaced it on the cradle. After I regained the courage to dial again, it took three calls before I found someone who would talk to me. The someone was her mother.

Her voice was thick, almost masculine, with the lingering warble of a Neapolitan accent. "This is Louise Lombardi. Whom am I speaking to, please?"

"My name is Marsh Tanner, Mrs. Lombardi. I met Rita at San Francisco General Hospital a few weeks ago. I was a patient there, too. We took lots of walks down the halls together. I liked her very much," I added, just in case it wasn't clear.

"She mentioned you," Mrs. Lombardi said. "She said you were a nice person." Her voice wavered only a second, then regained its steady timbre.

"She wanted me to come to Haciendas to see her," I said, struggling for control myself. "I was calling to set a date. Now they tell me she's dead."

The sigh was operatic, descending over two octaves. "She died four days after she came home to Haciendas."

"What happened? I thought her surgeries had gone well. She seemed so vibrant the last time I saw her." I thought of the staphylococcus that had threatened to engulf me after surgery, the deadly virus that lurks somewhere in the cracks and crevices of every hospital. "Did she come down with an infection or something?"

"It was not an infection, it was a knife. Some person stabbed her thirty times, stabbed and stabbed and stabbed. It is beyond thought how someone could do such a thing. It is beyond my faith that God would have allowed this to happen."

After a lengthy silence, I managed a bloodless platitude. "That's terrible, Mrs. Lombardi. I'm very sorry."

She continued as though I hadn't spoken. "To me, I could understand; I have made many mistakes in my life. But not to Rita. Not to someone who has borne so many burdens already."

The sigh became a sob, anguished and wrenching and universal; I was an inch from tears myself. "Why did it happen, Mrs. Lombardi? Was it a robbery or something?"

"No one knows why it happened. Rita had nothing. I have nothing. Everyone in Haciendas knows that no one in this family has anything worth stealing."

I asked a question I didn't want to ask, but the conditioning of twenty years wouldn't let me suppress it. "Could it have been a sex crime, Mrs. Lombardi?"

"She was not violated, thank the Lord for that small blessing; she was merely murdered. Now I must go. Friends have come to the house to console me. Now it is I who must care for them."

"One second, please."

"Yes?"

"I'm a private detective, Mrs. Lombardi. I've helped solve several criminal cases over the years. If I came to Haciendas I might be able to help."

"Help who?"

"Help find out what happened to Rita."

"We know what happened, Mr. Tanner. My daughter was slaughtered like a sheep in a pen."

"Then maybe I can find out why."

"How will that help?"

The answer didn't come as easily as it should have. "So you will know who did it and why," I managed finally. "So you will know no one else will suffer the way Rita suffered. So you can know the stranger you see on the street is not the one who murdered your child."

She hesitated, breathing in unnatural gasps for air. "I cannot stop you from coming to Haciendas, Mr. Tanner. But I have no money and my daughter was not an important person. There is no one here who can pay you to—"

"Rita was important to me," I interrupted. "I'll be in Haciendas by the end of next week."

"Come or not come, Mr. Tanner. It is all the same to me. Nothing you will do can change the fact that my child lies buried in the ground and that the Holy Spirit has chosen to forsake me once again."

"I can change the fact that the man who did it is walking around free," I said, but Mrs. Lombardi had already hung up.

It took two days to get through the backup at the office, which wasn't all that deep even though I'd been out of commission for almost two months, which told me more than I wanted to know about the state of my business. I made some calls and wrote some letters and arranged for Ruthie Spring to handle the pending matters that might fester in my absence.

It took another day to get my car serviced and another to deal with the police. They came in two shifts. First, two guys showed up on my doorstep at 10 A.M. on Thursday. They had cop written all over them—brown suits, brown shoes, and the brown butts of handguns sticking out of their brown belt holsters. They looked enough alike to be twins, except one of them had a scar across the bridge of his nose and the other had a chipped tooth. I hadn't noticed the tooth the last time I'd seen him, which was when he was lying flat on his belly on Twentieth Street, imploring Charley Sleet to spare his life.

"Figured you'd stop by sooner or later," I said. "Probably want to thank me for coming to the rescue out at the power station."

"Bullshit," they said simultaneously.

They barged inside and I returned to the couch and my coffee. They loomed over me like pistol-packing cougars, cool, confident, and menacing. "This place is a dump," the scarred one said after taking inventory.

"I would have redecorated, but I don't have your sources of income."

"What's that supposed to mean?"

I met his look. "It means I don't steal."

"Steal this, asshole." He flipped me the bird.

Since the one with the chipped tooth seemed slightly less inflammatory, I addressed my question to him. "What do you want?"

"We heard you kept your mouth shut when the A.D.A. came to call at the hospital."

"I did?"

"Yeah. You did. We came to tell you to keep it up, and that way we'll get along. Start barfing about what you think you know about Hilton and Mandarich and what went down on Twentieth Street, you could get in big trouble."

"Like the trouble Hilton and Mandarich got in?"

"Yeah," the scarred one muttered. "Like that."

I smiled into his bluster. "So what's the deal? Have you boys taken over the Triad operation? Or are you still flunkies like before?"

The scarred one made a fist and showed it to me. "You don't have Sleet around to hold your hand anymore, Tanner. So be smart and keep the Triad shit to yourself."

"Which reminds me, we haven't been properly introduced." I stuck out a hand.

"Ain't life a bitch," the scarred one said, and they sailed out the door like a stench.

An hour later, the second shift arrived. This round took place in my office—Assistant D.A. Jill Coppelia had made an appointment and this time she brought some brass with her. His name was Mark Belcastro and he was a shift captain out of the Central Division, where Charley had been assigned during the latter years of his career. Jill was crisp and cool in a blue suit with a white blouse; Belcastro looked to have bought his outfit from the same clothier who'd dressed Charley Sleet, which was somewhere down market from Sears.

They took seats in my mismatched chairs and looked around as though the office would tell them something important about me. After a while, Coppelia pointed to my painting. "Nice art."

"I like it."

"Good imitation of Klee."

"It isn't an imitation."

Her eyes bulged to the size of walnuts. "That's a genuine Klee? *The* Klee? *Paul* Klee?"

"So I'm told."

"You must have made a killing in this business." She saw my expression and reddened. "Sorry. Bad choice of words."

I shrugged it off. "The Klee was a gift from a client."

"You must have done a hell of a job. And he must have been a hell of a client."

"I did and he was." I leaned back in my chair and clasped my hands behind my head. "How can I help the San Francisco law enforcement authorities this morning?"

"The Sleet thing," Belcastro said.

"What about it?"

He shifted uneasily. "To get right to it, why did he kill those three cops?"

"I told Ms. Coppelia that I wasn't going to be a party to this. If Charley gets dragged through the City Hall mud, it won't be my doing."

Belcastro leaned forward and put his elbows on his knees. He was handsome in a weathered way, and had the muffled eyes of a nice guy. It's hard to stay a nice guy and be a career cop, though. I only knew two people who'd managed it and one of them was dead.

"Sleet's being dragged through the mud already," he said. "Every black eye in the department over the past ten years is being hung around his thick neck. They claim he stole cash from the evidence locker, they claim he sold drugs on the street, they're even claiming he sexually harassed female victims who came to the station to report a violation, for Christ's sake. Motherfuckers couldn't hold his jock on the best day they ever had."

To get that angry, Belcastro must have known Charley and liked him. Which was enough to make me like Belcastro.

"All of which has what to do with me?" I asked affably.

"We figured you might want to put a stop to the bullshit," he said.

"How?"

"By pointing us toward the bad guys."

I looked at Jill Coppelia. "Is it true about the frame they're hanging on Charley?"

She nodded. "It's true. In spades."

I thought of the cops who had paid me a visit and of what they and their buddies were doing to Charley's good name. I decided that telling a part of my story wouldn't make things worse for anyone but them.

"Charley killed the first cop—Walters—because Walters got Charley's partner killed on the job way back when Charley was a rookie."

"Rather a slow brand of justice."

"After the tumor took hold, Charley wouldn't or couldn't wait for the system to work any longer. He knew he was going to die and decided to set things right before he did."

"How about the other two?"

"Hilton and Mandarich were top dogs in a group of rogue cops called the Triad. They've raped and pillaged their way through the city for years. Charley said some of them were second-generation scum."

"The survivors were in this group, too?"

My memory of the threats of the morning was fresh enough to make me as definite as gravity. "For sure, and there were lots more besides them. The powerhouse where they died served as their hideout. Like Jesse James and the Daltons, except these guys were the posse, not the outlaws. Ironic, don't you think?"

Belcastro didn't bother to wrestle with the rhetoric. "Where did you get this information?"

"From Charley."

"Do you have independent evidence that what he said was true?"

"Not a scrap."

"So you wouldn't have much to tell a Grand Jury."

"Nothing that wasn't hearsay."

"Grand Juries can consider hearsay testimony."

"That's one of the things that's wrong with them," I said, then looked at Jill Coppelia. "But prosecutors can't get convictions if that's all they've got to offer in criminal court."

"We're considering impaneling a Grand Jury to investigate all forms of police corruption in the city," she said stiffly.

I smiled at the extravagance of her ambition. "That sounds like lifetime employment."

"Would you cooperate in the investigation?"

"I already have."

"How so?"

"I told you everything I know."

They looked at each other and held a silent meeting. "When did you first hear of this Triad outfit?" Belcastro asked.

"The night Charley died."

"Did he give you any other names?"

"Nope."

"Did he tell you about any specific crimes they'd committed?"

I searched what was left of my memory. "He said the Triad had murdered a guy named Chavez in the Mission, a guy named Jefferson in the Fillmore, and a guy named Pearlstine in Lake Merced."

Coppelia and Belcastro looked at each other again. "That would explain some things," Coppelia said to her mate.

"What else?" Belcastro asked me.

"That's it."

"You're sure?"

"I'm sure."

The two exchanged looks once again. I started to wonder if they were lovers.

"We need to get this under oath," Belcastro said finally.

"No, you don't," I said.

"Why not?"

"Because I'm always under oath."

I stood up and walked to the door. "It's been a pleasure to discuss these matters, but I have business to attend to. It would be swell if I could hand you a case against the Triad on a silver platter, but I'm afraid you'll have to do some policework to flesh it out."

"That's okay; we're pretty good at it," Belcastro said.

"Not as good as when Charley was alive."

As they were going out the door, Coppelia told Belcastro to go down to the car and wait for her. He hesitated, then frowned, then did as he was told.

"How are you feeling?" she asked after he had disappeared down the stairs and she had looked at me for several seconds.

"Fine."

"For real?"

"Yep."

"Good." She glanced at the Klee and then back. "We won't be filing charges against you. I just wanted you to know."

"Thanks. I appreciate it."

"Excusable homicide; no question."

"That's the way I saw it. The way Charley saw it, too."

Her look softened. "I imagine you're being punished anyway."

"Only after midnight," I said, but I didn't want to get into it. "I appreciate your seeing it my way."

"We try to do the right thing." She smiled and touched my forearm. "Most of the time."

"I know you do."

"Well . . ."

"Well . . ."

"I'll probably be talking to you if this corruption thing gets underway."

"I'm going out of town for a while. Maybe we could have dinner when I get back."

"Maybe so. How long will you be gone?"

"I don't know."

"Where are you going?"

"Little place named Haciendas; down by Salinas somewhere."

"Vacation?"

"Business."

"What kind?"

"A friend of mind was murdered."

Her brow lifted. "Another one?"

I nodded.

"Sounds like it could get dangerous to know you."

She didn't seem daunted by the prospect.

An hour later, the doctor gave me a clean bill of health, though with a stern caution about cholesterol and triglycerides. An hour after that I was packing my bags. An hour after that I fell asleep in my chair during a rerun of *Law and Order*.

My dreams were all of Rita Lombardi. And in all of them she was dead or dying.

CHAPTER FIVE

The first thing Friday morning I took Highway 101 south out of the city, through San Jose and Gilroy and into the Salinas Valley, which cut a verdant swath between the Santa Lucia mountains to the west and the Gabilan range to the east. The turnoff to Haciendas was south of Prunedale and north of Salinas. When I took it, I was plunged into the world of modern agriculture, into a land of warm sunny days and cool foggy nights where the breezes off the Pacific Ocean to the west met the high heat of the Central Valley to the east to produce a climate particularly suited to delicate crops like strawberries and raspberries and lettuce and artichokes, which could grow to juicy ripeness without being burned on the stem.

Mrs. Lombardi hadn't been enthusiastic when I'd called and told her I was coming. In other circumstances, I might have taken the hint and stayed away, particularly since I didn't have a client and the bank balance was low already because of my enforced inactivity. But in the last few months I'd lost two people I'd cared about, which reduced that particular population by 20 percent, which left a taste in my mouth I wanted to be rid of. It was too late to help Charley Sleet, at least until the D.A. and the police department decided what they were going to do about the gang called the Triad, but Rita Lombardi was someone I could help, if not her flesh, at least her spirit.

Maybe it's because I grew up in the Midwest amid a populace and a geography with a similar orientation, or maybe it's because in my college years I was a big reader of John Steinbeck, but I've always loved the Salinas Valley. When I first started going down there, usually on my way to L.A. or to the Monterey Jazz Festival, the enterprises were mostly truck farms owned chiefly by immigrants, particularly the Japanese, who grew various kinds of produce on small plots of land and marketed them mainly out of roadside shelters that attracted city dwellers eager for the kind of food that tasted the way food used to taste when you grew it in your backyard. Now it's increasingly corporate, much of the land owned and operated by giant agricultural combines or multinational conglomerates eager for diversification. That's not necessarily bad, I guess, except accountability for misdeeds tends to disappear somewhere in the middle of the organization chart.

Technological progress has changed farming as much as any other enterprise, perhaps even more so. Many crops are planted and picked by machines these days; even delicate produce like tomatoes are ripped from the plant by rotating scythes, deposited on conveyor belts, sorted by farmworkers clinging to the machines like barnacles, then dropped into trucks for shipment to the cannery. With many crops, the workers no longer pick, the workers tend the equipment—cleaning, sorting, repairing, and operating the ungainly devices that sweep through the fields like a rampaging rebel army and are beyond the budgets of all but the most affluent landowners.

An exception to the trend is the strawberry, which is still planted and tended and harvested by hand. On larger farms, most of the work is done by day workers, employees paid by the hour as they plant or tend the plants and who work nine months of the year on the farm, leaving them the time and money to return to their families in Mexico for Christmas. The smaller growers rely on workers hired and delivered to the fields by labor contractors, who often exploit them in a variety of ways, from docking their pay for specious reasons, to charging extortionate rents for substandard and unhealthy housing, to ignoring laws that enable workers to benefit from unemployment and workman's compensation insurance and receive increased pay for overtime labor.

But some of the owners follow a different plan, contracting with several families to work the entire season on the same parcel of land, two or three acres at most, families who, because of their intimate connection to the crop, from preparing the fields for planting to picking the fruit many months later, possess great pride of ownership in the harvest and work hard to produce fruit of the highest quality because they will share in the proceeds of sale. Maybe that's why strawberries still taste pretty good while tomatoes taste like a cardboard core with a waxed paper wrapper.

Strawberry growing is stooped, backbreaking labor that requires patience and strength and an almost mystical ability to withstand both the chill of the morning fog and the high heat of midday during the typical summer in the valley. These are the qualities that farm laborers have always had, of course, whether the crop was Kansas wheat or Washington apples, but they are qualities that in California are possessed almost exclusively by Mexican immigrants, who come to this country both legally and illegally for the express purpose of harvesting seasonal crops. Despite their importance, the workers are largely unappreciated by many though not all growers until, for reasons of labor strife or political engineering, they are no longer available and amenable, at which point the growers panic—fruit must be picked when it's ripe and strawberries should be picked every two or three days or the fruit begins to rot on the stem.

According to the papers, there's a union organizing effort going on with regard to the 25,000 strawberry workers in the state, an effort to do with strawberries what they did twenty-five years ago with grapes. The farmworkers' union points to a variety of abuses by the growers and to the meager incomes of the workers; the growers point to improved working conditions on their farms if not on all others and to the precarious profitability of their enterprise. Afraid of losing what little he already has and confused by the conflicting claims, the worker doesn't know where to cast his lot.

They were increasingly visible as I drove along the edge of the table-flat fields that stretched like green shag carpet toward the distant mountains, lines of workers wearing long-sleeved shirts and wide-brimmed straw hats with sweatshirts and sweaters, which had been removed when the morning fog receded, knotted around their waists. They bent over the amazingly uniform lines of squat green berry bushes for incredible lengths of time, pawing through the plants with both hands, selecting the ripened and well-formed berries, then placing them just right in the plastic pint baskets sitting in the three-wheeled carts they pushed along the furrows in front of them.

According to Rita, the biggest berries go on top, the smaller on the bottom, and the misshapen are tossed in a can on the back of the cart for transfer to the frozen market. In addition to picking, the workers are responsible for manicuring the plant, removing all rotting, diseased, and damaged fruit so the plant will stay healthy. When full, the baskets are put into cardboard flats carried on the cart. The flats go on the truck, where they are examined for quality and credited to the picker on the tally sheet, then hauled to huge sheds where the berries are cooled to thirty-three degrees and gassed with CO_2 to slow down their metabolism, then shipped in refrigerated trucks and airplanes to grocers throughout the country. Within three or four days, a berry picked in Watsonville or Salinas will be on sale in a market in New York City, in the same plastic basket that was filled in the field, thanks to a process that few consumers of the product are aware of. It was one of the marvels of the modern age and it depended primarily on the ability of a farmworker to spend ten hours a day bent over at the waist, often earning less than the minimum wage.

Another row, this one of cars and trucks and old vans and school buses, was parked on the dirt road that marked the boundary between the plots. A cluster of chemical toilets stood like sober chaperons among the vehicles, strapped to a simple trailer, ready to be towed to the next field when work on this one was done, their prosaic function enlivened by the colorful array of clothing hung on the side. According to Rita, toilets and water jugs were one of the few remaining achievements of the legislation passed during the days when Cesar Chavez marshaled so much public support for the plight of the farmworkers that even the corporate clients in the state legislature had to pay attention to their plight.

As I thought about Rita and her devotion to the workers, I couldn't help wonder if, as with many organizing efforts of old, the union campaign had turned violent. Which made me wonder if Rita Lombardi had been yet another young life lost to the eternal struggle between capital and labor. I hoped it wasn't so, but hoping doesn't change very much, certainly not the past.

Another field, another line of workers, another row of trucks and toilets. I turned off the air conditioner and opened the windows. Heat filled the car, more maternally than oppressively, bringing with it the smells of grass and soils and ripe fruit that displaced those of engine oils and leaking Freon. I took several deep breaths and relaxed. For now at least, the world seemed a healthier and more beneficent place. But I had a feeling I was about to learn that the countryside was as dangerous and corrupt as the more notorious urban landscape.

A billboard announced that Haciendas was home to 1,982 friendly souls and was a City on the Move. A small motel, a Union 76 station, two auto repair shops, and a farm implement dealer welcomed me at the fringe. In the center of town, a post office, fire station, police department, two *tacquerias* plus the Gelbride State Bank and St. Bonaventure's Catholic Church, were more established presences. Burger King was there; so was J. C. Penney, but Wal-Mart hadn't yet made an appearance, for which the local retailers must be giving thanks. The bars were called the Cantina and the Tractor Tavern; the café was called Shortcake's; the local wags seemed to be mostly Latino. The largest structure in town was a decaying brick building that had HACIENDAS COMMUNITY HOSPITAL etched above the door but which stood behind a sign that read FARM LABOR HOUSING—HOUSING AUTHORITY OF MONTEREY COUNTY.

I drove west to east, from one end of town to the other. It seemed a sleepy but highly functional place, with trucks loaded with produce passing through in one direction while school buses loaded with pieceworkers headed out of town in the other. The houses were small, the stores mostly geared to Latinos except for the chains. The brown faces were mostly men, lounging on corners, waiting for work. The white faces were mostly female, shopping or banking or hauling their kids toward summer fun. The offspring of the Latinos no doubt spent their summer bent over in the fields with their parents, which probably wasn't their idea of a vacation.

It was too soon to make judgments, of course, but there seemed to be a calm in the air in Haciendas, an aura of accommodation and cooperation between the various cultures and social strata, a tacit agreement about what would be said and unsaid, done and undone, punished and unpunished. Maybe it was the natural order of things, or maybe it was the result of an oppressive and authoritarian socioeconomic structure that brooked no dissent or disagreement, whatever the issue. Or maybe it was just that the summer sun had melted away the sharp edges of all concerned and bathed the populace in sweaty lethargy. In any event, I was prepared to believe that Haciendas was an oasis of multicultural serenity until I reached the east edge of town.

In contrast to Haciendas itself, the outskirts bulged with the mechanics of commerce. The massive cooling sheds and packing-houses and loading docks, interspersed with truck lots and rail yards and equipment dealers, were stark reminders of how big a business agriculture was. And the lengths of barbed wire that surrounded most of the installations, and the number of police and security cars that cruised up and down the road, were proof of how tense the atmosphere in the industry had become. All of a sudden it was easy to remember that Rita Lombardi had been stabbed thirty times in this self-same emotional climate.

Fremont Street bisected the highway four blocks east of the Catholic church. As opposed to much of Haciendas, it was a street flanked by trees, several large cottonwoods that shaded the pavement in welcome spots of charcoal gray amid the shimmering pastels of the rest of the town. But the street turned to gravel in the four hundred block and the trees gave out at the same place, as if nature itself were mourning Rita's passing.

Like most of the town, the Lombardi house was a simple bungalow, single story, painted a yellow that had paled in the sunlight to evoke the yolk of an old egg. The roof was blue shingle, the door red enamel, and the grass would turn green if it ever got watered. There were two vehicles parked out front, a ten-year-old Chevy Cavalier and an ageless Ford pickup. Another pickup was parked down the block, this one a brand-new Dodge Ram. The Cavalier was faded red, the Ford was deep green; the Ram was a bright white that made me squint in spite of my sunglasses. The vehicles were well used and unwashed. As I plucked my sodden shirt away from my damp back, I felt a lot like that myself. I circled the house, parked in the shade in the previous block, then went to the front door and knocked.

The man who answered was tall, handsome, Latino, and lost. He was dressed in Levi's worn to the white and a T-shirt with a woman's face on it—at first I thought it might be the singer Selena, but when I looked more closely I saw that the face was Rita Lombardi's, smiling and saucy and shaded by her birthmark, balancing precariously on two metal crutches while pointing toward the camera as if to forbid the photographer to snap the shutter. The photographer must have been Carlos Reyna and he must have had the shirt made up in tribute to his deceased financée. The sight of Rita's laughing eyes in such a ludicrous venue made me quake and turn away. If I had been uneasy before, now I was uneasy squared.

Her boyfriend seemed to be holding it together except for his eyes. They were red, rubbed and random, and seemed to beg me to be something I wasn't and to bring with me something I lacked. I told him my name and that I was expected by Mrs. Lombardi.

"Why?" he asked.

"Why what?"

"Why are you here?"

I forced myself to look him up and down. "Nice picture," I said. "You must be Carlos."

He crossed his arms as if to keep the image his private property. He projected arrogance and strength, and was imperial in look and bearing, but something in his eyes said it was mostly a pose. "That's me. So what?"

"You and Rita were going to be married."

"Yeah."

"She loved you very much."

"Yeah."

"She talked about you a lot."

"When?"

"When she was in the hospital."

He nodded as though I'd confirmed a conspiracy. "You're *that* guy."

"Marsh Tanner." I held out a hand.

He took it and squeezed it hard. "Carlos Reyna."

"Is Mrs. Lombardi in?"

"She's on the phone."

"Then I'll wait."

Despite the introductions and our common grief for Rita, Carlos stood like a sentinel, blocking my path to the presumably cooler interior, watching me wilt in the glare of sunlight that was the primary fuel in his world. As the heat of noon threatened to bring me to a boil, I decided to see what would happen if I kept my mouth shut. It's often the best way to get information—some people are comfortable with everything but dead silence.

"So you think you're going to drive down from the big city and poke around a few days and find the guy who did it," Carlos said after a while. "Like maybe we're too dumb to find him ourselves."

"I don't think that. It's just that sometimes an outsider can see things that loved ones can't."

"Things like what?"

"Motives. Moods. Machinations."

Carlos frowned. "Yeah, well, you don't need to bother; I'll take care of it myself." His tone left no doubt that he planned to be judge and jury and to issue a sentence of death at the first opportunity.

"I'm sure you can, Carlos, but why don't we work together? You know the town; I know the business. It might save time if we teamed up."

"What is this business? The strawberry business?"

"The detecting business," I corrected. "I'm a private eye. I find criminals for a living."

It was only a tiny part of my living, of course, but Carlos just needed to believe I could help him get where he wanted to go and that I would get out of his way when he got there. The latter part wouldn't happen, but Carlos didn't need to know that yet.

He cocked his head. "You going to pay me to work with you?"

"Not unless someone pays me, which Mrs. Lombardi says they aren't likely to do. So I was planning to work for free. I figured you'd do the same, since you were the guy who loved her."

"Yeah, well, I don't want someone ripping me off. Selling stories to the TV and the grocery store papers behind my back."

Hard Copy and O.J. have eroded our moral fabric. Truth and justice now go to the highest bidder—unless it's bought and broadcast, it isn't real. Pretty soon the problem witness won't be the one who sold her story to the trash media, it'll be the idiot who turned them down and was impeached on grounds of feeblemindedness.

I slapped him on the shoulder. "No TV and no tabloids, Carlos. So what do you say? Will we help each other out?"

He looked up and down the block, as though an answer might have been burned into the yards by the sun. When he saw the white Dodge Ram, he frowned. "The son of a bitch."

I looked at the truck myself. "Who?"

Carlos shook his head and looked at me. "I got things to do in the fields. If I can find the time later, we should talk. What do you plan to do first?" he asked, still dubious of our shaky alliance.

"I'd better begin with Mrs. Lombardi."

Carlos cocked an ear toward the house. "She's on the phone with Mrs. Gelbride."

"Who's Mrs. Gelbride?"

"The boss's wife."

"Boss of what?"

Carlos waved his hand. "Everything."

I smiled. "How did he manage that?"

"By having all the jobs."

I thought of the logos I'd seen on the trucks I had passed on the road, the initials GB and F intertwined in a leafy vine. "Gelbride Berry Farms," I said.

"Yeah. Gus Gelbride. His wife called Louise to express her condolences."

"That's nice."

Carlos glanced at the Ram once again. "Yeah."

"Gelbride is a pretty big operation, I guess," I said, just to keep things going.

"They own from the top to the bottom—the land, the nurseries, the cooling sheds, the truck lines and rail spurs, plus the bank and the pharmacy and funeral parlor, too. You want a job, a loan, a pill, or a casket, Gus Gelbride is the man to see. Gus or his son. The asshole."

"The son's not a nice guy?"

"The son is a fool, but Gus doesn't see it. Gus thinks he's *muy* macho, but Randy's the main reason the union came back to the valley."

"Why?"

"To put a stop to his labor practices."

"Sounds sort of medieval."

"I wouldn't know about that. I just know Mrs. Gelbride called to say how sorry she was about Rita."

"Did they know each other?"

"I don't know about the missus, but Gus knows Louise from way back. Her husband was a foreman at the farms and Louise used to work in the sheds during the pick. That was before she got sick."

"Sick how?"

Carlos placed a finger on his breastbone. "Heart. She's too heavy and she can't get around much any more. She was counting on me and Rita to care for her, but now there's just me, and I got my own people to look after. But I'll manage," he said, giving me a better idea why Rita had been in love with him.

"Do you work for the Gelbrides, Carlos?"

Carlos shook his head. "I'm an independent grower. I have a contract to grow for the Gelbrides, but I work for myself. Hire and fire my own people. Plant what and how I want. Apply the pesticides and fertilizers; pick when I choose."

I wiped my brow and sighed. "Is there a cooler place I can wait till Mrs. Lombardi gets off the phone?"

Carlos looked back at the house, as though inspecting it for the first time and finding it wanting. "Not really," he said. "She won't be much longer—Mrs. Gelbride is a busy woman. But they deserve some privacy."

"Maybe I'll wait in the shade by the car. After I see Mrs. Lombardi, I'd like to talk to you."

Carlos looked at his watch. "I got to be in the fields pretty soon. I could meet you at the Cantina at five. It's cool in there," he added as a major inducement.

"Five it is. I don't suppose there's a motel in town?"

He shook his head. "Nothing for Anglos—the only one we have is mostly for migrants. Salinas is closest. Or you want something fancy, you could drive over to Monterey."

"I don't do fancy," I told him.

I started to walk toward the car. Ten steps later I tripped over a rock, aggravating my wounds, sending another slice of pain through my innards. Sweat salted my eyes and trickled down my flanks—I felt as if I'd taken a shower in sulfuric acid. My head throbbed and my back ached—I felt old and decrepit and foolish.

Halfway across the street, Carlos called my name. "She's finished," he said, and waited for me to join him.

"How's she been holding up?" I asked as I climbed the steps to the door, gingerly, still waiting for the pain to subside.

"She is strong," Carlos said as he held the door for me. "And she has lost loved ones before. But one day she will fall. If you see it start to happen, you need to tell me right away."

With that, Carlos ushered me into the house. It was tidy but cluttered, everything in its place but lots of things in lots of places. Mrs. Lombardi was a collector. She collected sugar bowls and decorated plates and commemorative medallions and ice blue perfume bottles, and that was only the living room. The paraphernalia seemed to give her comfort, though, because despite the tragedy she had suffered, she appeared to be calm and on an even emotional keel, wanting to please, hoping to help. I was feeling guilty for interrupting the evolution of her grief even before I sat down.

"Welcome to my house, Mr. Tanner."

"Thank you for seeing me, Mrs. Lombardi. I'm sorry for intruding."

"Not at all. Father McNally will be here at noon, but until then I'm happy to speak with you." She looked at Carlos with fondness. "Go, Carlos. The workers need you more than I do now. I'll be fine."

"Okay, Mrs. Lombardi. Do you want something before I go?"

"No, thank you. Unless Mr. Tanner would like some tea."

"No, thanks. But a glass of water would be nice."

She nodded. "People from the city always need water."

Carlos fetched me a glass. I downed it before he was out the door. When I looked up, Mrs. Lombardi was watching me.

"You were right," she said. "I cannot be at peace while the man who killed Rita goes free."

CHAPTER SIX

With Carlos Reyna departed, the energy level in the house dropped by 80 percent. I was impressed with the young man, with the depth of his grief over Rita and his obvious devotion to her mother. I was sorry Rita hadn't lived to make a life with him.

Mrs. Lombardi and I sagged into our upholstered seats and regarded each other with equal shares of melancholy. She was a vast vat of a woman, younger than I'd assumed at first glance, perhaps because she dressed the part. Her gray-black hair was gathered into a large bun; her tiny black eyes were wedged deep behind slits of pink flesh. Two doughy cheeks cascaded into a swollen neck that deprived her of chin. Her upper arms trembled as she moved and her bulbous chest rose and fell like industrial bellows. A blue print dress, as tailored as a beach towel, fell over her like a giant tablecloth above black leather shoes with heels the size of tuna cans. She breathed with difficulty—wheezing asthmatically after the slightest expense of effort. Although it was cool in the house, a small fan oscillated like an obedient pet on the floor right in front of her. I worried that for different reasons Mrs. Lombardi wasn't far from joining her daughter in the grave.

"You have a nice house," I began.

"Thank you."

I gestured toward the shelves on the walls. "You like to collect things, I see."

"Yes. Very much."

"Are they souvenirs of your travels?"

Her smile was sufficiently lachrymose to be mystical. "I have never been north of San Jose or east of Modesto. I find my treasures in the flea markets. Times are hard; people have to sell precious things to feed their families. I enjoy myself by enjoying the mementos of other people's journeys. It seems heartless, perhaps, but I tell myself I honor their memories by preserving them."

"I'm sure you do," I said, though I wasn't sure I believed it.

She nodded ponderously, in a silence that became hermeneutic. I couldn't help but think of Rita, as engaged with the messy swirl of the world as her mother was removed from it.

"Have you lived in Haciendas all your life?" I asked when the hush became unbearable.

She shook her head. "Thirty years, almost. I came out from Chicago with my husband Franco after he returned from Vietnam and got out of the service. We came to Chicago from Napoli after we were married and we came West to make our fortune and to have a large family." She forced a smile. "It was God's will that we didn't have either. Now my only family is my treasures." Her eyes floated over the row upon row of painted plates, displayed in an ornate wall rack, each portraying a different national monument from a different state of the Union. The display was a shrine of some kind, though I wasn't sure to what.

"I was very sorry to hear about Rita," I said. "It must be hard for you to come to terms with it."

"The good die young," she said softly. "It is my only solace. Rita was so good, despite her handicaps, she seemed truly heaven-sent. But as with His only Son, God's plan did not allow my child to live a full lifetime."

"You seem like a religious person, Mrs. Lombardi."

"I am Roman Catholic," she said. In her world it was clearly answer enough.

"Was Rita active in the church as well?"

She nodded. "She was active in everything. If there was a group in Haciendas devoted to helping the less fortunate, Rita was an active part of it."

"Is that how she met Carlos?"

"At church? No. Rita was helping with what they called the second language program at the school. Carlos often brought his workers there in the evenings, so they could learn to speak better English."

"Was there any problem between Rita and anyone else in the program? A dispute of some sort?"

Mrs. Lombardi shook her head. "They loved her there. Everyone loved Rita." The precept seemed as sacred to her as those contained in the missal that lay beside her on the couch.

"Was Rita active politically at all? In the union movement, perhaps? Or in civil rights?"

She nodded. "She was like her father in that."

"How so?"

"Rita's father was a field foreman for Mr. Gelbride. Franco was like Carlos—the workers liked him because he treated them with dignity and respect and because he would take their complaints to the owner and be their advocate for better conditions. The same was not true of the men who came after him."

"Who came after him?"

"Several people, over the years. But Randy Gelbride is the one there now. Carlos says he is the worst of them all."

"He's the son of the owner?"

She nodded.

"What happened to your husband, Mrs. Lombardi?"

She closed her eyes. "He was killed."

"How?"

"He was hit by a truck as he was waiting to cross the big highway. They said he was drunk but he could not have been—he stopped drinking when he came home from the war. Rita told me he must have had a seizure." Her entire body swelled as she talked of the death, until she seemed twice her normal size and capable of levitation.

"When did that happen, Mrs. Lombardi?"

"Three years after Rita was born."

"So you raised her by yourself."

She nodded. "But I had help when I needed it. The church, the school, the neighbors, my friends. Rita never lacked for anything. Not anything important. Except a father."

"Tell me more about her," I said.

"She was a saint," Louise Lombardi said simply. "Even Father McNally said so in his eulogy."

"Did she go to college?"

"Two years at Hartnell College in Salinas."

"What did she study?"

"Accounting and social work." The phrase caused her to smile for the first time since I'd entered the room. "She didn't need to study social work. It came as naturally to her as breathing."

"Did Rita have any particular friends at college? Either students or professors?"

"There was a girl named Powell. Thelma Powell. She had a disability, too; a withered arm. But she could still drive, so she and Rita rode down to school together."

"Where's Thelma now?"

"I believe she is still in Salinas, working for one of the banks. Rita was lucky. Her disfigurements could be corrected. There was nothing they could do for Thelma's arm. Her mother took the wrong kind of medicine when she was still in the womb. Her mother suffers for it more than Thelma does. Every time she speaks of her child, she weeps."

I tried to narrow her focus to a single tragedy. "How about Rita's professors? Was there anyone she had a special relationship with?"

"Not in college, I don't think. But the English teacher at the high school was a good friend. Mr. Thorndike. Rita wrote many stories for his class. He wanted her to send them away to New York magazines, but she never would."

"Why not?"

"She felt no one would be interested in her thoughts."

"Everyone would be interested in her thoughts," I said, remembering my own reaction to them.

Mrs. Lombardi's smile became ethereal. "Everyone could see that but Rita. She was always surprised when people paid attention to her, and came to her for advice and asked what she thought they ought to do in their lives. It's what happens when you are disabled, I think. You believe the deformity applies to all of you, not just the crooked limbs."

Silence filled the room once more as we devoted even more thoughts to Rita. I was depressed by the absurd illogic of her death. It was time to get what I needed and leave.

"Based on the way Rita was killed, I'd have to say it looks personal, not random," I said, "that whoever did it was outraged at Rita for some reason. Do you know anyone who might have had reason to feel that way about her, Mrs. Lombardi?"

As she stiffened with anger, her upper arms trembled like vanilla pudding. "Of course not. There is no one like that in Haciendas."

"I was thinking of an ex-boyfriend. Maybe a guy she left for Carlos."

"Carlos was the first man in her life in that way."

"Are you sure?"

She thrust a lip. "A mother knows such things."

Not always, I knew, although maybe in this case. But I didn't accept it as gospel. "Did she have any trouble at her job? Or with any of the people she helped in the community? Sometimes good deeds are most resented by the people who benefit from them."

She closed her eyes and shook her head. "If there was anything like that, I didn't know what it was. Everyone liked Rita. It is what I always heard, from the day she started school. Rita is such a wonderful girl. It's a privilege to work with her in class. That was what they all said. I must have heard it a thousand times. I can show you her report cards if you want. Rita was always perfect."

Mrs. Lombardi's belated eulogy echoed through the house like a roll of distant thunder. I hoped it was true, what she said, that Rita truly had no enemies in life, that she was a blessing to all concerned the way she had been for me. It depressed me to realize that before I left Haciendas I was probably going to find out that the truth was more complicated than that.

I was about to ask if I could take a look at Rita's bedroom when someone knocked on the door. As Mrs. Lombardi struggled toward her feet, I motioned for her to stay put and hurried to answer it in her stead.

The woman standing on the stoop was taken aback. "Oh. I didn't expect . . . who are you, a policeman of some sort? I just stopped by to see Louise, but I can come another time if it's not convenient."

I told her I wasn't a policeman. "I'm a friend of Rita's," I added, because it was something I needed to keep saying.

The woman was short and stout and businesslike, with a high forehead and chubby cheeks and a determined look that indicated she dealt with adversity often enough and overcame it more often than not.

She wore a khaki pants suit that seemed far too coarse for the weather but it didn't slow her down. She strode past me at the pace of a troop on the parade ground at nearby Fort Ord and walked straight to the couch. She sat without invitation and took Mrs. Lombardi's hands in her own. "How are you, Louise?" she asked with a puff of gruff concern.

"I'm fine, Mona."

"Do you need anything? Anything at all?"

Mrs. Lombardi shook her head. "People have been very kind."

"A hot dish?"

"I have three casseroles in the fridge already. You work hard enough as it is. Let the ones with time to spare spend some of it on me."

Mrs. Lombardi turned my way. "Mr. Tanner, this is Mona Upshaw, one of my oldest friends. A saint, like my Rita."

"How do you do?" I said.

"Mona is a nurse. She was at the hospital when they brought Rita in."

Mona bowed her head. "It was the most difficult thing I've had to do in all my years of practice, to watch the monitors go flat as that dear girl left us."

"She was still alive when she got to the hospital?" I asked.

"Only technically, I believe. She hadn't quite bled out."

I stemmed a shudder at a fate I'd almost succumbed to myself. "Did she say anything about what happened to her?"

She shook her head. "I heard nothing myself and I asked the EMS team that same question, but she said nothing to them, either. I don't believe she ever regained consciousness."

"Where was she found, do you know?"

"Near the high school, is what the papers said. Apparently there was so much blood they assumed she was dead until they located a faint pulse."

"What does it matter?" Mrs. Lombardi interrupted heavily. "She's gone. That's all that matters now. She's gone and Franco is gone and I have no one left to care for."

Ms. Upshaw swiveled to embrace Mrs. Lombardi and began to comfort her with slow caresses and soothing words. Although I wanted to look at Rita's room and ask more questions about the last days of her life, now wasn't the time to do it. After saying what I could think of to say, which wasn't nearly enough, I bid the two women good-bye and let myself out the front door.

"One minute, Mr. Tanner."

Mona Upshaw was standing on the threshold, pulling the door closed behind her.

"You're the detective, aren't you?"

"That's right."

"Will you listen to some advice from an old friend of Rita's?"

"Sure."

She pulled the door closed and spoke in a rasping whisper. "Leave us alone, Mr. Tanner. There are things in Haciendas that should stay hidden, things no one needs to hear, things that will go to the grave with the only people who know of them if you leave them be. Let it happen, Mr. Tanner. Let time bury our secrets."

Before I could ask her if one of those secrets had gotten Rita Lombardi killed, she was already back in the house. When I turned toward the car, the heat hit me like a hammer.

CHAPTER SEVEN

It was time to talk to the cops. By the time I regained equilibrium and drove to the station, the sign on the bank said it was eighty-eight degrees and it was twice that in the car. The air conditioner in my Buick wasn't up to the task; neither was my deodorant. Since I was going to be even more offensive than usual, I walked through the door with a smile on my face, under the theory that you should never let them see you sweat.

The Haciendas police department occupied a fake adobe building that it shared with the fire department and the mayor's office: The town was so small, it seemed possible the same individual performed all three functions. As I walked toward the door, I could feel the heat invading my body through the soles of my shoes and the top of my head. If the currents ever met in the middle, my stitching might not withstand the collision.

I stopped in front of the first desk I came to, which belonged to a woman in mufti. She was sharp-faced and tanned to the color of khaki, with hyper-blond hair and hyper-red lips and a silver ring on each ear and each thumb. The wrinkles around her eyes and mouth were lighter than the rest of her skin, giving her a clownish aspect. It was a good bet that no one had ever told her that. It was also a good bet that I wasn't going to get anything helpful from

71

her, given what seemed to be a congenital dispassion—she wore her boredom like a badge.

She looked up from whatever her computer was telling her about the state of the world or at least Haciendas. "How can we help you, stranger?"

"How do you know I'm a stranger?"

She looked me over. "You ain't got enough color to be local, for one. For another, I seen every Anglo in Haciendas at one time or another—funeral, wedding, or right where you're standing—and I ain't seen you before or I'd have remembered."

I smiled. "I'll take that as a compliment."

She shrugged with aggressive uninterest. "Suit yourself. So what'll it be?"

"Information."

"Buying or selling?"

"Buying."

"We're not in that kind of business."

"It might be to your advantage to deal with me."

She cocked her head. "That's what they all say, one way or another, on duty and off. It seldom proves to be true." She surprised me with a smile that softened her features and doubled her attractiveness. "But maybe you're the exception."

I returned her grin. "Did you know Rita Lombardi wanted to fix us up?"

She frowned. "Say what?"

"Rita Lombardi thought you and I should go dancing with her and Carlos Reyna at a place called the Cantina."

"That poor girl." The woman stuck out her hand. "Sal Delder. I'm not much of a dancer so you didn't miss much, plus I've lived alone so long I lost the knack of smart conversation. You're the friend from the hospital, huh?"

I nodded. "Name's Tanner. Marsh Tanner."

"They fixed her up real good up there, didn't they?"

I nodded. "So you saw her after she got back?"

"She ducked in to say hello. And tell me to work on my fox-trot."

"She didn't say anything to indicate she was in some kind of trouble?"

"The opposite. She seemed happy as a bee on clover." Sal shook her head. "Life can sure turn shitty once in a while. Working in a place like this, that can be all of it you see. Weighs me down some, especially with something like Rita. What kind of information you interested in? As if I didn't know."

"The Lombardi case."

"Both? Or just Rita?"

"I didn't know there was more than one."

"We got a new one and an old one. Take your pick."

"The new one," I said. "For starters."

She lifted a thumb and aimed toward the back. "Man in charge is Sergeant Lopez. Office is that way, but he ain't here."

"Where is he?"

"Out on union patrol, I imagine, along with everyone else with a badge, making sure things don't get out of hand. Only one here is the chief."

"Then I'll talk to him."

She lifted a brow. "Got a good reason why he should take the time?"

"I'm a friend of the deceased, plus I'm a licensed private detective."

"That just might do it," she said with a grin.

She pecked some more strokes on her computer, pushed a button to clear the screen, then got out of her chair and went down the hall. Without her, the building seemed as hollow as a tire. Amazingly enough, despite the heat that made my shirt a soggy rag, I was chilly—the biggest item on the department budget must have been the air conditioning.

When Sal Delder returned she was followed by a man in a two-tone blue uniform that was two sizes too small in the chest and an inch too short in the inseam, with enough gadgetry hanging off the belt to outfit the Italian army. He was short and burly and buff, with his hair shaved to his skull and his sleeves rolled tight above biceps that had to have been acquired artificially. His neck was as thick as a stump and his chest was the size of a swamp cooler. In response to his persona, my gut gave off a quick twist of pain, as if to remind me not to give the man an excuse to punch me.

"PI, huh?" he said as he strolled down the hall to meet me.

"That's what the license says."

"Maybe I'd better confirm that you've got one."

I handed it over. He read it and looked up. "I'm Mace Dixon, chief cook and bottle washer around here. Call me Reb if you want; from Mason-Dixon and all that. Who hired you to come down and mess in our business?"

"No one."

His lip curled like an apple peel. "You some sort of Lone Ranger, riding around the country solving crimes without an invite?"

"I was a friend of Rita Lombardi's."

He squinted to get me in focus, then looked at Sal with a dubious frown. "Hard to see how that could happen."

"They shared the same hospital for a few weeks," Sal told him.

"Oh. Yeah. Heard they fixed her up real good, though it was hard to tell in the morgue what with all the . . . anyways, what you in the hospital for?"

"Gut shot."

"Yeah?"

"Yeah."

"Who shot you?"

"A cop."

His face hardened like baked clay beneath a hot pink glaze. "You out on bail, or something?"

"Nope."

"So it was an accident."

"Something like that."

"Guess that can happen in the big city. Down here, we don't put up with accidents."

74

"Glad to hear it. What can you tell me about the Lombardi case, Chief?"

He thought it over before he spoke. "Stabbed a couple dozen times, got her legs broke, found her over by the high school. No witnesses; not much physical evidence. Not much motive, either, at this point. Looks like it may take a while to sort out."

"When did it happen?"

"Last Friday night. After ten and before midnight."

"Where was she at ten?"

"Home. Lived with her mother on Fremont Street. Mother was asleep, but she got a call from a friend that confirms the time."

"Carlos Reyna?"

He shook his head. "Not that kind of friend. Woman named Powell from Salinas."

"What was the call about?"

"Girl stuff, is all she admits to. Mostly about the wedding the Lombardi woman was planning."

"And at midnight?"

"Body was found by a guy coming home from the swing shift at the cooling shed."

"Is that one of Gus Gelbride's operations?"

"Hell, son, you can say that about ever business in this town and then some."

"Including this one, Chief?"

The chief pinked up again. When he made a fist his bicep threatened to hop off his arm and slug me all by its lonesome. "You got no call to say something like that. Mr. Gelbride gets what everyone else in this town gets, which is the best effort I've got in me. I think maybe you should leave us be now, Mr. Tanner—I've told you more than you deserve already."

"You're right, Chief. And I apologize if you took offense."

He looked left. "With that and a quarter I can buy Sal a posy."

I guessed he was sweet on Sal but the sentiment wasn't requited. I'd been in that neighborhood myself, so I sympathized.

"Was there any connection between Rita and the guy who found her body?" I asked.

"Nope."

"Do you have any suspects at all?"

He looked me over. "I got one more than I had when you walked in the door," he said sourly. "Now I got work to do. You best get back to Frisco where you know how things work. Down here, you're going to be hip-deep in manure the minute you step out that door. And right at the moment, I wouldn't be inclined to haul you out of it."

I met his scowl with a sunny smile. "Thanks for the advice, Chief, but I'm going to be nosing around for a few days. Hope you won't have a problem with it."

His frown wrinkled everything from his chin to his cowlick. "Damn straight I got a problem. I told you to leave us be and go back to the big city. Why aren't you going to do it?"

I met his look and held it. "I came near dying in that hospital. For a while, the pain was so bad I decided that's what I wanted to do. Then Rita Lombardi came along and reminded me why I should try like hell to keep breathing."

"So you owe her."

"Big time."

He looked at Sal yet again. She smiled at him and shrugged, which I interpreted as a vote of confidence.

After the vote, the chief made his decision. "Don't get cute. Don't tell lies to folks about who you are and what you want. Report in whenever I tell you to and don't keep any secrets. And if I tell you to back off, do it, because it means we're breaking the case."

"I think I can manage that," I said, with my fingers tightly crossed at my side.

"Then we'll get along." The chief turned to go.

"Chief?"

"What?"

"The other Lombardi case."

"What about it?"

"Is it the position of the police department that Franco Lombardi was murdered?"

Chief Dixon crossed his arms and leaned against the wall, which made it give six inches. "Does it matter?"

"I figure it might somewhere down the road."

He thought it over, then nodded. "I'd only been here six months, just out of Shore Police with the Navy down in Dago. Some things about it seemed off plumb to me, so in my mind it's still open. But I'm the only one who thinks so."

"Who was the guy who hit him?"

"Man named Fitzroy. Dead himself a few years later; heart attack."

"Any connection to Franco Lombardi?"

"Not that I found. Except they work for the same man."

"Gus Gelbride."

"Around here, that's not much of a guess. Do what you got to do, Mr. Tanner. I got paperwork to do."

"I'd like to talk to you more about the Lombardi thing sometime."

"Not now."

"Then later."

"Anything's possible, they say, though in my experience it's not nearly true. Most things folks want ain't ever gonna happen and somewhere inside they know it."

The chief lumbered down the hall, a tough and candid man who seemed up to the task of warding off the pressures that would come to bear on law enforcement in a place like Haciendas. I decided it would be prudent to stay in his good graces.

Sal Delder walked with me as far as her desk. I bid her good-bye and pushed open the door.

"She wasn't who you thought she was," she said at my back.

I turned back. "What was that?"

"Rita Lombardi. She wasn't the saint people thought she was."

"Then what was she?"

"A revolutionary."

"Saints are the most radical revolutionaries of all," I said. By the time I found a motel room down in Salinas, my mood was as foul and apprehensive as it had been on the day I'd been shot.

CHAPTER EIGHT

I showered and changed my shirt, then called the machine in the office for messages. Ruthie had left one that said everything was under control more or less, except her phraseology was more scatological. The only other messages of interest were from Jill Coppelia and a lawyer named Knoblock. As I called the lawyer, the number seemed familiar and for good reason: Knoblock was a partner in Andy Potter's law firm and Andy was a friend of mine and a member of the poker group from time to time.

"Knoblock," he said gruffly.

"Marsh Tanner, returning your call."

"Ah. Mr. Tanner. How are you feeling?"

"Hunky-dory."

"I assume that means good."

"Good enough."

"Great. Well, the reason I called is, I don't know if you're aware of it or not, but some years back, this office drew up a will for your friend Charles Sleet."

I hadn't heard him called Charles since his wife, Flora, had died ten years ago. "I didn't know that. No."

"The terms of the will should be of interest to you. In fact, the terms are somewhat unusual."

"How so?"

"In essence, the will provides that the entire residue of Mr. Sleet's estate, after payment of debts and expenses and taxes, shall be bequeathed to the Tenderloin Children's Project."

"Great. They're a quality operation."

"So I've been told. But there is a condition precedent to that gift I need to apprise you of."

"Which means what?"

Knoblock cleared his throat. "Mr. Sleet's will specifically provided that you are entitled to select whatever assets you want from his estate and to keep them as your own, without limitation."

"Anything?"

"Anything at all—the house, his car, his bank account, his pension—anything and everything, if you so choose. As I said, it was quite an unusual bequest. So, as the co-executor along with Mr. Potter, whom I believe you know, I'm calling to ask you to make your selections as expeditiously as possible, so the residue can be transferred to the residual beneficiary without needless delay."

"I . . . what if I don't want anything?"

His voice cooled. "That's your prerogative, of course. Although I know Mr. Sleet hoped you would take something. A memento, if nothing else."

"It's a little like taking candy from a baby, though, isn't it?"

"How do you mean?"

"I mean whatever I get, the children's project loses."

"That would appear to be so. Yes. It's a zero-sum situation."

"How much are we talking about here, Mr. Knoblock? Not a lot, right?"

"The assets were valued at the date of death at six hundred and ten thousand dollars."

"What?"

"Six ten, Mr. Tanner. A sizable sum, though just below the level at which federal estate taxes would be incurred."

"Jesus," I blurted. "Maybe Charley *was* on the pad."

Knoblock's laugh was careful and controlled and his statement was meant to rebut my charge, whether or not it was serious. "Approximately three-fourths of the total is in real estate."

I was relieved. "Right. The house."

"And a second residence up near Rio Vista, I believe."

"A second . . . oh. The fishing cabin."

"Yes."

"Do you have any other questions about the assets, Mr. Tanner?"

"Not at the moment, I don't think."

"So when do you think you'll be reaching a decision in this matter?"

I was tired of his tone and tired of the suggestion that I pick over Charley's bones. "I don't know, Mr. Knoblock. I'm calling from Salinas; I'm involved in a case down here. I think I'd want to look at the house and his personal effects before I make any—"

"Of course. And I could make that arrangement at your convenience. Or you can use the key under the rock by the porch."

"I'll let you know when I get back to the city."

"Of course."

"That sadistic son of a bitch."

"Pardon me?"

"Just saying another form of good-bye," I said, and hung up.

Ten minutes later I'd pushed Charley back beneath my consciousness, so I called the number Jill Coppelia had left on my machine. When the person who answered said, "District Attorney's office," it seemed more a warning than a welcome.

I gave her Jill's name and a moment later she came on the line. "Good afternoon, Mr. Tanner."

"Good afternoon, Ms. Coppelia."

"How about Jill and John?"

"I go by Marsh, actually."

"So that would make it Jill and Marsh. If we were going to become less formal."

"Jill and Marsh. Sounds like a children's book."

"Jill and Marsh went to the farce—it has possibilities. Speaking of farces, we've done what you suggested."

"Which is?"

"Put our investigators on this Triad business."

"Good."

"One of them will probably be talking to you."

"Fine. I can't guarantee I'll be talking to him, however."

Her voice abandoned its coltish banter and fell toward asperity. "I hope you will, Marsh."

"I know you do, Jill."

She framed an alternate gambit. "What we want to know is, do you know anyone in the police department who has information about this Triad group? Anyone but the late Mr. Sleet, I mean?"

As it happened, I did. Charley's buddy, Wally Briscoe, had been part of the Triad himself, though less actively in recent years. I could give her Wally's name, and they could sweat him and eventually break him down, since backbone wasn't one of Wally's strong points. That would get them probable cause for some warrants and away they would go, straight to the Grand Jury. All I had to do was rat Wally out and things would take care of themselves. But I learned long ago that that's not my style. Not even when it would take the heat off dead friends.

"Sorry, Jill," I said. "You've got all you're getting from me."

"Because that's all you've got, or that's all you'll spill?"

"From where I sit, it doesn't matter."

"From where I sit, it does."

I laughed rather meanly. "Do what you have to do, Ms. Coppelia."

"You can be sure that I will, Mr. Tanner. The next hand you see may be carrying a subpoena."

She hung up in a huff. After I'd resisted an urge to call back and apologize, I got in my car and drove back up to Haciendas.

It was early for my meeting with Carlos, but bars are good places to hang out, especially in hot valley towns that have a lot of thirsty people in them, especially when you're getting the sense that the town is hiding a whole lot of secrets and that most of them have to do with a man named Gus Gelbride.

The ceiling of the Cantina hung so low I could touch it without standing on tiptoe. The floor was a series of rough-hewn planks that had been worn smooth by everything from line dancers to dead drunks and had absorbed spills ranging from beer to blood for at least forty years—it was so greasy from the leavings of its past it felt as if I were walking on ice. The dancers must have loved it.

The bar ran along the far wall, a simple ledge of polished cedar lit mostly by neon beer signs that hung above the booze on the back of the bar. The lighting made the bartender look more ghoulish than human, which didn't necessarily mean it made him look worse than he looked in the sunlight. The rest of the place was booths and tables and a wall of video games that emitted noises suitable for alien spacecraft, which was fitting since the clientele was straight out of the bar scene in *Star Wars.*

The guys at the bar were regulars, three Anglos and two Latinos drinking slow and steady and sweating it out the same way. Their eyes seemed to float on plates of buttermilk; their hands quaked like aspen as they raised the whiskey to their lips; their elbows were propped on the bar in a triangulation that would keep them secure on their stools. The whole time I was there, not one of them uttered a word or moved a muscle that didn't have to do with alcoholic intake.

The only other customers were three young women giggling at a corner table and an elderly couple holding hands across a booth. The young women were clearly talking about men. The grave intensity of the couple's engagement sparked the hunch that one of them had just learned he or she was dying.

I sat in a booth and waited to be served. Five minutes later, I was still waiting. I looked at the bartender until he looked at me. "Sherry don't come on till five," he explained over the tune in the jukebox, which was sung by Dwight Yoakam and involved a white

Cadillac. The scars on the bartender's face were from burns or the acids of acne. In the haze off the neon behind him, they looked like active arachnids.

I walked to the end of the bar and waited till he wandered my way. "Beer," I said. "In a bottle."

"Bud or Miller?"

"Miller."

He went to the cooler then slid one my way. I beckoned for him to come closer. "I'm meeting a guy named Carlos Reyna in a few minutes," I said.

"Yeah?" His eyes narrowed. "You union?"

"What if I am?"

He hooked his thumbs in the knotted towel that made do as his apron. A tattooed hula dancer gyrated near his bicep, decapitated by the hem of his T-shirt. "You're union, you leave," he said righteously. "I don't let politics come through that door. Especially not union politics."

"What's wrong with union politics?"

"Trying to destroy the Gelbrides, aren't they? Which means they're trying to destroy the town. Put us all out of business if they do and there ain't no kind of politics worth that." His wave encompassed everyone within a radius of a dozen miles.

"I'm not union," I told him.

"I better never hear otherwise."

"You won't. Can I buy you a drink?"

He shook his head. "Never touch it."

"Wise move. What kind of kid is Carlos?"

The bartender shrugged. "He's okay. Trying to make a buck like the rest of us."

"But not with the union."

"Naw, Carlos goes it alone. Admire the bastard for it, truth be known, even though the sad fact is he'll never make a dime."

"Why not?"

"The Gelbrides won't let him get far enough ahead to do anything but work for shares to pay off his debt. That way they can take him to court any time they have an inkling and slap a lien on everything he owns. It's the way they work; it's why Gus is still king of the valley."

"The Gelbrides are really that powerful?"

He nodded. "Maybe not statewide, but they're the cocks of the walk around these parts. Hell, they even got a deed of trust on *this* place. Which means I ought to be keeping my mouth shut." Despite his words, his expression didn't seem to encompass intimidation.

"If the Gelbrides keep everyone so far down, why wouldn't the union be a good idea?"

"Because any time the union takes over, the owner plows under the fields. Happened down in Oxnard and Santa Maria a few years back, and over in the Pajaro last season when the Milton place got certified. Will happen up here if they win."

"You're saying the Gelbrides will shut down their farming operation just to keep out the union?"

"That's exactly what I'm saying. Got developers lined up from here to Denver wanting to move into the place. Retirement communities is what they want to put in down here. Ever seen one of them? Might as well be buried alive."

"So a guy like Carlos has no chance to make it."

"No one in Haciendas can make it unless his name is Gelbride." His grin turned evil. "They've got it covered on both ends—Gus Gelbride is God and his son is the devil himself." With that he walked off, leaving me with images out of myth and hellfire.

Time drifted by, fuzzy and indistinct, the way it does in bars. People ducked in for a quick beer, then ducked out on other errands. The regulars stayed put, their intake as measured as an intravenous drip. I felt slightly drugged myself—the next time the door opened I didn't turn to see who it was.

She sat three stools down, wordless and impatient and intense. The bartender sidled her way in a hurry. "The usual, Larry," she said as he wiped a beer glass with an off-white towel and waited to speak until spoken to.

"Coming up."

Larry bent below the bar, found a thick tumbler that looked to be Waterford crystal, filled it with Absolut vodka and added a lemon twist, then put it in front of the woman. The only thanks she gave him was a deep drink of clear liquid, followed by a lick of her lips that on anyone else might have been suggestive but on her was just another letter in the No Trespassing sign.

She was dark-haired and dark-eyed and large but not fat, a big woman with a big thirst and maybe a big problem with booze. Her clothes were expensive—black linen slacks and gold silk blouse and jewels every place that would hold them—and she was clearly someone special—even the regulars seemed spry in her presence and the bartender was alert to her whims. She glanced my way once, with a look that advised me to stay put and let her drink, then returned her gaze to whatever was fascinating about the row of liquor bottles lined up like lollipops behind the bar.

She was the kind of woman who's intimidating to look at and even more so when she opens her mouth. It didn't make me timid but it did make me careful. "You must be Missy Gelbride," I said the next time Larry had business down-bar.

She rotated twenty degrees my way. "And you must be nobody."

"True, but I'm also a friend of Rita Lombardi's."

"Who?"

"Rita Lombardi."

"The dead girl."

"Right."

She shrugged. "Too bad, but she shouldn't have been walking around town all alone at that hour."

"Is that what she was doing?"

She gave me thirty more degrees of her presence. "How else would she end up at the high school?"

"I can think of several ways."

She shrugged with unconcern. "You get the prize for most creative. Larry, give the man some more of his poison."

I thanked her for the gesture. "I've been wondering if anyone in the Gelbride family was upset with Rita for any reason."

She took another healthy gulp of vodka. "Upset? Why would we be upset?"

"Because she was trying to improve the working conditions of your farmworkers."

Her laugh was cynical and cruel. "If we got upset at liberal crap like that, we'd never draw a peaceful breath." She knocked back the last of her drink. "Next time you see me in a place like this, remember I'm not there for a sermon."

She swooped out of the bar without paying for her drink, taking every eye in the place with her as far as the door, provoking an elaborate shrug from the bartender when she was safely gone.

Carlos Reyna came in when I was on my third beer. By then the Cantina had nearly filled with people off work, diluting the aches and pains of the day with the help of distilled spirits. There were men in suits and men in Levi's so filthy they could have come out of a coal mine. There were women of culture and women who could have been whores. There were three cocktail waitresses on duty and they needed two more. The music was country and twang; the smells were of fajitas and fries.

Carlos looked as if he'd picked a load of berries himself—his pants were dusty, his hands were stained red to his wrists, his straw hat was soaked with sweat, his skin was so hot it steamed in the cool of the air conditioning. But the smolder in his eyes was from something far more complex than weather.

"You look like someone who just lost his dog," I said.

"One of my families didn't come in today. I had to do their job."

"Does that happen often?"

"With Homero Vargas? Never."

"Can you give him a call?"

Carlos laughed. "Homero hasn't owned a phone in his life."

"I thought your workers made decent money."

"Some of them do, sometimes. But last year the rains came late and sliced open the fruit and the molds set in and ruined the berries. Last year no one made money, not even the Gelbrides."

"Would the union have made a difference?"

He wrinkled his lips. "Rita thought so. But the union can't change the weather."

"Did Rita work for the union?"

His voice firmed to match his jawline. "Rita worked for me."

"Could her death have anything to do with union activity?"

"I don't see how. She wasn't in the union and she didn't organize for them and no one thought otherwise."

"But she sympathized."

"She thought the union was the only force powerful enough to make owners like the Gelbrides change their ways. But even when Cesar was alive, the Gelbrides didn't change, except they had to put out toilets and keep kids out of the fields during school. So now they put the toilets out but they don't put shit paper in them. Like I said, nothing changed."

I shifted direction. "I was wondering how you felt about Rita's new look?"

Carlos frowned. "How do you mean?"

"I thought maybe you were worried you might lose her now that she was more attractive."

The implication made him angry. "She wore my ring. She said she was happy, happier than she had ever been." He frowned. "Why? Did she say something different to you?"

I shook my head. "Not at all. She was as eager to get married as she was to dance the night away on her new legs." I smiled at the image. "Did she get the job done? With the dancing, I mean?"

He shook his head. "She was waiting for you."

"I'm sorry." I let Carlos finish his beer then bought him another. "Did Rita seem worried about anything when she got back from the hospital?" I asked.

Carlos shook his head. "What can I say? She could walk without crutches for the first time in her life and she was going to be married. She kept singing stupid little songs all the time."

The image of Rita singing and laughing was as concrete in my mind as the barflies across the room. "Was there anything different at all in her life, that you know of?"

"Not yet, there wasn't."

I perked up. "What do you mean, 'not yet'?"

Carlos lowered his voice until it was just audible above the languid laments from the jukebox. "She said she was going to make big things happen."

"Happen where?"

"In the fields. She said things were going to be different real soon."

"Different for whom?"

"For the workers. And for me."

"How was that going to happen?"

Carlos shook his head. "I don't know. I guess she was going to push harder for the union. I guess she still thought that would matter."

His persistent pessimism was the only flaw I'd seen in Carlos's armor. It occurred to me that Rita might have gotten tired of the gloom and decided to look for someone with a more upbeat view of his life.

I was trying to decide how to get to the truth of their relationship when Carlos looked at his watch. "I have to find Homero. He may be sick. He may need help."

"Where is he?"

Carlos pointed west. "Twenty minutes from here. Up in the hills."

He got up and started to leave. "Let me come with you," I said quickly. "If he's hurt, you might need help getting him to a hospital."

"Okay," he said. "But when you see where we're going, remember it was Rita's idea, not mine."

CHAPTER NINE

We left the bar and climbed into Carlos's pickup, a dilapidated Ford long bed that had once been dark green but had been sun-bleached to the color of dirt. The bed was full of farming equipment, everything from rakes and hoes to white fiber dust masks and sets of muddy rain gear. Two of the devices looked like small wheelbarrows and another looked like a bomb but was probably a spray canister of pesticide or something similarly toxic. Several lengths of white plastic pipe were wound up next to a roll of plastic sheeting that had the sheen of a space suit. Several pairs of rubber boots covered in mud baked to the density of granite gave the impression that a war had recently been fought and lost somewhere in the vicinity.

Carlos ground the truck into gear and headed west out of town. A few blocks later we lurched to a stop. "I think I know what he needs," he said, and jumped out of the truck and trotted into a small market. A moment later he was back, toting a small white sack.

"Kaopectate," he said. "They get so hungry they eat green berries. Then they get sick. That plus the chemicals," he added ominously.

"What sorts of chemicals?"

"Pesticides, fungicides, herbicides—the fruit has lots of enemies. The only way to make money is to kill them quick."

"Is that why the women are wearing masks out there?"

Carlos's face closed like a fist. "They aren't masks, they are scarves. To protect from the dust. They have to be careful, is all," he said, and drummed his fingers on the steering wheel, impatient with me and my questions. A good man in a tough position, where the best path for himself and for his workers was seldom a clearly marked trail.

We left the town. For as far as the eye could see, the highway split flat fields of produce or ground that had already been picked and plowed and prepared for the next crop. Some of the fields were simply squares of flat soil; others were entirely covered with shimmering translucent plastic that looked like a lake of mercury. I asked Carlos what the plastic was for.

"The fields are replanted each year. When the old plants are ripped out, the soil is tilled, the beds are raised and shaped, then the field is covered with plastic and the soil is injected with methyl bromide and oxydemeton to kill the little ones: nematodes, cyclospora, mottle virus, verticillium wilt, xanthosis—plus pesticides for aphids and eelworms and spider mites. When the microbes and the pests are gone in about ten days, we take up the plastic and install drip irrigation pipe under the soil. Then we put down more plastic and plant the seedlings right through the plastic ribbons and begin to tend the crop."

"Why the second plastic?"

"It keeps the soil warm and moist—the best growing conditions for berries. And keeps out weeds and pests. We plant twice a year, in August and November."

"A lot of work," I said.

"And a lot of money. The average cost per acre is close to twenty-five thousand dollars."

I whistled. "How'd you learn so much about strawberries, Carlos?"

He laughed. "Experience. My parents were *braceros*. I worked in the fields when I was six. Plus I went to the Hartnell ag program for two years."

"Were you born in Mexico?"

"In the state of Jalisco. We moved to the States when I was ten, for the whole family to work in the *campo*. We lived in La Posada, the labor camp near the highway."

"You got a good education somewhere."

"My parents began as *braceros* then went over to Driscoll a few years later. They earned enough to buy a home in Pajaro and put us in school in Watsonville. I graduated from high school in 1987. My parents died the next year. Cancer. Both of them."

"I'm sorry."

"There are not many happy endings out here," he said, and turned off the highway onto a winding dirt road that took us toward the Santa Lucias along dry creekbeds and gentle hillocks. The truck bounced and bumped and assaulted its springs. Carlos's eyes blazed as bright as the sun that was starting to sink beneath the horizon ahead of us. If the truck had an air conditioner, it had surrendered in the last war. I wanted him to talk some more about Rita, so I asked him if he missed her.

"Like I would miss my eyes," he said. "She was so alive, so confident. Rita thought anything was possible if you set your mind to it. I need that," he added. "This business can make you loco."

"How?"

"The union says it's servitude. They say guys like Homero Vargas are slaves and I'm an overseer and the *patróns* like Gus Gelbride are the slave masters. I don't like that idea, but in some ways it is true."

"Do you use illegals in your fields?"

"You have to have illegals this time of year if you want the fruit picked in time. On my farm, that takes about sixty good workers. So in July and October I take who I can get." He laughed wryly. "Once in a while college kids come down from Stanford or Berkeley to work. Solidarity with the working class and all that; earn big money for school." He chuckled again. "They never last a day.

Bending over, sorting and packing the fruit, working ten hours in the sun, breathing the dust—they look at us like we're crazy to do this when they climb in their fancy cars and go back to the pretty campus. And maybe we are," he added after a minute.

"But the workers work for you, not Gus Gelbride."

"Right. I'm an independent grower." Each time he said it I was impressed by the gravity with which he pronounced his profession. I wish I still felt that way about mine.

"Whose idea was that? To have you employ the workers and not the Gelbrides?"

"It's what it says in the contract."

"What contract?"

"The one Gus's lawyer invented. It's based on the system they used over in Watsonville for a long time, only after a court decision in a case against the Driscolls, Gus's lawyer made changes. The purpose is to make men like me independent contractors, not employees. That way it is me, not them, who has to provide worker benefits." Carlos shook his head. "There is a twenty-page document we have to sign. Most of the growers can barely read. But they sign it anyway."

"What's the lawyer's name?"

"Grayson Noland."

"Where's his office?"

"Salinas, I think. I have never been there. They send someone out with the paper for me to sign and that's all I know."

"How much do your piece workers make?"

"I pay twelve cents a pint. That's two cents more than most, though the union is trying for fifteen. If they are fast and work hard, they can earn fifteen thousand a year. My regular workers earn three dollars an hour plus a bonus for picking. The ones who have homes and families in the area and stay with me the whole season can make thirty thousand a year."

"In a good year."

"Yeah. Not like last year."

"Rita told me you have a big debt to the Gelbrides. Because of the rains."

"Yeah. Plus costs keep rising."

"How does that happen, exactly?"

"I borrow money from the Gelbrides for the chemicals, for irrigation pipe, for plastic, for fertilizer, and for the new plants."

"How much do you have to borrow?"

"Two hundred thousand, sometimes."

"That's a lot of money."

"In a good year I pay it back from my share of the sale of the berries, no problem. But if it rains like last year, or freezes too late or too early, then I always owe more than I make."

"Seems like the risk of bad weather ought to be on the Gelbrides, not on you."

"It used to be that way, but not now. Not with the new contract."

"Why do you borrow from the Gelbrides and not from the bank?"

"The contract says I must."

"How much interest do you pay?"

"Eighteen percent."

I swore and shook my head. "No wonder you're in debt."

"That's what Rita said," Carlos murmured as he wrenched the truck around an abandoned hay barn. "But she said that wasn't going to happen anymore. That from now on it would be fair."

"Sounds like whatever she had planned wouldn't make the Gelbrides very happy."

"No one can hurt the Gelbrides," he said. "Not even Rita."

We drove into the hills, the dry grass a perpetual fire hazard to our flanks, the live oaks seeming to scream out for water even though they'd survived without it for scores of arid summers. I was soaked head to toe but Carlos seemed to stay cool even though he wrestled with the truck as if it were an alligator lunging up out of a Florida swamp. Just the thought of the swamp cooled me down a little.

"Rita said you want your own farm," I said after a while.

"Yes."

"How long do you think it will take?"

"I used to think ten years. That was my plan. To pay off the Gelbrides, work for Driscoll for a while, then have enough to buy fifteen or twenty acres."

"Who's this Driscoll you keep mentioning?"

"Driscoll Strawberry Associates, the biggest strawberry cooperative in California. If I work for Driscoll I can save maybe thirty thousand a year. I can live on five thousand easy."

"Do you think they'll hire you?"

He nodded. "Unless I get into trouble with Gus."

"That's why you stay away from the union people."

"That's one of the reasons," he said. "I just wish I knew what Rita was going to do," he added.

"How do you mean?"

"When she came back from the hospital, she said she'd learned something that would help us. She said they couldn't stop me from becoming an owner now. She even said the Gelbrides would cancel my debt."

"Why would they do that?"

"I don't know. But she was so certain, I began to believe her. I became excited. And impatient. It is not good for a Latino to be impatient," he added dolefully. "It is not our nature to want more than we have."

"What kind of information was she talking about?"

"I don't know. When I asked, she said I didn't have to do anything but wait. And then she died," he concluded mournfully, in as tactful a description of her fate as I could conjure.

A mile or so later we turned off the dirt road and headed cross country, down a steep saddle, then up a rocky draw. My teeth banged together like a Krupa rim shot; the previous portion of the ride seemed silky smooth by comparison.

"What kind of housing is way out here?" I asked.

"It isn't a house," Carlos said cryptically.

He pulled to a stop two hundred yards later, next to an abandoned Pontiac of early seventies vintage with a tire flat and the hood up. We got out and hiked for a half mile, up a crusty hillside and around a slick rock outcropping, until we came to a stop in front of a thin blue blanket that had been tacked to the side of the hill.

"Homero!" Carlos called loudly.

A moment later the blanket was drawn aside and a woman appeared from behind it. She looked to be forty but was probably much less. The baby in her arms was naked. Her dress was thin and shapeless, but flattering to her opulent figure. When she saw Carlos, her smile was as wide as the madonna's.

"*Ola*, Maria," Carlos said.

"*Buenos dias*, Señor Carlos. We were hoping you would come. Homero is sick and the car will not start. He is too sick to walk to town," she added, to make clear all the options were covered.

"Let me see him," Carlos said, then gestured toward me. "This is my friend. He came to help."

"*Buenos dias, señor*. Welcome to our home." She held back the blanket and we entered the small cave that seemed to serve as a residence for the woman and her family.

The sole interior light seeped from the mantles of a battered Coleman lamp, casting shadows all around, yet somehow making the place feel cozy. The floor was dirt, the walls and roof were lined with black plastic sheeting, the furnishings were little more than produce boxes and old mattresses. Most amazingly of all, the temperature was surprisingly cool.

There were four more children inside the cave, ranging from about three to about fifteen. The oldest, a barefoot young girl dressed in cut-off Levi's and a Pebble Beach T-shirt, was so impossibly lovely I couldn't stop looking at her. She was a child, I suppose, but I wasn't regarding her as such and she wasn't, either. Our eyes met, then hers slid away. It made me feel guilty, but not enough.

My look lingered so long, Carlos noticed. "Consuelo is the rea-son they live here," he whispered when he saw my fixation. "Rita thought it would be best."

I started to ask why, but from the back of the cave came a low groan and an agonized prayer for deliverance. Carlos rushed to the source of the suffering and knelt next to a man who was lying on a thin mattress, clutching his belly and moaning and writhing in pain.

"Homero," Carlos said. "It's Carlos Reyna."

Homero opened his eyes. "Señor Carlos. We prayed you would come."

"What's wrong?"

"My belly."

"The tourista?"

"No. A pain. Here." He pressed his hand over his lower torso. As Carlos bent to minister to him, I saw a photograph tacked to the wall with a nail. Even in the dim light of the cave I could see it was the same snapshot of Rita that Carlos had on his shirt that morning. The only other icons in the cave were a statue of Christ on the cross and pictures of Jerry Brown and Cesar Chavez hung on nails on the opposite wall.

Homero groaned again. Carlos looked back at me.

"Could be appendicitis," I said.

"You sure?" Carlos asked.

"Pretty sure. He needs to get to a hospital."

"We have no money for doctors," the woman began.

"I know someone at the clinic in Salinas," Carlos said. "She will help you." He turned to the wife. "I'll take Homero with me. You and the children stay here. I'll come back when he's been taken care of." He held up a hand to her protest. "We can't all go; there's not room in the cab of the truck and it isn't safe to ride in the back. Mr. Tanner can drive while I help Homero with the pain."

"We should leave now," I said, looking at the slant of light off the sweaty sauce that bathed Homero's contorted face. The fever danced as brightly as brush fire in his eyes, even in the gloom of the cave.

We carried Homero to the truck and wedged him in the cab. Carlos cradled him in his arms as I slipped behind the wheel and started the engine. At our back, Maria sobbed softly but the kids were silent and stoic.

Without thinking, I gave one last glance at the oldest girl, Consuelo. When she sensed my stare, she returned my look with an expression that could be interpreted as saying that if anything bad happened to her father, she would hunt me down and kill me.

The trip down the mountain was excruciating. Homero moaned with every bump. Carlos urged me to drive faster. There was so much play in the steering wheel I could barely keep us on the road even when I could find it. It seemed to take a day to reach the town, but it took only forty minutes.

We entered Salinas by a back road, drove through a neighborhood of small bungalows occupied by persons who seemed exclusively Latino and excessively devoted to cars, and pulled to a stop in front of a small white building with LA CLINICA DE SALUD DEL VALLE DE SALINAS painted above the door. It was a handsome new structure on North Sanborn Road, decorated in blue pastels and no doubt financed in part with federal monies that weren't fully budgeted anymore.

Carlos helped Homero through the front door, then I parked the truck. When I returned to the lobby there was no one in sight, not even at the reception desk in the center of the room. A stranger in a strange land, indeed.

A few minutes later, a nurse came through a side door. She was brusque to the point of insult. "Are you Señor Tanner?"

"Yes."

"Mr. Reyna said for you to wait here for him."

"Fine. Is the man with the appendix okay?"

"They are not okay," she said bitterly. "None of them are okay. But he is alive. For now."

She disappeared the way she'd come. A receptionist came in and nodded in my direction, then began talking on the phone in Spanish. Behind her were row upon row of medical files, a history of illness that for some reason seemed both universal and inevitable.

Ten minutes later, Carlos returned. "You were right about Homero—it is appendicitis. They are taking him to the hospital for surgery. I should go back to the cave for Maria. I'll drop you in Haciendas on the way."

"You're a good man, Mr. Reyna," I said.

"A thousand good men would not be enough for one like Homero," he answered bitterly. I led Carlos to his battered truck. Both of us stayed silent as he drove me back to the bar.

CHAPTER TEN

Carlos dropped me in front of the Cantina, then wheeled his truck toward the glowing horizon in the west, where Maria Vargas waited within her cave for news of her husband's health. Thanks to Carlos and his friend at the clinic, the news would not be as bad as it might have been. But that was little solace, at least not for me.

The music from the Cantina was gay and lively, almost manically so, as though to make light of the data I'd acquired during the day. Rita and Carlos should have been in there dancing, holding hands across the table, laughing with their friends, basking in the glow of young love, dreaming of a future full of hope and happiness. Rita should not have been dead and Carlos should not have had to spend the day prodding a social system to provide minimal medical treatment for a person who came to this country to work incredibly hard at an impossible job under conditions that most of America cannot imagine exist in this day and age. And the deepest sorrow is not that we can't imagine it, it is that we no longer try.

I leaned against the car and tried to decide what to do. My gut hurt from bouncing down the mountain in Carlos's truck, my head hurt from the assault of the sun, and my spirit ached from the sense that things were happening in these farmlands that I should do something to stop. The exploitations seemed akin to the

Jim Crow era in the South, where one class of people was considered less than human by another class and thus beyond the reach of both the law and the largesse of the majority. It was unhealthy then and is unhealthy now, making us less honorable than we should be as a people, making us hardened against any ethic that teaches us to act to the contrary, in order to avoid feeling ashamed of what we have done.

I wanted to go back to Salinas and drink my way out of my depression but I couldn't justify the indulgence because I hadn't made any progress toward what I'd come to Haciendas to do. I'd learned a lot about Carlos Reyna during the course of the day, but not that much more about Rita Lombardi, except that she seemed to have acquired some magic powers up in the hospital that were going to make big changes out in the field. Other than a new pair of legs, I had no idea what that might be.

I flipped open my notebook and went over my notes. The first name that jumped out at me was Scott Thorndike, Rita's high school English teacher, the man who felt she had talent as a writer. I got out of the car and went into the Cantina and found a local phone book, but there wasn't a listing under that name. When the bartender saw the scowl on my face, he asked if he could help me.

"I'm looking for a man named Thorndike," I yelled over the noise of the bar.

"The teach?"

I nodded.

He pointed left. "Above the laundromat around the corner."

I leaned closer, so he was the only one who could hear me. "Do you know him?"

He nodded. "Comes in for a beer after work some days. Sits in a booth and writes in a notebook. Women buy him drinks; far as I know, it doesn't get them much except 'thank you.' "

"How old is he?"

"Thirty-five, give or take."

"He have a steady girl?"

The bartender shrugged. "Not that he ever brought here. Course that doesn't mean there isn't one."

"Anything going on between him and Rita Lombardi?"

He shook his head. "Rita's Carlos's girl. Or was," he amended soberly. "Rumor has it Thorndike and Missy Gelbride get together Monday nights over in Carmel. Meet at the bar in the Pine Cone Inn, is what I hear, then go off to make out in some motel. But gossip is all it is."

A waitress called his name and he looked to his right. "They're backing up on me," he said, and went down to mix drinks. When I could see a path to the door through the crowd, I went outside and shivered. The fog had rolled in and the temperature had dropped thirty degrees. I went to the car for a jacket, then walked around the corner to the laundromat.

It was full, with both singles and with families making a ceremony out of doing the weekly wash, most of them Latino but not all. Several families huddled around cars in the parking lot, eating fast-food meals while waiting for the wash to dry. Others sat inside, the heat of the dryers an antidote to the foggy cool of the evening, reading or watching the TV that the management had placed high in the far corner of the room. Someone had a radio tuned to a Spanish language station. Someone else had a baby who was crying. And beyond it all, a steady stream of cars crammed full of teenagers swaggered through the city streets. Chopped low and lightly muffled, scraping along the pavement as their occupants slumped in their seats and scoped out the action, the cars were the only menacing elements I'd seen in Haciendas, other than the barbed wire fences around the cooling sheds east of town and the white Dodge pickup I'd seen lurking near Mrs. Lombardi's house when I first got there.

A door to the left of the laundromat led to the apartments upstairs. I expected it to be locked, but when it wasn't, I shoved my way into the stuffy foyer, climbed a steep set of charmless stairs, and knocked at the first door I came to.

The man who answered was tall and exceedingly slim, with clear blue eyes separated by an aquiline nose that suggested a hatchet had been buried in his forehead. His cheekbones were high and prominent, pink ledges below his azure eyes. The cheeks themselves were recessed as though scooped out with a spoon; the chin was sharp and thrusting. His clothes—a rumpled chambray work shirt and faded Levi's with tears at the knees—hung on him the way they would hang on a nail. His belt was cinched to the last hole; his shoes were huaraches that curled under his heels at the back.

He looked at me over a pair of wire-rimmed eyeglasses that seemed to magnify his bloodshot eyes. "Yes?"

"Are you Mr. Thorndike?"

"Yes."

"My name is Tanner. I understand you knew Rita Lombardi."

"Yes, but what does that—?"

"I'd like to talk to you about her for a few minutes, if you don't mind."

He frowned in deep vertical divides that slit his features like the scars of a knife fight. "Are you the police?"

"No. Just a friend."

"Then why are you—"

"I'm also a private detective."

"So this is a business call?"

I waited till I had claim on his eyes. "I spent three weeks with Rita in the hospital. If you knew her at all, you know it's a lot more than that."

He nodded in agreement, then looked at his watch. "I guess you can come in. I'm supposed to meet someone at nine, but since it's Rita . . ." He shrugged and stepped back and I joined him in his apartment.

It was as much a library as a home, with books piled on and around every surface—books squeezed into brick and board shelves, books stacked on the hardwood floors, books tossed atop the waist-high refrigerator, books abandoned on the unmade bed.

Next to the bed was an upholstered armchair worn to the nap, a green-shaded banker's lamp that lit both the desk and the chair, a metal trunk that served as both coffee table and footstool, and a file cabinet that looked to have been dropped off a truck and sold for a substantial discount. A spiral notebook lay open on the desktop, its pages blackish with handwriting courtesy of the golden fountain pen that lay atop it. Beside the notebook, a computer that seemed jealous of its venerable neighbor was animated by a screen saver starring the Simpsons.

The kitchen was barely that: the table folded out from the wall, the stove had only two burners, and the basin seemed attached to the wall as an afterthought. The bathroom was presumably beyond the door by the fridge, but that may have been the clothes closet with the toilet down the hall. In sum, it was a scholar's refuge, a monastic's cell, an ascetic's bed-sitter, except the prints on the wall were geometric abstracts by Still and Diebenkorn and Rothko and the books I could see were mostly modern novels.

Thorndike motioned for me to sit on the overstuffed chair, then took the typing stool for himself. His look was open and earnest or a good imitation of such traits.

"If you were told I know something about Rita's death, I'm afraid they misspoke," he began. "It was a tragic event, of course; I still haven't absorbed it. And so brutal. I keep thinking of the assault on the *Pietà* some years back, so senseless and so incongruous. But I know nothing about Rita except what I read in the papers or hear at the bar."

"What do they say at the bar?"

"They think it was about sex."

"Committed by whom?"

"Anyone from Randy Gelbride to Carlos Reyna to a gang rape by field workers." He shook his head. "I'm sure when I'm not present, I make the list of suspects as well."

"Do you give the stories any credence?"

"None whatsoever."

"Would you say Rita was sexually promiscuous?"

"Of course not."

"You're certain?"

His jaw firmed. "Absolutely."

"It sounds like you knew her quite well."

His eyes found the window, then glazed with reminiscence. "She was my student when she was in high school. Sophomore English and Creative Writing senior year."

"What kind of student was she?"

He looked back at me. "She was the best writer I ever had. Also the best person."

"So you held her in high esteem."

"The highest."

"Did it go beyond that?"

"How do you mean?"

"In the years since her high school days, did you and Rita become romantically involved?"

"Of course not. For one thing, she was crip—" He reddened and snipped off the word, as though he was about to utter blasphemy.

"You were saying she was crippled," I reminded when he didn't go on.

"Yes." He drummed his fingers on the desk, as fast as a Gatling gun. "It's shameful, isn't it, that I would let a superficial blemish override all her other qualities, but I . . ." He shrugged to let me complete the rationalization for him.

"Maybe it was an easy out," I said.

"How do you mean?"

"Lots of teachers have gotten into lots of trouble sleeping with their students. Maybe her physical abnormalities gave your sub-conscious a way to keep that from happening."

I'd offered him a life raft and he took it. "I like to think I would have drawn that line anyway, but yes. That made it easier."

"When did you see her last, Mr. Thorndike?"

He thought it over. "Two days before she died, I think. She came by to show me her new look. She was ecstatic, needless to say. We had a glass of wine to celebrate."

"Did she say anything at all to indicate a problem in her life?"

"Quite the contrary, as a mater of fact. She was eager to be back in Haciendas and working even harder for changes in the fields."

"What kind of changes was she talking about?"

"I don't know. We didn't talk business very much, we mostly talked literature."

"Like what?"

"My specialty is modern fiction, with an emphasis on the novelists of central California—Steinbeck, Saroyan, writers like that. Rita had reread *East of Eden* in the hospital and we talked about it quite a while."

"What kind of writing did Rita do herself?"

"Short fiction, mostly. Contemporary themes."

"Such as?"

"Women's issues; social issues; cultural disparities."

"Did she write about the farm workers ever?"

"Sometimes. And sometimes about the Anglos who see the Chicano workers exploited but allow the system to continue delivering its cruelties anyway."

I smiled at the similarity to my own musings only minutes earlier. "How long have you lived in Haciendas, Mr. Thorndike?"

"Ten years."

"It must seem foreign to you. Why do you stay?"

"It is foreign, as you say, but that's why I find it fascinating. A feudal empire, complete with vast land holdings and immense wealth overlaying the attendant oppressions and deprivations and class distinctions, all of it operating out in the open, within the context of a twentieth-century democracy. The logical absurdities and moral inconsistencies are rampant—I hope to write a novel that captures it all one day. It would be a postmodern *Mayor of Casterbridge,* if I can bring it off."

I wished him well and he thanked me. "It would help if you told me exactly what Rita said the last time you saw her," I said.

He frowned with thought. "She said something like, 'Now I have the power to make a difference. Now they must pay attention when I talk.' "

"What kind of power was she talking about?"

"I assumed she was talking about her legs. If it was something else, I don't know what it could be."

"Did Rita write anything recently?" I asked.

He nodded. "She gave me something she'd written after she got back from the hospital, a short story. I haven't had a chance to read it yet—no, that's not true. I haven't been able to bear looking at it yet, the memories it evokes are so painful."

"Do you mind if I borrow it for a while?"

He hesitated. "I don't know if that would be appropriate."

"Rita's dead, Mr. Thorndike. I'm trying to find out who killed her. You'll feel better if you do everything you can think of to help me."

"I guess it doesn't matter, anyway," he murmured, then went to the file cabinet and rummaged through it. When he returned to the desk, he was holding a small sheaf of papers in a manila folder.

He handed them over. "Please give it back when you're finished. If it's as good as her other work, I'm going to submit it to some journals. *Granta*, maybe. Or *Grand Street*."

I promised I'd bring the story back within a few days. Thorndike looked at his watch for the fourth time. "I really do have to go."

"One last thing," I said.

"Yes?"

"Did you ever hear Rita Lombardi discussed by any member of the Gelbride family?"

He looked at me and reddened. "What makes you think I'm in a position to know something like that?"

"Just a piece of gossip I heard."

"Well, I'm not. And even if I was, I haven't."

"I'd appreciate it if you keep your ear peeled."

"I . . ."

"You might even make inquiries. See what kind of reaction you get from the Gelbrides when you mention Rita."

"That is beyond your province, Mr. Tanner. I'll do nothing of the sort."

In the echo of his injured innocence, he walked to the door and waited for me to use it.

CHAPTER ELEVEN

I went back to my car. It had been a thousand degrees inside the Buick at midday, but now it was borderline freezing, courtesy of the surge of fog that had invaded from the west, spilling over the mountaintops like fluffy gray bunting installed to insulate Haciendas against the heat.

The noise skipping out from the Cantina was still a raucous blend of laughter and Latin music but at double the decibels of before. The cars crawling down the streets were still stuffed with kids on missions that would include a lot of macho and a little mayhem before the night was done, but now a black and white police cruiser was parked at the curb in the next block, ready to referee. Somewhere in the distance, a train called out a mournful farewell as it rocked and rolled toward Fresno. Except for the kids, the air was tranquil and inviting. But in any neighborhood in the country these days, kids make life edgy and capricious.

The streets were empty of foot traffic except for a trio of young girls in tight pants with flared bottoms and loose tops cut off just below their breasts, strolling toward a corner market, attracting goofy stares and inelegant propositions from the guys cruising by in the cars. Although the girls feigned disgust at the extravagant attention, they clearly reveled in their newfound seductiveness, arching their backs and swinging their hips just a little more provocatively whenever a low rider slid by. In their semi-innocent, semiwanton aspect, at the exact point of transition from childhood to womanhood, they reminded me of Consuelo Vargas.

I wondered if Consuelo was still in the cave in the hills or if she came to town on Friday nights to join with girls like the trio I was watching to test the reach of her sexuality in a rite of passage as old as the species. I guess I hoped not, because it was a time that got many a girl in a lifetime of trouble before they learned how to evade it, but also because it would have disappointed Rita Lombardi and Rita obviously had some special connection to the Vargas family, especially to Consuelo. It had occurred to me that the bond between the women might have something to do with Rita's death, but I still couldn't see the connection. Feeling as old as the species myself, I started the car and drove to Salinas and holed up in my dreary motel.

There was nothing on TV but reruns and a baseball game, which for some reason have come to seem like reruns themselves. I'd bought a book of pulp fiction and a local newspaper on the way into town, but they didn't interest me, either. When I called the office for messages, there was nothing on the line but an electronic insult. As I lay back on the bed I wondered who had reclined there the evening before and what kind of troubles had lain down with them. In the nature of a last resort, I went back to the car and got the envelope Scott Thorndike had given me and returned to the bed to read Rita Lombardi's most recent short fiction.

It was a love story, essentially, structured along the lines of *Romeo and Juliet,* in which a young man and young woman from different and hostile worlds try to find happiness despite the forces that pull them apart. The issue that separated the lovers in Rita's story wasn't family or culture, however, the issue was eyesight.

The girl was blind; the boy was not. In their younger years the boy had acted as her guide and protector and as her mentor at the mall store where they worked, reveling in the role above all others in his life. But midway through the story, the girl's eyesight was restored, through the miracle of corneal transplants. Her disability removed, she became accomplished and assured, enrolling in computer college at night and being promoted as the boy's superior at the store in the mall.

Predictably, the boy traveled in the opposite direction, losing his job, falling into debt, taking to drink and to petulance, until the contrasts were so formidable they reached the point of anger and then of breakup. At the lowest point, the girl's newly acquired power of eyesight enabled her to save the boy from certain death by shoving him out of the way of a speeding car that was running a red light. The mix of melodrama and serendipity broke the psychic stalemate, freeing the boy to admire the girl's achievements and see her love for what it was. According to the author, they lived happily ever after.

The story was derivative and simplistic but the prose was lyrical and expressive; the insights sharp and telling; the characterization crisp and vivid—Rita's talents as a writer were obvious to me and had been even more so to her teacher. But I was more interested in the story line than in the symbolism or the syntax.

The parallels to Rita's own disabilities and to the repairs she'd experienced in the hospital were obvious. The implication that Carlos Reyna had been threatened by Rita's newfound physical and social attainments seemed a postmortem finger of suspicion that pointed only his way. Much as I wanted to view Carlos as a good man because of the way he spoke about Rita and the way he treated the Vargas family, perhaps that was merely a cover for the panic he felt when he sensed he was losing his fiancée, if not to another man, then to another way of life. I hadn't even asked Carlos where he was the night Rita was murdered. In the morning I was going to have to remedy the oversight.

I woke in a postcoital sweat, the product of a vaguely remembered romp with a woman who looked enough like Jill Coppelia to make me wish it hadn't been a dream. After washing off that and other residues, I ate a quick breakfast at the ersatz diner down the road, hatched a plot over a Belgian waffle, then spent the rest of the breakfast amassing the courage to pursue it.

Back at the motel, I put in a call to Jill's office, realizing belatedly that no one would be home in the bowels of the government—there's no sense working for peanuts if you've got to work weekends to boot. I cursed the forces of evil that had nipped my plan in the bud and got ready for another day in Haciendas.

Halfway to the car, I remembered the card Jill had given me the last time I saw her, when she'd estimated the origins of the Klee in my office. The front side was nicely engraved with the seal of the county and the title of Assistant District Attorney but on the back was a handwritten number and the word *home* scrawled above it. I smiled and returned to my room.

It took her a long time to answer. When she did, she was puffing and panting and not in the mood to chat.

"Hi," I said. "It's Marsh Tanner."

"Who? Oh. The detective with the art."

Her detachment was enough to deflate me—the plan hatched over the waffle was already close to abandonment. "Sounds like my painting made more of an impression than I did," I grumped like a professional sourpuss.

She laughed. "Your painting is world-class."

"And I'm not."

"Let's just say I haven't had the opportunity to make that assessment."

A sudden crash was followed by a curse, followed by dead silence. "Sorry," she said finally, gasping for air. "The grocery bag fell off the table and I was afraid the wine might have broken. But it's fine. Wine bottles are pretty sturdy, I guess."

"They design them to stand up to falling down drunks."

She laughed easily and happily. The plan was revived, at least temporarily.

"I suppose that's it," she said, then spoke with inflated formality. "Are you calling to convey official information in aid of our investigation of police corruption in this city, Mr. Tanner?"

"No, I'm calling to ask you to dinner."

She gave me time to make it a joke. "Really?"

"Absolutely."

She was flustered and showed it. "I don't . . . I mean I'm not . . . Well, sure. I guess that would be okay. I'm sure it would be nice, in fact. Are we talking tonight?"

"Yes we are. Unless you have plans."

"No, I don't think so. Do you have somewhere specific in mind?"

"I was thinking about Salinas."

"Hmmm. I don't know it, I don't think. Wait. Is it that place in the Outer Mission everyone's talking about?"

The plan was going to take work. "It's not a restaurant, it's a town."

She paused again to sense my seriousness. "*That* Salinas?"

"Yep."

"Why there?"

"Because that's where I am."

"Doing what?"

"Working on a murder case."

"Oh. Right. You told me about that, didn't you? A friend of yours was killed or something."

"Right."

"Is it going to have anything to do with my office, at some point?"

"Not a chance."

She paused to put it together. When she did, she didn't seem to like it. "Let me get this straight. You want me to drive all the way to Salinas for dinner?"

"It's outrageous, I know. Completely out of the question."

"Wouldn't Carmel be more exciting? At least from a culinary standpoint?"

"It would be. Indubitably."

"But you're sticking with Salinas."

"Yep."

"Why?"

"I'm not a Carmel kind of guy. But we could go to Carmel on Sunday. For brunch or something. They eat lots of brunch in Carmel."

"So now it's a weekend, not just dinner."

"If you want it to be."

Her breath sang like a teakettle. "That's kind of an important decision, isn't it? I mean, weekends mean something. At least they used to."

"Still do, probably. But you don't need to decide now. You can play it by ear till after dinner."

"I'm not good at playing by ear; I like to have the sheet music." She hesitated again. "How far is Salinas from here?"

"Hour and a half. Maybe a tad more."

"What time should I be there?"

"Sevenish?"

"What kind of clothes?"

"Comfortable."

"This is strictly social? Nothing about the SFPD or Mr. Sleet?"

"Not a peep."

"I don't know. It sounds sort of . . ."

"Slick. Manipulative. Unfair. Underhanded."

"It's not underhanded," she corrected. "It's totally overhanded as far as I can tell. Which is to your credit, I suppose. And it's not that I—"

With a whiff of success in the air, I tried to make my proposal more palatable. "I don't usually do this kind of thing, Ms. Coppelia. In fact I never have, not with someone I've only known a few days. But I dreamed about you last night so I thought maybe we could . . . you know . . . get to know each other or something."

"You *dreamed* about me?"

"Yes I did."

"That's funny."

"Why funny?"

"Because I dreamed about you, too."

"You're kidding."

"I majored in psychology in college," she said with high seriousness. "I don't kid about dreams."

"It wasn't a nightmare, I hope."

"Quite the contrary."

"Good."

"Me, too. I hope. That you had a nice dream, I mean."

"The nicest," I said.

"Good."

"Though we probably mean different things by nice when it comes to dreams."

"Probably."

"But maybe not."

"No, maybe not." She tried and failed to stifle a giggle. "Oh, what the hell. I'll probably hate myself later, but I think I'll do it."

I strained to keep an adolescent flutter out of my voice. "I could come get you, if you'd rather. It's really not fair to make you drive all the way down—"

"It's all right. I haven't been out of the city in weeks. And you'd have to drive up and back twice if we did it that way. Where should I be at seven?"

I looked at my room, then went to the window and looked down the street. "Take the Market Street exit off 101, then left and left again at the light and drive to the Best Western a block down on the left. I'll be waiting in the lobby."

"Market Street. Best Western. I'll be there."

"So will I," I said, but she'd already hung up.

Five minutes later, I floated out of my motel and walked down the road and made a reservation for two in the Best Western, making sure the room had only a single queen-sized bed. Ten minutes after that I was pulling to a stop in front of Louise Lombardi's bungalow, doing what I should have done the first time, which was to look more closely into the final days in the life of her dead daughter.

CHAPTER TWELVE

This time there were no burly vehicles lurking outside Mrs. Lombardi's bungalow and no friends mourning with her inside the house. There was just a lonely, frightened woman, not wanting me there but not wanting to spend the day alone, either. When she invited me in, it was still a debatable proposition.

"I'm sorry to bother you again, Mrs. Lombardi," I said as she retook her seat on the couch and almost caused it to fold in half. "But I was wondering if I could have a look at Rita's room."

She blinked and frowned and coughed, in rolling ripples of excess flesh. "Her room? Why would you want to do that?"

"To see what might be in there that would tell me what was going on in her life just before she died."

"She was going to be married. That was what was going on. That was all she talked about."

Not to Carlos and her English teacher, I thought but didn't say. "I'm sure it was. But maybe there was something else as well."

"Like what?"

"I don't know. That's why I need to look."

She wasn't enthusiastic and I wasn't either, to be truthful—rummaging around in a dead person's effects is among the least dignified by-products of my profession. On top of that, rummag-

117

ing in Rita's effects reminded me that I had been urged to do the same with Charley's estate once I got back to the city, to pick over his property like a seagull at a landfill, to choose what could be regarded by some as souvenirs but by others as plunder.

She led me down a narrow corridor to a bedroom in the back of the house. It was tiny, maybe twelve feet square, separated from the only other bedroom by a thin wall of studs and sheetrock, making privacy nonexistent. I could imagine Rita living her home life mostly in whispered yearnings over the phone to her friends as her mother pressed an ear against the wall, living vicariously through the murmurs of her only child. I wondered who she listened to now.

"Do you mind if I poke around in here a bit?" I asked as Mrs. Lombardi puffed and panted at my side.

"Do you have to?"

"I think I do."

She sighed like a valve easing pressure off a boiler. "Very well. If you must. But please don't disturb anything."

"I won't."

For some reason, she turned huffy. "The police have already been here, you know. They took several boxes of Rita's things with them, so I don't know what you expect to find."

"The police make mistakes," I said, then looked at my watch in order to shove her off the dime. "If I can get started, I'll be finished in a few minutes."

"Don't you take anything from in there," she instructed adamantly. "Not one thing."

I gave her the promise she was seeking, knowing I wouldn't necessarily keep it, and stepped into the room. Behind me, the sub-flooring creaked like my knees in the morning as Mrs. Lombardi made her way back to her perch in the front room. There are a lot of extremely obese people around these days, most of them women, most of them doing nothing to change the picture except aggravating it. Some people say it's glandular or genetic, but I think it's a symptom of depression, a lack of esteem so fathomless as to foster public self-destruction.

As Mrs. Lombardi's footsteps retreated down the hall, I stepped into her daughter's room and inspected it. It was a child's domain in many ways, with frilly pink pillows and wallpaper with Pooh characters frolicking over it, and a throw rug bearing the image of Snow White. The books were girlish classics—Alcott and Austen and Browning, with Kingsolver and McMillan and Watters thrown in as contemporary spice. The music was lots of Celine Dion and Boyz II Men, the art on the wall was magazine photos of Princess Di and posters from movies like *Roman Holiday* and *Sabrina*—Rita obviously had an affinity for Audrey Hepburn.

Taken together, the accoutrements of Rita's home life seemed aggressively sunny and intensely romantic, as if her physical handicaps had provided more than enough dark clouds so the optional additions should foster the opposite climate. I'd have done the same in her shoes, I imagine, though with David Lodge and Richard Russo and Dan Hicks and Mose Allison and posters of Marilyn Monroe.

I eliminated the periphery first. Nothing in the closet, or the dresser, or the bathroom yielded anything but the trappings of an ascetic existence, with the exception of Rita's wedding dress, white and lacy and beaded and heartbreaking, hung on a padded hanger on the back of the closet door like a vestment of hand-carved ivory. I touched it for a moment, long enough to envision Rita walking down the aisle and Carlos in his tux eager to receive her at the altar. It took an effort to jerk myself back to the reality of the tiny bedroom and its hidden treasures, which at this point meant the desk.

It was piled high with paper and not a sheet of it was anything but adult. There were government reports on pesticide dangers, a bulletin on accounting methods for depreciation in small businesses, communiqués from the farmworkers union about violations of the wages and hours act, and clippings about union protest marches at stockholder meetings of corporations that had agricultural subsidiaries that employed farm labor. One of the drawers contained several snapshots of Rita and Carlos and of Rita and a woman I didn't recognize but guessed was her friend Thelma Powell, stacked and ready to be pasted in a small blue photo album that was in the drawer as well. Other than that, the contents of the desk were mundane.

Various notes to herself were pinned to the corkboard on the wall above the desk—reminders to get the dry cleaning or call the dentist or meet with the priest, presumably about the wedding arrangements, plus a snapshot of Carlos looking as handsome as Valentino in his Sunday suit. The only oddity was a snapshot of Missy Gelbride, current and candid, climbing into a Mercedes convertible parked in downtown Haciendas, right in front of the laundromat, which meant right in front of Scott Thorndike's apartment. Jealousy? Blackmail? Curiosity? Or worship of the princess of the valley in the sense that she worshiped Princess Di and Audrey Hepburn?

Having found nothing helpful in my first pass through the room, I cast about for secret sources—loose floorboards, hollow walls, the bottoms of drawers and the backs of pictures, shoe boxes stuffed in the back of the closet, canisters afloat in the toilet tank. But nothing suggested a lead until I glanced at the closet a third time.

Hanging on a ceramic hook on the front of the door was a backpack. Although it didn't bulge with content, it seemed to fall from the hook in an odd shape, stiff on one side, slack on the other. I took it down and looked inside. The main compartment was empty, but when I felt around the edges there was a hard surface toward the bottom that seemed not part of the original design. When I looked closer, I found a zipper. So I unzipped it.

Some sort of electronic datebook was secreted in the bottom pocket of the pack. Made by Rolodex, it was the size of a trade paperback only thinner, with a hinged top and a battery pack and instructions printed on the inside cover. I turned it on, read the instructions, pressed some tiny buttons, and eventually found what amounted to Rita's appointment calendar, reduced to a digital readout.

I scrolled to the month of August and saw an impressive variety of names listed beside the dates and times of their meetings with Rita. Most of the dates were with Carlos, of course, and most of the rest seemed clearly about business, with people like the departments of Agriculture and Immigration and a trucking line that, like everything else in Haciendas, was owned by the Gelbrides. But in the last week of her life, she had met with at least four people who might have had other agendas.

One of the appointments was with Scott Thorndike, the teacher who wanted Rita to publish her fiction in prestigious magazines, no doubt the meeting Thorndike had already told me about. One was with Grayson Noland, a name I finally remembered as the lawyer who'd drawn the contract for Carlos to grow berries for Gus Gelbride. One was with someone with the initials J.R. And the last was with Mona Upshaw, the nurse who had been on duty at the hospital the night they'd brought Rita in, who had asked me to let Rita's secrets slip quietly into the grave with her.

After a second's consideration of the criminal consequences of disturbing evidence, I put the device in my pocket and headed back to the living room. But it occurred to me as I was leaving that meetings scheduled in the days immediately after her death might be as important as the ones before, so I returned to the bedroom, activated the device again, scrolled forward in time, and looked at the result.

Opposite the date blocks for the remainder of the month were two entries: One was with a woman named Liz Connors, a name I didn't recognize; the other said simply Gelbride—Mother. There was no notation to indicate the subject matter of the first meeting or whether the latter session was with Mrs. Gelbride or with a Gelbride to talk about Mrs. Lombardi.

I slipped the device in my pocket and found Mrs. Lombardi in her usual place, a cup of tea steaming beside her on the occasional table, her eyes roaming as intimate as a caress over the collectibles lining the walls. "I found some names in Rita's calendar I'm not familiar with," I said. "I wonder if you can help me."

She shrugged infinitesimally. "If I can."

"Liz Connors."

She frowned. "I don't know."

"How about someone named J.R.?"

She smiled. "That's Randy Gelbride. When he was in grade school, they all called him that."

"Why?"

"It had to do with that character in *Dallas*. You know, the TV show? Because that's they way he acted, I guess. A big man impatient to take over for his father."

"Do you know why Rita would be meeting with him?"

"No."

"Do you know why Rita would be meeting with Ms. Upshaw the day before she died?"

"Mona?"

I nodded.

"No."

"No idea at all?"

She shook her head. "Unless it was to do with me. Mona is worried about my health. I keep telling her I'm fine, but she worries. She wants me to go up to Stanford for a physical examination."

Mrs. Lombardi looked down at her bulbous torso as if onto a separate being, one in which she took a maternal concern. Causing people to worry seemed to be her proudest accomplishment. My guess was that Rita's meeting with a Gelbride was on the same subject—her mother's well-being.

She was eager to have me on my way. "Where does Ms. Upshaw live?" I asked before she could invite me to leave.

"On Del Rio Road." She told me how to get there. "I'm afraid I need to rest now," she said. "If I don't get my sleep, my blood pressure acts up."

"One last thing and I'll be off."

"Yes?"

"I was wondering about Rita's surgery."

"What about it?"

"I was wondering who paid for it."

Her eyes disappeared like raisins pressed into a mound of white flour. "That's none of your business."

"So it wasn't health insurance."

She struggled to her feet. "Please leave this house. Now. I'm afraid I must insist."

I stayed seated. "There's some indication that Rita was going to meet with one of the Gelbrides a few days after she died, and that the reason for the meeting was you."

"That's crazy. Why would they talk about me?"

"I was hoping you could tell me."

"I know nothing about it," she pouted, both repelled and attracted by the possibility it was true.

"Maybe Rita wanted Gus to pay for some medical work for you. Just like he had done for Rita."

"You don't know what you're talking about," she grumbled.

"I'll find out sooner or later. You might as well tell me now."

"I'll tell you nothing," she said, her voice climbing toward hysteria. "You are no longer welcome in this house. I wish you had never come."

"I'm sorry you feel that way, Mrs. Lombardi."

"And I am sorry for *you*, Mr. Tanner. That you make it your business to pry into private matters, that you intrude where you're not wanted, that you open old wounds and make mothers who have lost their husband and their only child even more unhappy than they are already."

If she had one of her painted plates in her hand, she would have thrown it at me. There was nothing for me to do but apologize once again and leave, taking with me a private plea of guilty to most of the charges she had made about me.

Ten minutes later, I pulled into the parking lot at the headquarters of Gelbride Berry Farms, about a mile east of Haciendas, and parked next to a white Dodge Ram pickup just like the one I'd seen near Mrs. Lombardi's house the morning before. Before I got out, a security guard came out of a gatehouse and approached the car. Behind him, a fence of shiny new razor wire encircled the entire compound, which included the low brick headquarters building, a dusty lot filled with flatbed trucks, Caterpillar tractors with steel tracks instead of rubber tires, stacks of cardboard strawberry flats and lengths of irrigation pipe, and a square stucco building, huge and gray and windowless, that loomed over the rest of the compound like a brewing storm.

The guard tapped on the window. "What can we do for you, mister?"

I rolled it down. The air was still cool from the morning fog, a misty veil that made everything indistinct and out of focus. "My name's Tanner. I'm here to see Mr. Gelbride."

"Would that be Gus or Randy?"

"Gus," I said, then amended it. "Either one."

"Do you have an appointment?"

"Yes, I do."

He raised a clipboard and consulted it. "Don't have you on the sheet."

"Someone must have made a mistake."

He licked his lips and grinned. "If they did, it would be the first time. What's your business?"

I smiled. "Confidential, I'm afraid."

He smiled back. "You from the government, by any chance? Labor? EPA? Immigration? Agriculture? OSHA? Any of them?"

I shook my head.

"You a cop?"

I shook my head again.

"Then it's hard for me to see a reason why I need to let you in here."

124

I looked at his uniform and then at the fence that stretched toward the horizon beyond him, the fence that suggested prison breaks and border crossings. "What are you guys hiding out here, anyway?"

He fidgeted. "How do you mean?"

"All this security. It's like you're running a nuclear installation or a meth lab or something. What's so secret about strawberries? My grandma used to raise them in the backyard."

"We get people coming around to cause trouble."

"What kind of trouble? Labor trouble?"

"That's part of it, but there's lots of it I don't know." He wrinkled his nose and shrugged. "Anyways, I don't make the decisions, I just carry them out. And right now my job is to tell you to move along."

"How can I see Mr. Gelbride?"

"Call for an appointment."

"How likely am I to get one?"

"Not very, unless you got something he wants."

"What does he want?"

The guard smiled. "Peace and quiet, mostly."

I returned his smile. "He's not going to get it till he talks to me about Rita Lombardi."

"That may be, mister, but it's not going to happen today. Now move along."

I turned the key and started the car and began to back out of my space. As I looked in the mirror to make sure I was clear, a man stepped in my path and blocked it. He was tall and powerfully built, with broad shoulders and a thick waist and skin tanned like butterscotch and stretched like cowhide. His smile was more sneer than grin, as if he were wearing a rubber mask that had crinkled and curled in the heat. His straw hat hid everything above his cruel brown eyes.

"What we got here, Mr. Gilstrap?" he asked the security guard.

"Man wants to see you or your daddy."

"What about?"

"Didn't say. Got no appointment, so I told him to move along."

I got out of the car and leaned against the rear fender and smiled at Randy Gelbride. "Actually it was Mr. Gelbride the younger I wanted to see most. J.R., as they used to call him in school."

Gilstrap started to say something else but Randy waved him off. "Is that so?"

"Yep."

"What would you want to see him about?"

"To tell him I'm a private detective from San Francisco looking into the death of Rita Lombardi, and that I'd like to ask him some questions about it."

He nodded his head in mock seriousness and referred to himself in the third person, the way Richard Nixon used to. "What makes you think Gelbride the younger knows anything about that subject whatsoever?"

"Nothing, except he had an appointment to see Rita a few days before she died. Plus, I'll bet he knows something about everything that goes on around here. Plus, he seems to be trying to avoid me."

The man laughed and waved toward the guard and the fence. "You think all this was done to keep out grungy private eyes from the big city?"

"I can't think of any other reason, can you?"

Randy looked at the guard and then at me, then pointed toward the white Dodge truck. "Hop in. I got a few places to go this morning; we can talk while I take care of business." He stuck out a hand. "Randy Gelbride."

I shook it. "Marsh Tanner."

"Climb aboard."

As I did as he asked, I noticed a small handgun strapped to the bench seat just beneath his left leg. It was an exact fit with the mood of the place, and it didn't make me more comfortable.

CHAPTER THIRTEEN

Randy started the truck and roared off down the highway toward the east. The rising sun was still elbowing its way through the fog, creating an ambiguous aspect, half cheerful, half gloomy. My attentions still split between Rita Lombardi and Jill Coppelia, I felt that way myself.

In contrast to Carlos Reyna's rig, this one rode as smooth as a sled, complete with leather seats and air conditioning and cupholders every six inches. After a screech of brakes and a lurch to the left, we abandoned the highway in favor of one dirt road after another, passing slow-moving trucks stacked with everything from boxes of strawberries to crates of broccoli, past row upon row of nursery buildings covered with translucent cloth roofs and designed on the model of Army barracks, furthering the sense that I was in the middle of some kind of absurdist battle in which the munitions were fruits and vegetables, not rifle bullets and mortar rounds.

I kept a lookout for Carlos Reyna and his workers, but it would be a long shot if I spotted him. Most of the fields were shielded from the road by rows of corn stalks and sunflowers, much the way timber companies leave a stand of trees along the roadside to camouflage the clear-cuts being committed beyond the screen. It was an odd sensation, the benign and even salutary sight of such magnificent fertility coupled with the sense of skulduggery fostered by the elaborate security and secrecy. The implication was that something illegal or at least inappropriate was going on in the fields despite the surface serenity, as if the Mafia or the Colombians or the CIA were using American agriculture as a front for criminal enterprises. Since that was probably not the case, it was puzzling why growers like Gus Gelbride chose to foster such suspicions.

I didn't voice my thoughts, but Randy drove as angrily as if I had, wrestling the wheel as though it were an animate adversary, fishtailing down the road as if we were racing off-road in Baja. Although roadside signs repeatedly warned that dust could harm the plants, we were creating a cumulus brown cloud that blotted out most of the world to our rear. Again, the image was of warfare, the aftermath of aerial bombardment, the accompaniment to a mechanized assault.

After five minutes of strife with the roadway, Randy swung onto a narrow dirt levee that rose three feet above the plane of the fields and separated two large plots of strawberry plants. Some twenty yards from the end of the levee he skidded to a stop and got out of the truck. A dozen other vehicles were parked there already, plus the ubiquitous portable toilets towed on a trailer behind a baby blue school bus that had presumably hauled most of the workers to the job.

Halfway into the field, a line of pickers worked a double row of strawberry plants. They were tended by a small truck stacked high with cardboard flats stamped with the Gelbride Berry Farm logo and supervised by a row boss who stood at the head of the row being worked, arms crossed, alert for problems. The only sound came from a portable radio hung from the side of the toilets. The tunes were sung in Spanish and were decidedly upbeat, in contrast with the drudgery they accompanied.

As I followed Randy into the field, I recognized the supervisor who roamed over the area as Carlos Reyna. When he saw Randy he frowned, and when he saw me with him he scowled even deeper, to the point of hostility. He made me feel like a traitor and I didn't like it.

"We got a problem out here, Reyna," Randy was saying as he eyed the row of workers.

Everybody but Carlos was bent over a plant, but Carlos stood tall and proud and just a little arrogant.

"What problem would that be?" he asked Randy, meeting his eye, aping his bearing.

Randy walked to the row of pickers and inspected them one by one, as if they were seasonal crops themselves, coming to the end of their useful life. No one looked up; no one said a word. When he didn't see what he was looking for, he looked back at Carlos. "Where is he? I know he's out here, the fucking greaser."

When Carlos didn't respond, Randy walked down the row of pickers once again, an inspection as totalitarian and demeaning as a Marine boot camp. He hesitated before the last picker in line, started to say something but didn't, and continued walking until he came to the portable toilets.

With a sudden burst of fury, he banged on a blue plastic door. "Come out of there, you brown bastard, or I'll dump it over and you can roll around in tamale shit the rest of the morning." He banged again. "Tuck it and zip it, asshole."

A second later, the door to the toilet opened and a young man stepped out onto the dirt with as much dignity as he could muster, which wasn't a whole lot. He was short and handsome, with quick black eyes and small brown hands and a look on his face that spelled trouble. He wore a red flannel shirt and a hooded gray sweatshirt and a bandanna knotted around his head so that a short black drape fell down the back of his neck.

As he stood facing Randy, he pulled a hat out of his back pocket and put it on over the bandanna. The hat was red with a black eagle on the front. If I remembered my history, it was the symbol of the UFW.

Randy looked him over with contempt verging on odium, then turned toward Carlos. "Hey. Reyna. How long has Morales been working your crew?"

Carlos hesitated, then yelled back. "Just this morning. One of my regulars is in the hospital."

"With what?"

"Appendicitis."

"He blaming it on us?"

Carlos only shrugged.

"Well, Morales is out. Now. I see another one of these union guys out here and you and I are going to square off. Got it, Carlos?"

Carlos only looked at him. "He's a good worker," he muttered finally.

"Worker, hell. He's not here to pick fruit, he's here to stir things up. You keep telling me you aren't taking your crew to the union, Carlos, but this don't look antiunion to me, this looks like you're a fucking sympathizer."

Carlos met his eyes without saying another word. Finally, he looked at the young union man and shook his head. The man tugged his cap lower on his head and walked to the end of the field, watched in awe and trepidation by his fellow workers.

When he got to the raised road he took off his hat and waved it from side to side. "Viva la Raza!" he yelled, and then, "Viva la Huelga!" With that, he climbed into his truck and drove off, the cloud of dust at his back a symbol of his own brand of disdain.

When he was gone, Randy Gelbride looked at Carlos. "I see him in my fields again, I'll kill him. And you, too, if I think you hired him on purpose. Now get these assholes back to work."

Randy stomped back toward the truck, but veered off as he reached the end of the line of pickers. He said something I couldn't hear to the worker at the far end, then cocked his head and waited for an answer.

The worker was a woman, bent over the berries, not working, just hiding. After Randy spoke to her a second time, she straightened up and turned his way, but as far as I could tell she didn't say anything in return.

I hadn't recognized her because she was swaddled in three layers of clothing, but the worker was Consuelo Vargas, eldest daughter of Homero and Maria, her lovely face covered by a red scarf knotted behind her neck like an outlaw's mask, her blooming curves buried beneath her baggy sweater and loose slacks.

Randy was talking, she was listening, but there was nothing between them but tension, sexual on his part, something close to homicidal on hers. Randy asked a final question that went unanswered, then uttered an epithet that caused Consuelo to place her palms over her breasts, as though she feared assault. I started to move toward them, and Carlos did, too, but Randy swore again for effect, then walked back toward his pickup.

Halfway there he turned and yelled toward the truck where the picked fruit was being tallied. "Hey. Gonzalez. I seen lots of cat faces in her box. Dump them out. All of them. Everything she picked this morning. Go on. Do it before I do it for you. We don't ship ugly berries from this farm."

Randy watched with satisfaction as the checker on the truck reviewed his notes, then began dumping boxes of berries onto the dirt. I glanced at Consuelo Vargas. Her hands were over her eyes and she was sobbing. Her mother ran to her side and comforted her. Randy Gelbride climbed back in his pickup and slammed the door.

After a moment's debate, I walked to Carlos's side and asked if he was all right.

He thrust his jaw. "I'm fine."

"How's Homero?"

"He's okay. But he needs rest."

"Is he still in the hospital?"

He nodded. "I take him home tonight."

"To the cave?"

He glanced at Randy's white truck, then nodded.

"Randy is why Rita sent them up in the hills, isn't he?"

He nodded again.

"Has it worked?"

"So far," he said. "No one's told him where she is."

At my back, I heard Randy start his engine and honk. "I was talking to him about Rita," I said by way of explanation. "She had an appointment with him just before she died and I wanted to ask about it. I didn't know what he was going to do when he got here."

"It's all right."

"I'm sorry."

"*Da nada*," Carlos said, then lowered his voice. "He killed her," he whispered. "I know it. When I can prove what he did, I will kill him as well. Slowly. So he suffers."

I started to caution against it, but Carlos turned toward his workers and began to speak to them in Spanish. They straightened to hear his counsel, then bent over the plants once again. I walked back to the white truck and climbed in.

"You know Reyna, it looks like," Randy Gelbride said to me as I slammed the door.

"He was Rita Lombardi's fiancé."

"Yeah. So I heard. I were you, I'd try him out as a suspect."

"Why?"

"I knew Rita from day one. She had a mouth on her but she was smart. Too smart to end up with a beaner, even one as sharp as Reyna. I figure she wised up and dumped him and he couldn't handle it. These guys don't like to lose face, you know? The macho thing, plus they treat their women like shit even when they work their asses off for them."

I doubted Randy was objective on any subject, particularly one encompassing women or Mexicans. He just seemed to be playing the most popular sport in Haciendas, which was accusing others of murder.

"What connection was there between Rita and Gelbride Berry Farms?" I asked.

"What makes you think there was one?"

"Your mother called Mrs. Lombardi to console her over her loss."

Randy shrugged. "Louise used to work for us. From what I heard, she was a shitty employee—fat and lazy. But Mom likes to think the best of people. Lucky for us, she keeps her nose out of the business."

"Do you know anything about what happened to Mrs. Lombardi's husband?"

"Franco? I was just a kid when it happened, but what I heard was he got run down one night. Drunk. Wandered onto the highway. Probably banged by a beaner rattling around in one of those pickups without brakes. They drive them till they rot, then fix them with baling wire and duct tape and drive them another five years. Amazing thing is, they always keep running."

I thought of the snapshot tacked over Rita's desk. "Were Rita and your sister friends?"

"Missy? Shit. The last friend Missy had was our dead dog. I think Sparky killed himself to get away from her." His scorn seemed even more marbled than the version he directed at Morales and the union.

"Does Missy work for the company?"

Randy sneered again. "Thinks she does. But we just ignore her."

"Who's we?"

"Me and the old man."

"Is Grayson Noland active in the business?"

"Noland eats shit," Randy growled a little too intensely to let me believe his next statement. "Me and the old man run the business. No one else."

"Why did Rita meet with you the day before she died?"

He looked at me for the first time, and almost drove us off the road. "Who said she did?"

"Her datebook."

"Yeah, well, it was just more bullshit."

"Union bullshit?"

"The UFW? Fuck no. Rita was too smart to get mixed up with them. Lesbians and Jews is the only white people who buy into that crap."

"So what did Rita want from you?"

He kept his eyes locked on the road. "None of your fucking business."

"The cops don't know about the meeting yet. I could forget to mention it if you tell me what happened."

His laugh was imperious. "You think I give a shit what the cops in this burg know or don't know?"

"Usually not, I'm sure. But you might if it gets you mixed up in a murder case. Chief Dixon doesn't act like he's been bought and paid for."

He threw me a glance the way he would give me a tip. "The whole town's been bought and paid for, Mr. Detective. If you're smart, you'll keep it in mind."

I smiled. "Where were you the night she was killed, Randy?"

He shrugged. "With a woman, I imagine."

"What woman?"

"Who knows? They got different names, but their snatches look all the same."

"I imagine you keep some sort of list, don't you? And some sort of scoring system? You seem like that type of guy."

"That's for me to know and you to find out."

I shifted gears. "How much does Carlos Reyna owe your company?"

Randy shrugged at its insignificance. "Seventy grand, last I looked."

"How much is he likely to clear this year?"

"Above expenses? Maybe twenty."

"So he'll still owe you."

Randy grinned. "One way or another, he'll owe me till the day he dies."

"You plan to file suit to collect the debt?"

"Not if he keeps in line."

"By that you mean he keeps union workers out of the fields."

"That. Other things," he added cryptically.

"And if he gets out of line?"

"We take everything he has and run him out of the state. Any more stunts like bringing guys like Morales to the farm, that's just what we'll do."

The smile on his face was adolescent and infuriating. It would please me no end to pin Rita's killing on him but at this point I couldn't see how to make it happen.

As we got out of the truck, I grabbed his arm. "If anything happens to the Vargas girl, I'm going to come after you first, Randy."

"Yeah?" he sneered. "You and what army?"

I looked at the fields surrounding the Gelbride compound. "The one out there," I said, gesturing toward the verdant workplace. "Where all the armies come from."

CHAPTER FOURTEEN

When I got back to town I looked at my watch—six hours till my tryst with Jill Coppelia. I was hot and bothered for the next five minutes, until it occurred to me that the reason Jill was coming to Salinas might not have to do with romance, it might be to serve a subpoena.

I stopped at the first phone I came to, called the hospital and asked for Mona Upshaw, learned she hadn't come in that day, and followed the directions Louise Lombardi had given me to her house. Nurse Upshaw had implied there were secrets in Haciendas that no one need know, information that would be more harmful to unearth than to let Rita's killer go free. Since I hadn't learned the secrets on my own, it was time to go to the source.

Del Rio Road was on the south end of Haciendas. Once, it had served as the southern boundary of the town, but now it was too near a mini-mall and a car wash and a park that had been given over to kids and their attendant gang graffiti and skateboard ramps.

Mona Upshaw's house was the only bright spot on the block, a long low ranch home with stone accents and a redwood fence that protected a small Japanese garden from the ravages of drive-bys and random vandalism. I walked through the gate and up to the door and knocked, then noticed the bell and pushed it. The chimes that echoed back at me sounded monastic and melancholy. I knocked as loud as I could, then followed the narrow flagstone pathway that took me to the back of the house.

The patio was small but attractive, a core of stone and flowers amid a circle of well-trimmed shrubbery. The decor included a brick fireplace and portable gas grill and tasteful lawn furniture lounging comfortably in the shade of a large yellow umbrella. Everything was as neat as a pin as befit a registered nurse, except the back door was standing wide open. I stuck my head inside and called her name. What answered wasn't the voice of Mona Upshaw, what answered was the unmistakable vapor of death.

I went inside, wishing my spare gun was in my pocket instead of my car, alert for sounds, alert for the macabre manifestation of murder. As I moved through the kitchen and dining room, I was dimly aware of a tidy, efficient abode, the lair of a woman who knew what she liked and needed and could afford to accommodate both elements of a placid existence. The only thing I found that was ugly and inappropriate was her body.

She was on the floor in the tiny foyer near the front door, face down, dressed in a nurse's uniform that had once been pristine but was now soaked in the blood that still seeped out of the many stab wounds that someone had put in her back. There was no sign of a weapon, no sign of forced entry, no sign of a struggle, and no sign that Mona Upshaw had any idea she was about to draw her last breath until that was what she had done.

I tiptoed around the fringes of the blood pool but saw nothing helpful so I went back to the living room, found a phone, and called it in. I told whoever answered that I'd be waiting out back, under the yellow umbrella.

Before I left the house I took a quick inventory. There was nothing anywhere that was not a fit with the home of an aging professional who was determined to live with as much dignity and elegance as she could accumulate. But as I moved toward the small study Mona had made out of the second bedroom, I began to wonder. Nursing is a good job, but nurses aren't doctors and Mona Upshaw lived very high on the hog. The furnishings were expensive. The art was original; the electronics near top of the line. She had a TV the size of a refrigerator and a chair covered with leather so soft it seemed liquid. The crystal was just that, the china was French, the flatware was solid silver. You could live pretty well on a nurse's salary in Haciendas, but not that well.

When I got to the study I went straight to the desk. It didn't take long to learn two things. First, Mona Upshaw had an investment portfolio worth almost a million dollars. And second, it was she, not Gus Gelbride, who had paid for Rita's surgery. The bill from the hospital was the size of the Haciendas phone book and the net amount due was $123,595.67.

I was about to pry for more information but I heard a car slide to a stop in front, so I hurried out the back and was basking in the shade of the yellow umbrella when a cop came down the path. He was Latino and large. His gun was drawn and his eyes were shifty and scared, always a potential disaster.

I made sure my hands were visible. "I'm the one who called it in," I told him. "She's in the house, by the front door."

He looked around the yard. "She dead?"

"Yes."

"You touch anything?"

"No."

"Anyone else been in there?"

"No one except the killer as far as I know."

"Stay put," he ordered, and eased into the house. When he came back he was talking on his radio, telling the dispatcher what he'd found. "The chief's going to want to see this, Sal," he concluded, then signed off.

I waited.

"You a friend of hers?" he asked.

"No."

"What are you doing here, then?"

"I came to ask Ms. Upshaw some questions."

"That's who lives here? Upshaw?"

"Mona Upshaw. She's a nurse in Salinas."

"So she's the one who's dead then."

"Right."

"What kind of questions you ask? You a salesman or something?"

I smiled. "Why don't we wait for Chief Dixon?"

He stiffened at the insult. "What?"

"If I'm going to tell my story, why don't we wait for the chief, so I won't have to tell it twice."

"You know the chief?"

"A little."

As he pondered his next move, an ambulance turned into the block, siren blaring, then strangled into a brusque silence. The cop went out front to direct them. When he came back there were two EMT guys with him.

The three of them went in the back door. By the time they came out, Chief Dixon was on the scene, still popping out of his uniform, still regarding me with a mix of respect and resentment.

He took a chair under the umbrella and sighed. "You found her?"

"Yep."

"How'd she die?"

"Stabbed a couple dozen times. No weapon in sight."

"You searched the place?"

"Not really."

He shook his head with disgust. "Put a scare into anyone when you showed up?"

"Nope. I'd say she's been dead for a few hours."

"Robbery or rape?"

"No sign of either."

"Gang stuff?"

I shook my head.

"You here on anything hot?"

"Not till I found the body."

He squinted into the sun that had driven away the fog and was broiling my back. "The fact she was stabbed and the fact that you're here make me think the killer might be the guy who killed Rita Lombardi."

"It's a possibility," I agreed.

The chief crossed his massive arms. "So what's the connection?"

"Ms. Upshaw was on duty the night they brought Rita to the hospital. I figure maybe she heard something or saw something that might be a lead to her killer."

He wrinkled his nose. "Mona was an upstanding citizen. If she'd heard or seen something important she would have brought it to us to look into."

"Maybe she didn't know what was significant about it."

The chief's smile was as tolerant as a teacher's. "When I got sick of Gifford and his sidekicks telling me things I already knew, I used to play euchre with Mona on Monday nights. Sharp as a finishing nail. If she couldn't figure out what it meant, she'd go to someone for help."

"Maybe she was warned not to talk. Maybe it took her time to work up the courage."

"You're reaching, Tanner. This may qualify as a big lead up in the city, but down here we call it slim pickings." He stood up and walked toward the house.

"Mind if I look around in there, Chief?"

He stopped and turned back. "Look for what?"

"Some link to Rita Lombardi."

"They knew each other forever. Plus Mona was best friends with Louise. A link wouldn't necessarily be significant."

"Rita had an appointment to see Upshaw the day before she died."

"To do what?"

"I don't know."

"How'd you find out about it?"

"It was on her appointment calendar."

The chief chased unwelcome thoughts through his brain. "Which you saw where?" he asked.

"At the Lombardi house."

The chief turned toward the house. "*Lopez*. Get out here." The summons was at the pitch of a foghorn.

The original cop responded, tugging his belt above his waist as he came out the door, his eyes alert for danger and pointed solely at the chief.

"You remember a datebook of some kind over at the Lombardi place?"

Lopez shook his head. "There was nothing like that over there, Chief."

Dixon looked at me. "Where was it?"

"Backpack, in a sort of secret pocket. It's an electronic gizmo, like a little computer." I reached in my pocket and pulled it out. "Looks a lot like this."

The chief glared at me and then at Lopez and then back at me. When he held out his hand, I gave it to him. In turn, he passed it to Lopez with a piece of advice. "You want my job someday, Hector, keep better tabs on your crime scenes."

"Yes, sir."

"Go back tomorrow and get the job done right."

"Yes, sir."

Lopez almost saluted but not quite. When he had gone back inside, the chief looked at me thoughtfully. "We'll be here all afternoon, so you'll be in the way. You come by tomorrow, you'll probably be able to look around some. Meanwhile, it's under seal. I find out you broke it, I'll lock you up for interfering with a police investigation."

"Yes, sir," I said, mimicking Sergeant Lopez.

"So that's it?" he asked.

"There's one more thing."

"Make it quick."

"Has Randy Gelbride ever been charged with a sexual offense in this town?"

The chief uncrossed his arms and looked beyond me, at the crowd that had formed on the curb. "What makes you ask something like that?"

"Randy seems to take a proprietary interest in some of his female workers. *Droit du seigneur* and all that."

"I don't know about that French bullshit or whatever it was, but Randy's randy. I'll give you that."

"But he's never been charged with a criminal offense?"

"Got a hell of a lot of speeding tickets. And there's been some talk about the other stuff, I won't deny it. But the Gelbrides always handled it in-house."

"You mean they bought the girl off."

The chief shrugged. "Could be. Could be other things. Unless it lands on my desk in the form of a complaint, it's none of my business. Or yours," he added pointedly.

"You know a family named Vargas, Chief?"

"Hell, there's a dozen families named Vargas within the sound of my voice."

"This family lives in a cave."

"Yeah?"

"Yeah."

"Then they're outside my jurisdiction. Now get lost," he added, but since there was a smile in his voice when he said it, I risked one more question.

"Could Rita's killer have been a woman, Chief?"

He thought it over. "Only if she was berserk."

I thanked him for his time, then got in my car and drove to the Catholic church.

St. Bonaventure looked older than the town itself, though in slightly better condition. Although not on the historically validated list of California missions, it had the same look and feel as the more famous churches in San Juan Bautista and Carmel, with a red tile roof above a creamy adobe shell that rose to a bell tower high over the sanctuary. Inside, the dark oaks and pastel ceramics of the nave made way for white plaster walls at the altar, a match with the tallow of the altar candles and the statuary of the crucifix and the Virgin Mary. The statues of Christ and the Virgin were tied to hooks in the walls with fishing line, in case an earthquake occurred while God was otherwise occupied.

A single figure knelt at the chancel rail, a woman in a long black dress with a black mantilla draped over her head; otherwise, the church was unoccupied except perhaps by the Holy Ghost. It seemed impossible that I would know the lonely worshiper, but something in the arc of her shoulder and the cut of her hair seemed familiar. I tiptoed down the aisle until I could see her in profile.

Maria Vargas, hands clasped, eyes squeezed tight, was giving thanks for her husband's survival, maybe, or praying for the deliverance of her daughter from what must have been her many pursuers, the most potent of them being Randy Gelbride. It was tempting to interrupt her prayers to ask her some questions, but even I'm not that big a jerk, at least not unless I want to be.

I tiptoed out the side door and walked to the rectory next door, where the priests worked and lived. It was a match to the church in design, but smaller in scale and more secular in function, as demonstrated by the poster that was taped to the front door advertising a raffle to pay for new pews.

The hallway was tiled in blood-red tile squares and beamed with heavy cedar; the walls seemed as thick as the walls of a jail. My shoes made sounds of muffled drums as I looked for Father McNally's office, which turned out to be three doors down, identifiable from the name painted above the door in block letters. I knocked and waited, then stuck my head in.

The man who looked up from the desk was younger than I

expected, taller and more athletic as well. He examined me closely, trying and failing to peg me as a parishioner, then stood up and extended his hand. He wore a simple black cassock topped by a clerical collar and his hair was cut within a quarter inch of his skull. His lips were thick and sensuous and there was a gap between his teeth that gave him a boyish charm, but his eyes were solemn and serious, as if they had borne witness to all the pain in the parish.

His grip was as firm as a stevedore's. "I'm Father McNally," he boomed as I tried to escape his hand. "How may I help you?"

I clasped my hands behind my back, rubbing them to ease the pain. It was an effort not to bow my head. "My name's Tanner. I'm a private detective from San Francisco. I'm looking into the death of Rita Lombardi."

He nodded. "I see. It was a terrible tragedy, of course. In many ways the worst of my priesthood. What brings you to St. Bonaventure?"

"I'm hoping you can help me out."

"I can't imagine what kind of help that might be."

"I was wondering if Rita committed any sins of the kind that could have gotten her killed."

He blinked. "Did you know her, Mr. Tanner?"

"Yes."

"Then you know her only sins were not seen as such in the eyes of the Lord."

"How about in the eyes of the strawberry growers?"

He smiled. "That I cannot say."

"Was Rita fearful in her final days? Or angry? Any mental state that might point to her killer?"

"Why do you think I would know such a thing even if it existed?"

"You must have heard her confession many times. Plus you met with her two days before she died."

Father McNally rubbed his skull with his left hand, then gestured toward the only chair in the room. "Please. Sit down, Mr. Tanner. This may take time."

I did as he asked and he took a seat across the desk from me, then crossed his arms on his chest and leaned back in his chair. He was ruggedly handsome and seemed gentle and sincere and intelligent as well—even the good Catholic women of Haciendas must be having second thoughts about the celibacy thing.

"Of course anything Rita might have told me would be covered by the priest-penitent privilege of confidentiality," he began softly.

"While she was alive, at least."

"And after, Mr. Tanner."

"Even if it protects her killer?"

"I'm afraid so." He made a steeple of his fingers and regarded me over the top of it. "However, I believe I can ethically reveal in this instance that Rita demonstrated none of the emotions you listed. Instead, she was quite euphoric."

"Because of the wedding."

"That. Other things as well, I believe."

"What other things?"

"Her surgery, for one. Do you know about that?"

I nodded.

He smiled. "God does seem to work through the AMA at times."

"Were there other reasons for her euphoria, Father?"

"I don't know."

"Or won't say?"

"In this case, I can truthfully plead ignorance."

"Was there a problem with Carlos Reyna, Father? Was she having second thoughts about the wedding?"

"None that she expressed to me. And she would have, I believe."

"Was there a problem with any of the Gelbride family? With Randy in particular?"

"Everyone in Haciendas seems to have issues with a Gelbride. I know of nothing special between Rita and Randy, other than the normal business disputes."

"Which are?"

He met my eye and spoke with brisk precision. "The historic exploitations of the farmworker."

"Was there anything special going on in that area at the time of Rita's death?"

He pondered in the light of the afternoon sun. "On second thought, I believe there was one thing."

"What was it?"

He pursed his lips. I bet myself that at some point in her young life, Rita had had a crush on him. "I believe I should keep that in confidence," he said at last.

"Was it about a young girl named Vargas? Was Rita asking the church to protect her in some way?"

Father McNally looked at Christ on the cross, tacked to the wall by the door. "You seem to know enough already, Mr. Tanner. You must be good at your job."

"If you can help Consuelo Vargas the way Rita wanted, you'll be good at yours as well."

He looked away. "We do what we can. It is seldom all that's needed, unfortunately. Now I'm afraid I must ask you to go. I schedule an hour of meditation at this point in the afternoon. To review my day. To make sure I have not strayed from God's path."

I stood up. "As far as you know, the wedding plans were on schedule?"

He nodded. "The wedding, plus she wanted to meet later to talk about baptism."

"Rita hadn't been baptized before?"

"Of course she had. I checked the records myself."

I took a deep breath. "So that means she was pregnant."

The priest closed his eyes as if in pain. "I can't believe that is so, even though it does seem indicated." He opened his eyes and shook his head. "If she strayed in matters of the flesh, it only shows the power of sin in the world. Rita was truly a child of God.

And like our Lord and Savior Jesus Christ, she was taken from this earth before her time, for reasons we can only guess at."

His tribute seemed to echo off the mountains and return for an encore. "Was Mona Upshaw one of your parishioners, Father?"

"No, but I have met her many times. Why?"

"She was murdered this morning."

He bowed his head. "How terrible. But surely it has nothing to do with Rita."

"I was hoping you'd let me know." I smiled. "You wouldn't have to violate the confessional; I'm pretty good at deduction."

"I'm sure you are," he countered stiffly, then ushered me out the door.

CHAPTER FIFTEEN

I was waiting in the parking lot when she came out of the church, removing the shawl from her head and stuffing it in her handbag as she walked toward the main street. She was swaddled in a daze of some sort, as though the Holy Ghost had taken possession of her senses and was guiding her Himself.

"Mrs. Vargas?"

She stopped, startled and afraid; her hand flew to her throat and clutched it as though she were choking. I expected her to calm down when she saw who it was, but she seemed even more alarmed than before as she focused on my face.

"I'm Marsh Tanner," I said. "A friend of Carlos Reyna's. I was at the cave with him last night when your husband got sick."

She nodded when I finished, but I had no idea how much of it she had understood. "Do you speak English, Mrs. Vargas?"

She held up her thumb and forefinger a millimeter apart. "*Un poco,*" she said.

"I was also a friend of Rita Lombardi's," I said, playing my only two wild cards up front.

"Señorita Rita. *Sí.*" Even through her fear, she managed a smile at the alliteration.

"Carlos told me that before she died, Rita was helping your daughter, Mrs. Vargas. Keeping Consuelo out of trouble, was what he called it."

She shook her head adamantly. "Consuelo no bad. Consuelo *es bueno.*"

"*Bueno.* Right. I'm sure she's not a bad girl; that's not what I meant. But what kind of trouble was Rita protecting her from?"

Mrs. Vargas shook her head again, eyes wide with panic, breaths quick with distress. "*No sé. No sé, señor.*"

"Was she guarding her from Mr. Gelbride? Was that who was bothering Consuelo?"

The reaction to the name was electric. Mrs. Vargas shook her head once more, this time violently and conclusively. "Señor Gelbride no hurt Consuelo. You leave now. You no talk to Carlos no more."

As I puzzled over her defense of the man who'd just brutalized her daughter in the field, Mrs. Vargas hurried away as fast as she could, walking toward the center of town where people like her would be there to shield her from people like me. She was clearly fearful to the point of flight, but I didn't know why. Perhaps she'd seen me that morning and thought I was allied with the Gelbrides and that, therefore, her job was at risk. Perhaps she was afraid I'd make more trouble for her rather than less if I kept pressing for truth about Rita, or perhaps she had a guilty secret of her own of some sort, something that had contributed to Rita's demise. Given the barriers that lay between us, the chance that I would learn the source of her fears from her bordered on infinitesimal.

When Mrs. Vargas had disappeared down the street, I looked at my watch for the two hundredth time. Four o'clock. Well, three-thirty. Three hours plus change till my dinner with Jill Coppelia. If I went back to Salinas and looked up Rita's best friend, Thelma Powell, there would be time to shave and shower after I finished the interview and by then Jill would be pulling into town. Good plan, Señor Tanner; eliminate the dead time, when the mind makes even serendipity seem suspect and erodes resolve like a Santa Ana wind.

I took the Main Street exit toward downtown, then stopped at the first phone booth I came to. A T. Powell was listed, with a number but no address. When I dialed the number, I got a machine. In my profession it's seldom an advantage to let them know you're coming, so I hung up without leaving my name. Since Mrs. Lombardi had said Thelma Powell worked in a bank, I drove to the center of town to find one.

Downtown Salinas was being revived—gonfalons proclaiming it Old Towne were hung on every lamppost and a streamer stretched above the street proclaimed its Uptown Style; Downtown Charm. Here and there a storefront sported a new face, but the inevitable knot of transients already occupied the public benches.

Parts of it were inviting. Main Street itself was lined with dozens of leafy trees that gave it a cool, bucolic aspect. The thru traffic had been routed away from the core and the sidewalks were broad to encourage meandering. A second streamer advertised an upcoming Scottish Festival, suggesting multicultural conviviality. But except for an elaborate clothing store on the corner, the commercial establishments were mostly unexceptional, as though both the existing owners and the national chains were waiting for the benefits of the revival to kick in before risking further capital. A chicken or egg thing, I imagine, but the elaborate new malls I'd seen on the north edge of town weren't waiting for anything but customers.

I parked at an angle along with the rest of the cars and walked to the tallest building in sight, which housed the Coast Federal Bank. I went inside and stopped at the first free teller I came to. "I'm looking for a woman named Thelma Powell," I said. "I was told she works here."

The teller brightened. "Thelma? Sure." She looked left. "She's back there, the blonde in the blue dress."

I looked where she pointed. A blonde in a blue dress was sitting at a desk that was one of a covey of identical work stations clustered at the far end of the room. Whatever business was conducted in the vicinity wouldn't be private for an instant, which I suppose was the idea. If you have secrets, you don't get loans.

"You must be buying a new car," the teller said after I thanked her. "What kind are you getting?"

"Cadillac," I said.

"Really. We don't get many of those anymore. Most people favor the Lexus."

"Too tiny," I said gruffly, adopting a pose for no reason except burlesque. "Me and the missus like lots of leg room."

She nodded to confirm my good taste. "You're a big man so you need a big car. Thelma can finance you fine, I'm sure."

"Hope so," I said. "Not that I ain't got the net worth, but most of my cash flow's tied up in coffee futures." I waved farewell to the teller and went back to the bowels of the bank, feeling out of place and poverty-stricken.

Thelma Powell was young and pleasant-looking, though too overweight and too moon-faced to be beautiful and too open and friendly to be intriguing. Her hair was short, with the color and body of yellow thread. Her dress was blue with red buttons and her left sleeve was missing an arm. Not a complete arm, just the musculature from the elbow down, the part that would make it a forearm instead of a withered stick of bone and skin that culminated in a tiny stump in the manner of a peg leg. I tried to notice it without noticing, and it was kind of Thelma Powell to let me believe I'd gotten the job done.

"Yes, sir?" she said as I loomed over the desk. "How can I help you?"

"My name is Tanner. I'd like to talk to you for a minute."

"Of course. Sit right down and we'll—"

"It's not business," I interrupted, then lowered my voice. "It's about Rita Lombardi. Maybe you could go on break for a few minutes."

She frowned in puzzlement, then looked at the clock on the wall. "It's not really break time, but . . ." She looked up at me and nodded as if to confirm a hunch. "You're the man from the hospital."

"Right."

Her expression turned grave. "I'm very glad you're here. And I do want to speak with you." She looked at something I assumed was her appointment book but was in reality a stuffed bear that looked like Rita's Brownie.

When she saw me notice it, Thelma smiled. "She gave it to me before she died. She said I needed it more than she did. Typical Rita," she added in a heartfelt tribute. "Always thinking of others." She grabbed her purse. "Tell you what. We'll just go outside and appraise your car."

"But I—"

"I know. You're not buying a new car today. But we'll pretend you are and that way I can leave the office for half an hour while I look over the trade-in."

She got up and went to one of the enclosed offices along the back wall of the bank and poked her head in the door and told a fib. A moment later she returned. "What kind of car are you thinking of purchasing, Mr. Tanner?" she asked, loud enough for the entire environs to overhear.

"Cadillac," I intoned again. "I buy American. Always have; always will."

"Good for you," she said and took my arm with her one good hand. "The new Deville is a wonderful vehicle. I'm sure we can put together an attractive package."

We walked out the door like Bruce and Demi on the way to Planet Hollywood before Bruce and Demi split up, then crossed the street and walked till we were out of sight of the bank's front door. "How about some coffee?" she asked after a glance back the way we'd come.

"Great."

She led me to a coffee house named the Cherry Bean that featured a variety of fresh brews and some secluded booths in the back by the roasting machine and bags of beans from Guatemala. Thelma ordered a cappuccino and I ordered a double espresso in the hope that there was much to be done before I slept and I wanted to be awake enough to enjoy it. As I made an effort to keep my mind off Jill Coppelia and on the business at hand, we made small talk at the counter until the drinks were ready, then repaired to a booth by the rear door.

"I haven't slept since she died," Thelma began after she licked foam off her lip and put down her cup, her voice low and urgent, as though we were discussing high treason. "It's so terrible. I see it happening, over and over and over. The knife, the blood; everything. I cry out in the night; I wake myself screaming."

"Who do you see doing it to her, Thelma?"

Her eyes shifted warily, as though she herself were under suspicion. "I don't know. Some faceless creature, I guess. Some monster."

I gave her time to calm down. "You see quite a bit better than that, I think."

She paused, then nodded, then looked around the room and whispered. "It's Randy Gelbride. He's the one I see. Every single dream, it's Randy." She rubbed her bad arm with the opposite hand as though a brisk massage would restore it. "God. I can't believe this has happened. I can't believe the valley has turned into some sort of *slaughterhouse.*"

"Why is he doing it, Thelma? Why is Randy killing Rita?"

"Because she hates him."

"Why does he care what she thinks?"

"Because she's stopping him from getting what he wants."

"What does he want?"

"He wants to take over the business from Daddy and he doesn't want to wait much longer to do it."

"And Rita's in the way of that?"

"I think so."

"How?"

"I'm not sure. She just made vague references to making changes at the Gelbrides'."

"It sounds like she had something on Randy. Something she could use to force him out of the business."

"Maybe she did."

"Any idea what it was?"

She lowered her voice again. "Randy likes young women, apparently."

"Are you talking about Consuelo Vargas?"

She nodded. "Randy wants to add her to his list."

"List of what?"

"Women he's deflowered, I guess. Spoiled. Abused. Whatever he does to them, it must be hideous. Rita says some of them never recover. They go back to Mexico to live in shame for the rest of their lives."

"But Randy must have pursued lots of women over the years. Why did Rita care about the Vargas girl?"

Thelma shook her head. "I don't know for sure. She's very beautiful, Rita told me, almost magically so. And smart. Rita was trying to find a way to make sure she stays in school and goes on to college. When Randy set out to debase her, Rita swore she'd stop him. Oh. And it had something to do with Gus."

"Randy's father?"

She nodded. "Rita was going to get Gus to stop Randy from molesting the Vargas girl, I guess."

"How?"

"I don't know. But she seemed pretty confident that she'd get the job done."

Thelma finished her drink and wiped foam off her lips. "Rita said Consuelo was like a fawn in the forest, about to be devoured by a lion." Thelma began to cry. "Now Rita has been devoured herself."

I gave her time to compose herself. "What was the connection between Rita and the Vargas family?"

"They worked for Carlos. That's all I know."

"Did you ever meet Consuelo?"

"No."

"You said Rita hated Randy. Did she have problems with him besides Consuelo?"

Thelma shrugged. "They've hated each other since Randy was in third grade and Rita was in first."

"Why?"

"Because they have opposite views on practically everything. Because Rita used to be friends with Missy and Missy and Randy despise each other. And because Rita was crippled so he couldn't browbeat her the way he did the rest of the kids."

"What happened between Rita and Missy?"

Her voice hardened. "Missy turned into a drunk."

"And there was no other issue of late? Except for Consuelo Vargas?"

"Not as far as I know. Except for the usual quarrel over the conditions in the fields."

"Was anything else going on in Rita's life before she died?"

Thelma sniffed and blew her nose on her hankie and pulled herself together. "The wedding, of course. She talked a lot about that. I was going to be maid of honor. I already bought my dress. I look stunning in it, if I do say so myself."

The tears reappeared with full force, eroding her makeup, tarnishing her eyes. I patted her hand. "I'm sorry to put you through this, Thelma."

"No. I want to. I haven't been able to talk to anyone else about her death and these feelings need to come out so I can get past it. Rita said you were a good listener, so it might as well be you who puts up with me." She tried to assemble a smile out of a host of contrary emotions. "If it's all right with you."

"It's fine."

I waited for her to calm once again. "So things were still fine with Rita and Carlos."

"Yes. Of course."

"How about the union? Was Rita active with the organizing campaign?"

"She talked to them a lot, I know that. She had lots of ideas she wanted to discuss."

"What kinds of ideas?"

"I don't know specifically. Benefits for the workers, basically, I guess. I'm not really into agriculture."

I smiled. "You're into cars."

She grinned. "Only at the office." She glanced at the clock and got ready to leave.

"Who did Rita talk to at the union?" I asked quickly.

"A woman named Connors at the UFW office in Watsonville. She was one of the leaders, I think."

"How about a lawyer named Noland? Did Rita mention him?"

"I know who he is but I don't think Rita ever mentioned him. Oh God. She was so *happy* since she got back from the city. The wedding, the operation." She put a hand on her stunted arm once more. "I knew how she felt, exactly. It was the way I would feel if they could ever . . . but they can't, so it doesn't matter, I guess."

"It matters."

"To you. To me. To Carlos and Mrs. Lombardi. But the rest of the world couldn't care less about us. We're nothing to them down here. Less than nothing, in fact."

"Why?"

"Because of the way we live."

"How do you mean?"

"People in the big cities think we're racists, that the valley is like the South way back when, that we live off slave labor only this time it's brown skins, not black."

"Are they right?"

"About some of us, they are. There are bad people around, no question, narrow-minded brutes. But not all of us are like that, not nearly. Latinos are treated with respect by most of us. The city council has several Latino members; so does the school board and the Chamber of Commerce. There are all kinds of social programs for disadvantaged workers, too. And some of my best friends are Latino." She put her hand to her mouth. "I can't believe I said that. Even though it's true." She looked at her watch and then at the door. "I should get back to the bank before it closes."

"Is there anything else you can tell me about Rita's death?"

"I don't think so. Except she was certain she was going to do big things, now that her legs were fixed. I was so proud of her; it was like she was Joan of Arc or someone, going off to battle the growers."

I refrained from mentioning their common fate. "Can I have a number where I can reach you in case something comes up that I need help to decipher?"

"You sound like there's some secret code out there that has the answer to everything."

"I get the feeling this whole place operates by code."

Instead of disagreeing, she dug a card out of her purse and wrote on the back. "My home number. I'm usually there if I'm not at work. The cats depend on me to entertain them, which is where I'm going in half an hour." She found another smile. "I hope you enjoy your Cadillac, Mr. Tanner."

"Thanks for giving me such a good deal, Ms. Powell."

Out on the walk, we went separate ways.

CHAPTER SIXTEEN

I looked at my watch. Four-thirty. Damn. Still time to kill before Jill. I walked back into the Cherry Bean and asked for a phone book.

Grayson Noland's office was on Alisal, the street that crossed Main in the center of town, only few blocks from where I was. I noted the number and walked west until I found it, across the street from the county courthouse.

The courthouse was an eclectic structure incorporating a variety of neoclassic motifs in the color and texture of sandstone, attractively landscaped and substantially expanded to fit the needs of the booming populace of the Central Coast. A variety of people eddied through its walks and pathways, none of them looking particularly abandoned or confused, which made it a different kettle of fish from the courthouse I'm most familiar with.

The law office of Grayson Noland had been built to match the courthouse, with columns, courtyards, fountains, gardens, and several pieces of statuary thrown into the mix as accents, all featuring nude women and dramatic gestures. Mr. Noland was obviously making a tidy living representing the Gelbride family interests, tidy enough to suggest that the courthouse was merely an annex to their empire.

There were ten lawyers listed on the door, but the building

seemed bigger than that, possibly because they used a lot of para-legal personnel, or maybe they had an indoor pool and tennis court. Grayson Noland's name came first, which made it unlikely I'd get in to see him, but it was worth a shot, especially since the alternative was feeling foolish at being as eager as an adolescent to see what would happen when and if Jill Coppelia showed up.

The receptionist was young and attractive and artifically happy to see me. When I told her my mission, she said she'd have to check Mr. Noland's schedule and apologized for making me wait. She punched a button, murmured some words in her headset, then told me someone would be with me shortly.

The someone was a stumpy, pugnacious woman whose job was to run interference for her boss, which was fitting since she looked like a fullback. "Mr. Tanner?" Her voice was already dubious, as if I didn't have a right to my own name, let alone to disturb her employer.

"I'd like to see Mr. Noland for a minute," I said.

"And what is the nature of your business?"

"Murder."

"I . . . what did you say?" Her left hand flew to her sternum, to make sure everything was still in place, to make sure I hadn't shot her.

I grinned into her overreaction—Mr. Noland must not do crim-inal defense work. "I'm in the murder business," I said. "The solv-ing part, not the committing part."

"I see," she managed. "But what—"

"Specifically, I'm in the business of the murder of a woman named Rita Lombardi."

"I see," she said again, ill at ease with issues more volatile than rules against perpetuities and covenants running with the land. "I remember reading about it in the *Californian*. A tragic event, I'm sure, but of course it is impossible that Mr. Noland had anything to do with Ms. Lombardi's unfortunate demise or any trouble she might have been experiencing at the time she was killed."

Her essay made me laugh. "That's not what her appointment book said."

"How do you mean?"

"I mean Ms. Lombardi had an appointment to see Mr. Noland two days before she died. I'm surprised you don't remember—you look more competent than that."

She blushed. "I was on vacation last week but I'm sure nothing ... that is, I'm quite confident that—" She broke off the disclaimer as though it had burned her tongue. "Just a moment, please."

She fled down the hall, her gait somewhere between a gallop and a waddle. I was left to admire both the receptionist and the art on the walls, the latter a series of semiskilled renderings of idyllic landscapes and breaking waves. I made a mental bet that the artist was connected to the firm by marriage.

The fullback returned. "Please follow me," she said without preamble, then went back the way she'd come.

She led me to the office in the far corner of the building, which we entered without pause. "Mr. Noland; Mr. Tanner." With that terse introduction, she left me alone with her boss.

He was sandy-haired and pink-skinned, too chubby and too oily and too expensively dressed in silks and linens in pastel shades that made it look as if he'd just driven in from Beverly Hills or La Jolla. His forehead was flushed and freckled and the flesh of his neck dripped over his shirt collar like wallpaper coming loose from its glue. He was not a handsome man, had no doubt been a homely kid, and had been making the world make up the deficit for the last fifty years.

"Mr. Tanner, is it?" he asked, his fingers pawing through papers on his desk in order to let me know that he had better things to do with his time than speak with me. On the wall behind him, a version of the Ten Commandments in elaborate frame and calligraphy shared space with his law degree from U.C.-Davis, a citation for some form of public zealotry from Rotary International, and two paintings of Point Lobos just like the ones out front. The only book on his desk was a Bible but if he was a Christian, I was an astronaut.

"What brings you to our fair city?" he asked.

"Rita Lombardi," I said.

He kept pawing the papers. "Ah, yes. An unfortunate thing. Extremely unfortunate." He looked up. "May I assume you're connected with law enforcement in some capacity, Mr. Tanner?"

"In the capacity of observer and critic and occasional competitor."

He frowned. "I don't understand."

"I'm a private eye."

His expression turned massively condescending, which was good because it pissed me off and I'm a better interrogator when I don't give a damn about feelings. "Employed by whom?" he asked.

"My conscience."

"I'm afraid I don't—"

"I was a friend of Rita's. I feel the way you'd feel if someone ripped your wife's art work off the walls and burned it in the yard."

The pink turned two shades darker, to the tint his wife had employed to evoke the setting sun. "Of course. I didn't mean to imply . . . how may I help you?"

"How well did you know Rita?"

He raised a sun-bleached brow. "Why are you assuming I did?"

"Because you saw her two days before she died. In this office. On official business."

"What makes you think that?"

"Informed sources."

"I see." He put down the papers and looked at me. "I did meet with her briefly, as it happens. But it had nothing to do with her death, I assure you."

I smiled. "I'll be the judge of that. Did you know her other than professionally, Mr. Noland?"

"What are you implying?"

"I don't know yet."

"Well, I didn't know Ms. Lombardi at all, I'm afraid, other than that one encounter. But people say she was a very nice person."

"What people are those?"

He shrugged. "People around town. You know. The people who keep track of such things."

"Your clients, you mean." I glanced at the plaque on the wall at his back. "Or maybe you're making a theological reference."

"I don't understand."

"God keeps track of who's naughty and nice, don't you think? If He does anything at all, that's what He spends His time doing. Seeing who measures up to the ethic."

Noland was off balance—it always disturbs people when you take their spiritual poses seriously. His voice dropped the lilt of paternal patronizing and took on the throb of the legal eagle. "What do you want to know, Mr. Tanner? I have other business that is quite pressing."

"Tell me what you and Rita talked about when she came to see you."

"I'm afraid that would be privileged information."

I shook my head. "Only if she was a client, and that seems unlikely. Unless you can show me a receipt for a retainer."

Noland leaned back in his chair and closed his eyes, as if he could think his brand of thought only in total darkness. "I suppose there's no reason to dissemble in this instance. It was a rather absurd conversation, really."

"Absurd how? Why was she here?"

"She seemed to believe I negotiated the contract between her employer, a Mr. . . . ."

"Reyna."

"Yes. Carlos Reyna. The contract between Mr. Reyna and Gelbride Berry Farms."

"Did you?"

"No. I have never met Mr. Reyna nor any other independent grower for that matter. I am, however, the primary drafter of the basic contract for agricultural goods and services that the Gel-brides negotiate with all their share farmers."

"What did Rita want you to do with the contract?"

"As I understood it, she wanted me to change it."

"In what way?"

He sighed and chuckled dryly, as though we were discussing *Seinfeld.* "It was really quite remarkable. She wanted certain costs of production to be borne by the Gelbrides, not the IGs. She wanted the growers to be free to borrow elsewhere than from the Gelbride State Bank and to sell fruit other than through the Gelbride coop-erative. She wanted certain financial guarantees in the event of a bad crop year and guarantees that all state and federal laws would be obeyed to the point of allowing independent observers to come on company property to ensure compliance. And she wanted an independent accounting of income and wage allocations at the Gelbrides' expense." He shook his head in mock befuddlement. "What she wanted was pie in the sky, in other words."

"She wanted you to make these changes for Mr. Reyna?"

"For all the Gelbride growers." The pulp in his lips disappeared in an expression of distaste. "Hence my use of the word *absurd.*"

"Why did she think you'd agree to do this? Because you're such a nice guy?"

"My interpretation was that she was making some sort of threat."

"Threat?"

He nodded.

"How could Rita be in a position to threaten you or the Gel-brides?"

His grin would have peeved a weasel. "She couldn't."

"But she must have had something in mind; she wasn't a fool-ish person."

"She just said she was giving me a chance to make the changes on my own. If I didn't, she would make them over my dead body, which was exactly how she put it."

This time I was the one off balance. "She was threatening violence of some kind?"

"That's the interpretation I put on it. Wouldn't you?"

"Did you take her seriously?"

"Yes."

"Why?"

"Because I assumed she was speaking for the union or some other group hostile to the Gelbride family. Even if she were acting alone, anyone can be violent with a gun in her hand. So I've been taking precautions."

"What kind?"

He opened a drawer in his desk and pulled out a pistol and held it up. It looked like a nice little Llama 9mm semiautomatic, retailing for close to a grand. "I have identical weapons in my car and home. I've advised my clients to arm themselves similarly."

"By clients you mean the Gelbrides."

"Primarily."

"Don't you think that makes for the chance of an unfortunate accident somewhere down the road, Mr. Noland?"

"You may see it that way," he answered prissily. "I see it strictly in terms of protection and prevention."

I borrowed the feral smile he had used on me. "Protection from the ghost of Rita Lombardi?"

"And from those allied with her cause."

"What cause was that?"

He mounted his soapbox. "To destroy the system of agricultural production that has prevailed in this valley for the last hundred years. The system that puts on the table of the average American the best food products in the world at a price that is the envy of our competitors, foreign and domestic."

"The system that made you rich, you mean."

"Please, Mr. Tanner. Don't expect me to apologize for my success or for that of my clients. This nation was founded on the principles of Christian capitalism. I know of nothing that makes profit immoral. Now I'm afraid you must excuse me."

He fiddled with a file but I ignored it. "A couple of points. How much did the Gelbrides net from their operations last year?"

"Last year was a bad year. The weather was horrible."

"So how much?"

"I'm not at liberty to say, of course."

"But they made money."

"I'm sorry, I can't tell you anything on that score."

"Will the Gelbrides plow up the fields if their workers vote union?"

He looked up. "Don't take me for a fool. You know that question involves private client communications. I wouldn't last a day in this business if I discussed such a subject with you. Now really, I must insist that you leave. Otherwise I will summon security."

"One last thing. Did Rita's visit have anything to do with a young woman named Consuelo Vargas?"

Noland turned his chair toward the wall, as though the Commandments had something to do with any of this. "The name came up. Yes."

"In what connection?"

"Ms. Lombardi had some hysterical fantasy about Randy Gelbride and the Vargas girl. A sexual assault that was purportedly imminent."

"What did Rita want you to do?"

"Put a stop to it, apparently."

"What did you tell her?"

He paused, then swiveled my way, then shrugged. "That no one has any control over Randy anymore. Not even his father."

"How did Rita react?"

"She said if Randy harmed Consuelo, it would destroy the Gelbrides forever."

"How so?"

"She didn't say. Because she couldn't, of course. Her threat was juvenile posturing, no more. Gus Gelbride is the most powerful man in this county."

"I take it you represent the father, not the son, Mr. Noland."

"Who I represent is none of your damned business. If you don't leave this minute, I'm calling the police."

Noland reached for the phone and I stood up. "Lots of things point to the Gelbrides in Rita's murder, Mr. Noland. If they did it, I'm going to find out and take it to the police. You might want to consider whether you want to go down with them."

"Now you're being absurd yourself," he said, but the quiver in his lower lip belied his words.

"By the way," I said. "The bit about the morality of profits and capitalism?"

"Yes?"

I pointed to the Bible. "You might want to reread that one of these days. Particularly Matthew Chapter Nineteen."

CHAPTER SEVENTEEN

I took Alisal back to the Best Western, unpacked, shaved and showered, smeared on deodorant, brushed my teeth, gargled with mouthwash, brushed my teeth again to be rid of the taste of the mouthwash, sucked on a Breath Saver I'd bought in the lobby, and started to get dressed. I don't know how to pack effectively, though, and I don't own the right kind of luggage, so everything in my suitcase was wrinkled: I looked like I'd wadded up my best shirt and spent the day with it in my pocket.

I called the front desk and asked if they had an iron I could borrow. They said they'd send it right up. A minute passed, then four more. I called again. They said another room was using the iron, but it would be available shortly. I went from having time to spare to running late.

I began to sweat, hot pebbles forming atop my forehead and along my forearms as though my flesh had a fresh coat of varnish that was beginning to blister in the sun. Increasingly desperate, I spread my shirt on the bed and tried to smooth it out with my hands, which seemed at least as hot as steam irons, but apparently they were not. I did the same with my trousers, tucking the cuffs under my chin and pressing the wrinkles against my torso and thighs, but that was similarly ineffective. I sweated some more, to the point that I decided to take a second shower. This time the deodorant was applied in three layers—my underarms would itch for a month.

When I emerged from the shower the iron and board were in my room. I set up the board as fast as I could, creating a racket in the nature of a fusillade. I ran the iron over my shirt and pants in a hurry, pressing in as many wrinkles as I removed, burning my hand as I made a mad grasp to keep the shirt from falling to the floor, knocking the iron off the board and spilling its store of steaming water into the carpet in the process. By the time I was finished I'd uttered every swear word in my vocabulary and was bathed in a sticky subdural substance that made sweat seem sweet by comparison.

When I was dressed I looked in the mirror: I looked like a drunk who'd tried to sober up and had decided to hell with it. With one last look in the mirror and an appropriate curse at its contents, I left the room, only to turn back when I was halfway to the elevator in order to unplug the iron. By the time I got to the lobby I was ten minutes late and two degrees below boiling.

But of course Jill wasn't there. By the time she arrived twenty minutes later, I'd looked at my watch two hundred times, looked into the parking lot half that often, drunk two cans of vending machine pop while convincing the East Indian desk clerk I was either insane or a criminal masterminding a heist. At seven-thirty, convinced she wasn't coming and that I'd been an idiot to expect her, I strolled toward the elevator with as much nonchalance as I could muster after having made it abundantly clear to all and sundry that I'd been stood up.

"Sorry I'm late," she said at my back, sounding far more coy than sorry, sounding expectant, sounding even eager, maybe. "Traffic backed up south of Gilroy. A truck turned over—tomatoes all over the place."

When I turned to look at her, my arms inched across my body as though I were stark naked and my voice became as tremulous as hers. "Hi there," I ventured.

"Hi."

"Glad you could make it."

She looked around the lobby. What she saw didn't obviously impress. "I hope you weren't waiting down here all that time."

"Five minutes," I lied. "No problem. I was running late myself."

"Good."

She was wearing black slacks and a gray print blouse and black shoes with no heels that looked something like the loafers I was wearing myself. Her hair was tousled in a blowzy way, scraped haphazardly across her forehead and over her ears. Her face was ruddy from the drive, giving her a carnal blush; her blue eyes seemed double the wattage of my own. I was thankful as hell that she'd come, though it was clear Jill was reserving judgment.

I shuffled from one foot to the next, then back to the first. "Shall we go straight to dinner or do you want to go up to the room and . . . freshen up, as they say? I can give you the key and wait here, if you want."

She shook her head. "I can do all that needs to be done when we get to the restaurant."

"Fine. What kind of food are you in the mood for?"

"You choose," she said.

"I don't do decent food all that often. I still look forward to macaroni and cheese."

She grinned. "Me, too."

"Kraft? In the blue box."

She nodded. "To die for. How about Mexican? I'm sure there's some great Mexican food in this town."

"Mexican it is," I said, and led her out of the lobby and toward my Buick. Thanks to a brochure in the room and some consultation with the desk clerk while I was waiting, I'd made a mental list of the decent restaurants in each of three categories—Mexican, Chinese, and Italian. The Mexican place was on John Street. I got there after only one wrong turn and two curses at my fellow drivers.

Conversation along the way was immaculately inoffensive—

the weather, the ride down, the geometric precision of the newly plowed fields, the contrast with life in the city, the preponderance of Latino faces in town. I was happy to be as trivial as Jill was and we arrived at the restaurant without major damage, except I'd forgotten to tell her how nice she looked, a defect I remedied as we waited for the hostess to take us to our table. She thanked me but didn't say anything I could interpret as a return of the compliment.

The restaurant wasn't quite full and the service and menu were adequate if not innovative. Jill ordered a chile relleno and I ordered a chimichanga. We both ordered margaritas, which came in stem glasses with salted rims with the circumference of Frisbees. We sipped and smiled for quite a while, each thinking of something to say and editing out most of the product. I was glad she hadn't made the waitress amend the menu to fit some sort of nutritive eleventh commandment and she seemed pleased to be the most stylish woman in the place.

"I almost didn't come," she said after a third pass at her drink.

"I wouldn't have blamed you. It was presumptuous of me to ask."

"It's not that, it's just that with the police investigation and all, I realized this might compromise my position at some point. Give me a conflict of interest of some kind."

"I doubt if it will come up, actually."

"Just in case, can we keep this our little secret?"

"Sure."

Pause.

"So how's the work going? Down here, I mean?"

"Slowly."

"Is it really a murder case?"

"Yep."

"Has there been an arrest?"

"Not even close."

"No suspects?"

"Several. But they're mostly big agricultural wigs who are

untouchable in this part of the state unless they're caught with a corpse and a smoking gun and their name scrawled in blood on the wall."

"Are you giving up?"

"I don't give up."

"I didn't think so."

Pause.

"Have you changed your mind about contributing to our investigation?" she asked.

"Is that some kind of quid pro quo?"

"For what?"

"For this."

"It probably should be, but no. I shouldn't have brought it up. Forget I said anything."

Pause for the food and a second margarita.

"So tell me about yourself, Ms. Coppelia," I said when I realized it was my turn to move the boulder.

"My life story in a hundred words or less?"

"Take two."

"Let's see. Born and raised in Santa Barbara. Father a lawyer; mother a realtor."

"Which has to mean you were rich, given it was Santa Barbara."

"Not rich, not in Santa Barbara terms, at least. But comfortable."

"House on the beach?"

"Near."

"Private school?"

"Public."

"BMW in high school?"

"What are you, some sort of sociologist?"

"Just revisiting some stereotypes."

"So I'm a stereotype now?"

"The fact that you're here means you're far from it. But maybe back then. Just a little."

"If it pleases you to think so, be my guest."

"Sorry. So you followed in Daddy's footsteps."

"Eventually."

"Do I sense some past indiscretions?"

"I went though a rebellious phase, if that's what you mean."

"Tell me what makes for rebellion down Santa Barbara way."

"What on earth have you got against Santa Barbara?"

"Nothing I don't have against Sausalito."

"Whatever that means. I did some drugs, did some sex, did some living off the land till I ended up in a Portuguese jail on a trumped-up charge involving prostitution and hashish. That straightened me out real quick, let me tell you."

"Pretty hard time in those foreign jails."

"Until Daddy pulled strings and got me out. Thank God he went to Harvard along with half the foreign service."

"Then?"

"UCSB. Major in art history. Law school at Hastings. Clerked a year in Nevada, then went with the D. A.'s office nine years ago."

"Your indiscretions in Portugal didn't keep you from taking the bar on character grounds?"

"Not after Daddy talked to the right people. It seems moral turpitude is an elastic concept."

Pause.

"How about the men in your life?"

"Now? None that matter in terms other than friendship or office politics. Before? Too many to count. Well, not *that* many, since I did in fact count them one night, but a lot if the measure is carnal knowledge."

"How about if the measure is transcendant devotion?"

"Once."

"Who?"

"Guy I met in Europe; a Swede who was the most gorgeous thing I'd ever seen on two feet and for some reason God gave him a brain to go with it. It must have been some kind of willpower test, which of course I failed. Plus he was funny, and he truly loved women. That was his expertise, in fact—Sven knew more about women than women do."

"But?"

"Turned out he was gay. Or said he was, at least. But not before I made a fool of myself for a month and a half."

"Sorry about that."

"You bet I was. And that must have been lots more than a hundred words. So how about you? This first date business is tit for tat, in case you haven't done it for a while."

"Me? Let's see. Age forty-nine. Iowa; Army; Vietnam. College; law school; law practice; private investigation. Parents dead; three siblings still in the Midwest. No marriages; one engagement. No money; one less friend now that Charley Sleet is dead. Watch a lot of TV, read a lot of books, go to a lot of ball games. Bottom line— bloodied but unbowed, and no sexually transmitted diseases."

"That wasn't even close to a hundred words."

"My life has been a very short story."

"Somehow I doubt it."

"Maybe a genre novel. But definitely not a best-seller."

"You seem at ease with women. Plus you're well preserved and kind of cute. Why only one serious relationship?"

"All my relationships are serious."

"But none of them worked out."

"Not enough to take a vow."

"Are you sorry about that?"

"Yes, in general. No, in any of the particulars."

"Have you given up the hunt?"

"Nope."

"Good. What kinds of books do you read?"

"Novels, mostly."

"What kind of novels? Detective stories?"

"Not since I've been a detective."

"Lawyer novels?"

"Not since I've been a lawyer. How about you?"

"For recreation? I read mostly women, like Anne Tyler and Alice Hoffman, some biography as well. And I hike and bike and take pictures of birds. And go to Tahoe to gamble every six months."

"Really?"

"Really."

"Why?"

"It gives me the illusion that I'm still rebelling against something, I think."

Pause.

"You like your job, Ms. Coppelia?" I asked.

"Most of the time."

"Going to leave the government for private practice some day?"

"I hope not."

"You can't get rich being an A.D.A."

"I don't need to get rich. I forgot to mention that Daddy died three years back. Despite our differences, he had a nice trust fund set up for me; the monthly stipend is embarrassingly large."

"Quite a guy, your daddy."

"I hated his guts."

"Ah."

"That's not the word for it."

"Should we talk about that for a while?"

"Not yet, we shouldn't," she said, and finished her chile relleno and drained her margarita.

I looked at her empty plate. "What now? Dessert? Movie? A nightcap somewhere? A tour of my sumptuous room?"

"Does your motel have those Pay per View types of movies?"

"I think so."

"What's playing?"

"No idea."

"But probably something."

"There's always something," I said. "Usually starring Schwarzenegger."

CHAPTER EIGHTEEN

While I was settling the bill at the register, a young man came in the front door, obviously looking for something or someone. When he got to the cashier, he stopped. "You know who owns that gray Buick out in the lot?"

"That would be me," I told him.

His grin was broadly wry and genuinely amazed. "You better get out there, mister."

"Why?"

"Someone just dumped it over."

"What are you talking about?"

He scratched the tip of his nose as words tumbled from his mouth like clowns. "Some guys drive up in a truck, one of those flatbed jobs that tilts back and makes a ramp? Then one of them gets in your car and drives it onto the incline, only with two wheels on and two off, which turns it over. Not an accident, but on purpose. Then he climbs out of the car, gets back in the truck, and they drive off like they did that kind of thing every day of the week. Damnedest thing I ever seen. Figured they were shooting a movie. They do that around here sometimes, except there weren't any cameras or trailers or groupies out there," he added, as though I'd already accused him of fibbing.

Jill was standing next to me, mouth agape or close to it. "What on earth?" she said.

I put a hand on her arm. "I'd better check it out. Stay here till I get back."

I went outside and looked. The truck and the two guys were gone, but the Buick was just as the kid said it would be, resting at a thirty-degree angle on its roof and hood, as helpless as a turtle flipped on its back, its wheels raised toward the sky like the hooves of a long-dead horse. The windshield was cracked, the front edge of the roof was caved in six inches, and the hood was dented in front from the weight of the engine, but otherwise nothing seemed different except for the paper flapping beneath the windshield wiper.

I bent down and pulled it free. It was a map of Northern California, torn from a road atlas and annotated. A Magic Marker circled Salinas and San Francisco and a big black arrow pointed from the former to the latter. I guess the message was that I was supposed to go home, the way the crow flies if possible. I went back inside the restaurant.

"Did they really flip your car?" Jill asked, the strings of a smile tugging her lips.

I nodded. "We're going to need a wrecker," I told her. "Then maybe a cab." I asked the cashier for a phone book.

"Are they still out there?" Jill asked as I was looking up the number.

"No."

"Why did they do it?"

"They want me to go back where I came from."

"Who's they?"

"I don't know. Probably one of the Gelbrides."

"Those signs I see all over? Some kind of farms or something?"

"That's them."

"You make enemies pretty fast, Mr. Tanner. Tough ones, too, it sounds like."

I closed the phone book and looked at her. "I think you should go back to the city tonight."

"Why?"

"It could be dangerous to hang around with me."

She smiled. "Okay."

"Okay what?"

"Okay I'll consider it."

The wrecker guy was certain he could do what I needed, which was to roll the car back onto its wheels, so certain I suspected he had done it before. It took him twenty minutes to get there and another thirty to get the job done with minimal damage to the rest of the car—all I had to do was shove when he had one side of the vehicle up on the hook and gave me the word to push. The next thing I knew it had flopped down onto its wheels, bouncing like a housebound child eager to go out and play.

Since I wasn't a member of AAA, the wrecker guy charged me a fortune. I got behind the wheel, slouched down in the seat to keep from bumping my head, and drove around the lot. Despite how it looked, the Buick ran as well as before or maybe better, but the top of my skull wanted to poke through the roof and the view through the windshield was fractured. I waved for the driver to go, then joined Jill at the door.

I'd spent the dead time telling her about Rita Lombardi and what she had done and why I was there. When I'd finished, she'd looked at me with a higher degree of concern. "You're a stranger in a strange land, it sounds like."

"To coin a phrase."

"Why don't you leave it up to the police?"

"For the same reason you shouldn't leave the Triad up to the SFPD."

When I reached the door I asked a question. "Are you going back to the city tonight?"

She crossed her arms and scowled. "I wouldn't have been a

prosecutor for nine years if I turned tail whenever someone tossed a threat at me."

"I suppose not."

"Actually, I find danger to be something of an aphrodisiac."

"Do you now?"

She poked me on the arm. "But at the moment I'm in the mood for more talk."

"Talk is a woman's favorite foreplay, someone told me once."

"Talk is a woman's favorite anything except new shoes," Jill countered. "Where can we find a cold beer?"

We went into the night and scrunched into the front of my caved-in car, looking more than a little ridiculous and feeling giddy and heedless as a result. We found a bar downtown, another in the Latino section, and a third in a mall so far north I wasn't sure I could find my way back to the motel.

By the time I did, I'd learned more about Jill's family in Southern California, and more than I wanted to know about her life as a single woman footloose in San Francisco—Jill was candid to a fault. She was bold, brave, and brash in her professional life as well, as proved by the fact that she was getting ready to take on the entire San Francisco police department in the aftermath of the death of my friend, Charley Sleet.

She was already feeling the heat from foe and friend alike, from everyone from the Chamber of Commerce to the Navy League to the PBA. But with the backing of her boss, a maverick former defense attorney elected two years earlier on a reformist ticket, she was determined to proceed to indictment and conviction via the institution of the Grand Jury. The first hearing was scheduled for the end of the month. Though I expected another entreaty that I join the fray in the form of turning state's evidence, all she seemed to expect was that I wished her well.

We got out of the car and regarded the motel, a boxy structure with a few halfhearted efforts at a federal design tacked on as cheap upgrades, the roar of traffic on Highway 101 a precursor of insomnia directly at its back. "Maybe we should drive to Carmel," I said. "This isn't all that romantic."

"It has a bed and a bathroom, doesn't it?"

"One of each."

"Then that's all the romance we need. We're not teenagers, after all."

"All teenagers need is a backseat."

We detoured past her car—a trim little Altima—to pick up her bag, then went up to the room by the side entrance so we wouldn't have to deal with the desk clerk. When we got to the room, she inspected it cursorily and nodded. "I've stayed in worse. The D.A.'s per diem barely covers a Motel 6."

"There's one across the street if you want to reminisce."

"This will be fine, thank you very much. I don't suppose you have the makings of a nightcap on hand."

Flushed with her decision to spend the night and relieved that it hadn't taken abject pleading to achieve, I held up a bottle of Ballantine's. "Don't leave home without it."

"A light one, please. Ice, no water."

I picked up the empty ice bucket. "Be back in a minute."

"Take three," she said, and grabbed her bag and went into the bathroom and shut the door.

I tucked the bucket under my arm and headed down the hall, my feet barely touching the carpet, my heart butting against my chest like a psychotic in a padded room. I started to fill the bucket right away, then decided Jill meant me to take her literally, so I lingered near the vending machine, examining the selections. It's amazing what you can get out of a machine these days—this one included toothpaste and shampoo and cherry-flavored mouthwash, as well as a dozen candy bars I'd never heard of before—whatever happened to Butterfinger and Clark bars?

My watch was getting worn out from being looked at so often. When my three minutes were up, I filled the bucket with a noisy crash of cubes, then returned to the room at the pace of a forced march, my heart doing enough calisthenics to suggest a tantrum. As I walked down the hall I tried not to overestimate what might lie in wait for me. It would be wonderful or awful, if past experience was any guide, and edgy and awkward until I was sure which direction it would take. I tapped on the door and entered the room.

Jill was nowhere to be seen. For a moment I was sure she'd fled, coming to some prim version of her senses, but then I heard water running in the bathroom. My own senses stuck on autopilot, I went to the basin, unwrapped the glasses, added ice and then booze, took a look, then gave one of them a bit of a boost.

As I was finishing the calibrations I heard a rustle at my back, slick and smooth, like a skater on fresh ice. I looked in the mirror. What I saw made me pivot so I could appreciate the image directly, rather than on the rebound.

Jill had changed from her travel clothes into a negligee—a black, floor-length number cut low at the bust and cinched tight at the waist, sexy but subtle, simple yet tantalizing. She met my look as squarely as a head-on collision.

"These moments can be awkward sometimes," she said, her voice throaty and resolute. "So I thought I'd make things easier." She turned in a dancer's pirouette. "You like?"

"Very much. But I'm afraid my silk pajamas are still at the cleaners."

"You've never owned silk pajamas in your life."

"True."

"But that's okay. Men look better in their birthday suits anyway."

I looked at the bulge around my middle. "You've been consorting with a better class of people." I held up the glasses. "Do we drink first? Or get right to the cuddling?"

"Drink please," she said.

I handed her a sweaty highball, then took the other for myself. She looked at hers and then mine. "This one is stronger," she said. "Are you trying to get me loaded? The negligee was to make it clear that wouldn't be necessary."

"I've found that as I've gotten older, liquor has a tendency to adversely affect my performance in certain venues."

She raised her glass. "To peak performance, by all means."

I tried to laugh but couldn't quite bring it off. "Not that there's any pressure or anything."

"Not yet, there isn't."

She giggled at her impertinence, then sipped her drink, then went to the bed and pulled back the covers and propped the pillows against the headboard. The art above her was a copy of a rural scene by Grant Wood. The barn looked like a battleship and the shocks of winter wheat looked like weapons of ancient combat.

"I used to love motels," Jill said as she slipped into the bed. "The anonymity. The freedom from responsibility of cleaning up after yourself. But now all I can think of is what kind of infectious organism the previous occupants might have deposited."

"That's a mood lifter."

She wrinkled her nose. "Sorry about that."

I started to stretch out next to her, but she stiff-armed me away. "No clothes allowed. It's nude or nothing, buster."

"You're not nude," I pointed out.

She crossed her arms, lifted her hips, and was out of her gown with a flair and a flourish that only women can manage with panache. "Any more complaints?"

I looked her over. "I believe those breasts aren't precisely symmetrical. Maybe I'd better take measurements."

She threw the nightgown at my face. "Finish your drink and get in and warm me up. I thought it was hot in this part of the state. I should have brought my pajamas."

I finished my drink in a single gulp and got naked without falling on my face, which is as close to panache as I come.

My gusto was soon tempered by my recent bout with a bullet. As I groaned involuntarily during a preliminary maneuver, Jill sensed what was happening and slowed things down, though almost to a fault. Her generosity was so comprehensive I worried that she was obtaining no pleasure herself from the exercise, that the thrall was traveling in a single direction. But my nerve endings must have cut a deal with my genitalia, because as we surged toward climax I kept my part of the bargain, or so it seemed to me.

When we collapsed into a panting clutch, Jill asked if I was all right.

"Fine," I said. "You?"

She kissed me on the nose, her breasts nuzzling like kittens at my neck. "You're a considerate lover, Mr. Tanner," she cooed.

"And you're an accomplished partner, Ms. Coppelia."

"I like making love. It's nice if it comes packaged with a deep and meaningful relationship, but I discovered that if I waited for that to happen, I only had sex once a decade. So I adjusted my standards."

"Good idea."

"I suppose you screw anything in a skirt."

"Only District Attorneys, as a matter of fact. You're my seventy-ninth."

She hit me with a pillow; I took it from her and hit her back. We kissed and cuddled and ten minutes later she was asleep, snoring softly at my side, as comfortable as if we'd been married for twenty years and she trusted me to put out the cat and lock the back door. Surprisingly, I found myself wishing it were so.

CHAPTER NINETEEN

We had breakfast in the ersatz diner next to the motel. Neither of us said very much, but if Jill was in the vicinity of where I was, her mind was arcing into the future, speculating, estimating, and plotting additional episodes that would be as golden as this one had been. But maybe that wasn't where she was at all. Maybe she was eager to get back to the city, to the comforts of distance and disentanglement, leaving the complications of me in her rearview mirror. I finished my pancakes, drank a third cup of coffee, and decided how I would finish the day.

When her mushroom omelet was gone, Jill looked at her watch. "Well . . ."

"Well . . ."

"I guess I should be on my way."

"We could go over to Carmel for a few hours. Wallow in cuteness. Walk on the beach. Spend lots of money."

"Been there; done that, I'm afraid."

"We could pick strawberries for ten hours at ten cents a pint."

"That's all they get? A dime for those little baskets that sell for a dollar in the market?"

"That's it."

"And your friend was trying to do something about that?"

"Yep."

"Is that why she was killed, do you think? Because she was agitating on behalf of the farmworkers?"

"I don't know," I said truthfully.

"She sounds like a wonderful woman. I think I'd better let you get back to work."

"It's Sunday. Even Sam Spade rested on Sunday."

"When you're as famous as Sam Spade, you can rest, too."

When we got to her car we looked at each other, then smiled, then embraced. "Thanks for coming down," I said.

"It was definitely my pleasure. Thanks for asking."

"And thanks for saying things like that."

"You're not a charity case, Mr. Tanner. And I'm not a social worker."

With that burst of chastisement, she got in the car and started the engine, then rolled down the window and leaned out. "Thanks for breakfast. And dinner. And the room."

"You're welcome."

"Good luck with the case. And the car."

"Thanks. You, too. With bringing down the bad cops."

"Thanks."

"I'd like to call you when I get back to the city."

"Please do."

"I had a nice time, Jill. A real nice time."

"So did I, Marsh. I didn't know Salinas was so sexy."

She puckered up and I bent down and kissed her lightly and somehow it was the most intimate moment of her visit. She put the Altima in gear and drove out of the lot and, after a brief wave in my direction, launched herself toward the stream of traffic heading north on 101.

I was more regretful at her departure than I expected to be, a spasm of tristesse that was far from usual in my experience. Beset by foreign feelings, I went back to the room and watched news-talk TV until my psyche had reassembled itself enough to get me back to business.

It was time to visit the union, so I took 101 north for almost ten miles, then took a left at the Watsonville/Aromas turnoff. Rita had been right—because of their surging profitability, every tillable pocket of land in the Pajaro Valley was given over to strawberries. In each of the fields I passed, the crop looked ready to pick, though there were few workers in sight, presumably because it was Sunday.

The highway eventually deposited me on San Juan Road, took me past the distribution and research facilities of Driscoll Strawberry Associates, the cooperative Carlos had mentioned as one of the pioneers in the strawberry business, then through the sleepy town of Pajaro and into the heart of Watsonville, a city of some thirty thousand people that was the core of the strawberry industry in the state. As I reached the center of town, I attracted a host of catcalls and giggles because of the risible state of my car. I felt like sort of a celebrity.

The UFW office was a block off the main drag in a narrow storefront that was part of a rustic mini-mall, which seemed less prosperous than its developers must have projected. The windows of the union office were plastered with flyers in both Spanish and English, urging support for the *campesinos*. The most arresting displayed bold white lettering on a red and blue background that read: "WHEN WAS THE LAST TIME YOU SAID . . . THIS IS WRONG."

Inside the door there was a small waiting room with a picture of Cesar Chavez on the wall and a display case full of caps and buttons and T-shirts on sale to union supporters, as though the UFW was a sports franchise out to milk its market for every last nickel it could generate. A young woman behind the reception desk asked how she could help me, then was immediately interrupted by a phone call. By the time she got back to me she'd answered two other calls, sold buttons to three kids of high school age who were poking and teasing each other during the entire transaction, and directed yet another visitor to an office in the back.

When she turned my way again, I smiled. "Busy day."

"Always."

"Even on Sunday."

"Especially on Sunday. It's the only day the workers have the time and energy to meet with us."

"Are you in the union yourself?"

She shook her head. "I'm a volunteer."

"Have you ever worked the fields?"

"In summers since I was five. When I went to college my father refused to let me pick fruit anymore—he said I was better than that now. So I work days for the union and nights at Long's Drugs. There is more honor working the fields," she added, "even if my father cannot see it." She looked me over. "Are you a reporter?"

"No."

"*La migra?* Immigration?" she explained when she saw I didn't understand.

I shook my head. "I'm looking for information about a friend of mine who was sympathetic to the cause and might have done some work for the union in recent months. I've been told a woman named Liz Connors knew the woman I'm talking about."

"What's the name of your friend?"

"Rita Lombardi."

"Not Latino."

"Italian, from Haciendas."

"Why do you need this information?"

"It might tell me who killed her."

That one knocked her off balance. "I see. *Uno momento, por favor.*"

She left her desk and trotted down the hall. After a minute she returned and told me someone would be with me shortly. Then she helped the four people who made up the line that had formed in her absence, in a language I couldn't interpret.

I took a seat on the battered couch and stared up into the chocolate eyes of Mr. Chavez. He was a saint, some people say, which doesn't mean he was perfect, it just means he was courageous and right—a soft and selfless man, intensely spiritual, who had given his life to aid an oppressed people whose simple aspirations were opposed by some of the most powerful political and financial interests in the state.

Chavez may have been less effective than leaders like Gandhi and King, perhaps, but the effort, not the result, is the measure of a man, and his effort had been superhuman at times, such as when he starved himself to the point of collapse in protest of the outrages committed in the table grape industry. In his latter years he had reportedly withdrawn into an almost mystical reliance on a higher power to deliver the workers from their oppressors and the union effort had suffered from his detachment.

But who could blame him? By then the crusading spirit of the sixties had given way to the self-absorption of the eighties. To the extent that the union relied on popular support for success, it was doomed to failure—the populace from which Chavez had formerly received both money and time was worshiping Madonna and reading Danielle Steele and clamoring to work on Wall Street. I remembered the only time I'd seen Chavez in person. He had seemed truly holy to me, a man of God and the people, a revolutionary in the footsteps of Christ himself. I doubted that I or anyone retained the capacity to see any leader in such a light again.

A woman came through the front door and stood before me as if she were auditioning for a remake of *Shane*. "You the man who was asking about Rita Lombardi?" she said.

She was in her early thirties, her skin browned like Thanksgiving turkey, her hair shaggy and short and dull brown, and her eyes dark and squinting, as though genetically forearmed against the sun. Her attire included cowboy boots, Levi's as snug as blue body lotion, and a denim shirt with sleeves rolled above her elbows.

I stood up. "I'm him," I said. "Marsh Tanner."

She extended a hand. "Liz Connors."

We shook. "You knew Rita Lombardi, am I right?"

"Yes, I did. It's horrible what happened to her."

"I'm trying to find out exactly what that was."

"Who killed her, you mean."

"Yes."

"I'm happy to help if I can. But I have to tell you I don't know anything significant. If I did, I'd have gone to the police."

"I'm still looking for motive at this point, so I'm wondering if Rita did much work for the union in the past few months."

Connors looked at me and then at the people still lined up at the front desk for purposes as much social as political or economic. "Why don't we discuss this outside?"

"Fine with me."

She led me into a small courtyard in the center of the mini-mall. It was too early for the shops to be open, so the bench was relatively private. When we sat side by side we were secluded by a variety of flora, most of which were prickly. "I could probably find you some coffee," Liz Connors began.

"I'm topped up. But thanks." I looked back at the flyers decorating the window. "How'd you get in the union business?"

"My parents were sixties radicals. Berkeley, mostly; Madison for a while. I was conceived in People's Park, so they claim, though for some reason I always had doubts about that and some of their other supposed exploits. Anyway, they went on and on about civil rights and social justice and economic tyranny, and for a long time I tuned them out, but lo and behold, I ended up buying into it, big time." She grinned. "Mom and Dad are appalled, of course. They still dress like hippies but they live in Mill Valley on my mother's inheritance. Trustafarians is what people call them behind their backs."

I laughed at the image and the nomenclature. "Have you always worked for the farmworkers?"

"I spent some time with the Native American Rights in Arizona when I got out of college at Reed. But it's too hot down there for Irish stock like me, plus the Native Americans don't like palefaces telling them what to do anymore. Even palefaces who agree that they've been screwed for two hundred years."

"How about Rita?" I asked again. "Did she work for the union at some point?"

Liz Connors shook her head. "Not in any official capacity."

"Then how did you meet her?"

"She came by the office not long after she started to work in the strawberry business. We traded information from time to time, about the latest atrocity in the fields, about more effective forms of advocacy, about workers who looked as if they had some organizing skills. When I was in Haciendas or she was in Watsonville we'd commiserate over a beer or a cup of coffee." She smiled sadly. "And dream of a brighter day for workers everywhere."

"But Rita wasn't doing anything specific? Organizing or recruiting or whatever?"

"Not for us, she wasn't. From what I could see, she was pretty busy keeping Carlos Reyna's operation afloat."

"You know Carlos?"

"A little."

"He a good guy?"

"His heart's in the right place, but his methods are mistaken."

"How so?"

She gazed across the mall, as if an explanation hung somewhere near the ice cream parlor. "Carlos believes he can go it alone, rise high enough in the system to offer a better way to the workers all by himself. But the owners won't cave in to Carlos Reyna, they'll only respond to collective pressure applied across the entire Salinas and Pajaro valleys."

"You think you can organize enough workers to bring that kind of pressure to bear?"

"I'm sure of it."

When her eyes dared me to deny it, I shrugged. "Good luck."

"We've got some things going for us, you know," she said defensively.

"Like what?"

"One, Chicanos are the only people who will do this kind of work full time. Two, when the fruit is ripe, it must be picked. A strawberry plant is not a warehouse—it's harvested or it dies. Three, some time early in the next century, Latinos will be the largest political force in the state of California. At that point, the legislature will support us, not our oppressors. And four, our cause is just and our hearts are pure and God is on our side." Her smile was part beatific and part insolent.

"You're an optimistic woman, Ms. Connors. I seem to be running into a lot of them lately."

She shrugged. "What's the point of being anything else?"

"That's fine, except I think you're leaving something out."

"Like what?"

"The degree of desperation of the workers. Seems to me most of them will be happy to keep taking crumbs because even a crumb is more than they had back home."

"That's true to a point. But fewer workers are illegal now, because of pressure on the Border Patrol to keep them out, because of the hardships of life up here, because of better conditions in Mexico. More and more of the strawberry workers are citizens, but to hold your head high in America you need to make more than five thousand dollars a year. Sooner or later they will see that the union is the only way they can become economic citizens as well as legal citizens."

"Apparently Rita was highly energized before she died. She seemed to think she was going to bring about some big changes in the system." I gestured toward the union office. "I figured she was thinking that the agent of those changes would come from here."

"In time it will, but Rita believed she would see major improvement in conditions right away, it had nothing to do with us. Like all revolutions, our struggle will take many years. A lifetime, probably."

"Do you know what the meeting with you was going to be about? The one set for the day after she died?"

She shook her head. "All I know is, she wanted one of our lawyers to be there, too."

This was new, so I perked up. "What lawyer?"

"She didn't mention anyone in particular, she let me choose."

"So the lawyer didn't know what she wanted?"

"No. After Rita was killed, I asked Jake—Bill Jacobs—if she'd talked to him privately, but he said she hadn't."

Liz Connors stood up. "Sorry I can't be more help, but I have to get back. We're taking a busload of foreign journalists out to a labor camp on San Andreas Road to see the abominable conditions for themselves. You're welcome to join us. We'll leave here about two."

"Do the camps have some connection with Rita?"

"Not that I know of. Not the ones over here, at least."

"Then I'll take a pass." I put out my hand. "Thanks for your time. And good luck with your efforts."

"Thank you."

"By the way. Do you know a family named Vargas? Homero and Maria and a daughter named Consuelo?"

"I believe Rita mentioned them once. But I don't remember why and I know nothing more about them."

"Does the Gelbride family do much business over here?"

She shook her head. "All their fields are in Salinas. This is Driscoll and Naturripe and Coastal Berry territory."

"Did Rita mention anything about Randy Gelbride in her talks with you?"

"Just that he trolled for young women in the labor camps over there, and she warned me to be on the lookout for him."

"So that's it as far as Rita's concerned?"

"I'm afraid so. Sorry I can't be more help."

"Well, thanks again."

Liz Connors turned away, then turned back. "If you find out that Rita was killed by a farmworker, please let us know right away."

"Why?"

"So we can prepare a counter-statement."

"A denial, you mean?"

"More like an explanation of how a person can be driven to a murderous sense of outrage by the system of labor employed in this valley. How a person may not be criminally responsible when that system deprives him of his dignity, his heath, and his ability to earn a living wage. And how such a system poisons the victimizer as well as the victim."

"But in this case the victim wasn't a grower, the victim was on the side of the workers."

"Craziness makes it impossible to recognize your friends from your enemies," she said. "It's why the workers in these valleys live in constant fear."

CHAPTER TWENTY

I drove back to Haciendas, my mind still oscillating between Jill Coppelia and Rita Lombardi. They were polar opposites in some ways—the former bold and erotic and naughty, the latter wholesome and generous and sweet—but they were alike in their bravery and their candor and their commitment to causes beyond their own self-interest. I guess that's what attracted me to both of them, because such people are becoming an endangered species.

Since it was Sunday, there weren't many options open to investigation, but one of them might be the police department. I pulled up in front of the multipurpose municipal building a little before eleven, the air still cool from the fog, the town still sleeping off the night before, memories of my time with Jill still buoying my spirits and rewriting my fantasies.

The officer who was occupying Sal Delder's chair told me the chief was in back in his office. Because he offered no indication that it was unusual for Mace Dixon to be working on Sunday, the chief kept inching up in my estimation.

After getting clearance to pass, I headed toward the back of the building. The door was open so I tapped on the jamb and looked in. "Tanner," he pronounced when he saw me. "Stumble over any more corpses?"

I shook my head. "I was wondering if you'd made any progress with the last one."

"Mona Upshaw? Afraid not. She was a saint, according to everyone who knew her."

"I hear the same about Rita Lombardi."

"Guess it's still a hazardous occupation."

"Maybe that's how they're connected," I said.

"I don't get it. Some sort of church thing, you mean?"

I shook my head. "Maybe they were both trying to help the same cause."

"What cause was that?"

"A family named Vargas."

The chief flexed his bicep, checked to be sure it retained its impressive dimension, then looked back at me. "Who are these Vargas people you keep talking about? I know a dozen families named Vargas."

"This is Homero and Maria. And a daughter named Consuelo, who looks like a young Rita Hayworth."

The chief leaned back in his chair. "That one."

"That one," I agreed.

"Come to think of it, the Lombardi girl did talk to me about her."

"Talked in what way?"

"She told me the girl might need police protection."

"From whom?"

The chief paused. "This doesn't go out of this room."

"Fine."

"I mean it, Tanner."

"So do I."

He thought it over, then nodded. "Randy Gelbride was the name she mentioned."

"Police protection from what?"

"Sexual harassment, it sounded like. Maybe even assault. Like father, like son," was what I thought he muttered next.

194

"What does that mean, Chief?"

"Nothing."

"It didn't sound like nothing. It sounded like genetics."

"Forget about it."

"Gus Gelbride assaulted some woman sexually?" I persisted.

The chief reddened like a raspberry and shook his head. "No fucking comment."

"Okay, let's take the names out of it. Sexual advances by growers toward female field workers aren't uncommon, are they?"

"Unfortunately no."

"Had Rita ever talked to you about the problem before?"

"No."

"But she did with the Vargas girl."

"Yep."

"So why her?"

"I don't know."

I reminded him of our pact. "It stays in the room, Chief."

He rolled his eyes in exasperation. "Look, Tanner. It pisses me off to no end that two women have been murdered in this town and I have no idea who did it, but I still don't know what was going on with Rita Lombardi and the Vargas girl."

I didn't know whether to believe him but I also didn't know how to make him tell me more if there was more to tell. "What did you tell Rita you'd do about the Vargas situation?"

"I told her there was nothing much we could do without locking Randy up before he did something wrong and we wouldn't do that because it's called preventive detention and we don't operate that way in this county."

"At least not with the Gelbrides."

The chief slapped his hands on the desk simultaneously, creating a minor earthquake. "You keep implying there's more than one kind of justice in this town. I don't like it. I don't like it enough to tell you to get the fuck out of my office."

I stayed put. "If apologies are in order, I apologize."

"That's no apology, that's lawyer talk. Hit the road, Tanner. I got better things to do with a Sunday than listen to you insult me."

"I take back what I said about the Gelbrides."

"Fuck you. Get out of here before I have Lopez put you in a cell." He picked up some paperwork to give his fury something to work on but me.

"A couple more things and I'll be gone," I said peaceably. "Do you know of any connection between the Vargas girl and Nurse Upshaw?"

"Not a one. You through now?"

"What about my original hunch?"

"Which was what?"

"That Nurse Upshaw might have heard or seen something important the night they brought Rita in."

"We're not idiots, Tanner. We talked to everyone on duty down at Mercy that night. No one heard anything because there was nothing to hear—the Lombardi girl was a heartbeat away from being DOA."

"How about what they saw?"

"How do you mean?"

"I don't know. I thought maybe they might have seen someone odd down there that night. Someone out of place."

"The killer, you mean?"

"Why not?"

"In my experience, life's seldom that simple. Plus it's a hospital. Sooner or later we're all going to be in there for something, so who's to say what's out of place?"

I walked to the door, then turned back. "What did Rita say when you told her you couldn't stop Randy Gelbride from tormenting the Vargas girl?"

"She said she'd have to stop him herself."

"What do you think she meant?"

"No idea."

"There are people who think Rita was threatening to make trouble for the Gelbrides."

"What kind of trouble?"

"Trouble you stop with a gun."

"That's pretty hard to visualize."

"Would give a Gelbride a motive for getting rid of her if the trouble was big enough to shut them down."

"I need more than guesses, Tanner."

"You're saying you've got no leads at all?"

"Not any worth mentioning, which I wouldn't necessarily if there was."

Which meant the chief wasn't playing square. Otherwise he would have told me about Mona Upshaw's surprising bank balance and the evidence that she'd underwritten Rita's surgery, the kind of connections that lead to relevant evidence in a murder case. So all bets were off. Somehow it made me relieved.

"How about you?" the chief went on sarcastically. "I figured a private eye from the big city would have the Lombardi thing wrapped up by now."

I sent his words back in the same envelope of condescension. "In my experience, life isn't that simple."

"So you've come up empty?"

I shrugged. "I hear a lot of bad things about the Gelbride boy."

"So do I."

"But no charges have ever been filed?"

He shook his head. "Lots of conversation, though. Words to the wise, you might say."

"Is he wise enough to take them?"

"Not so you'd notice. Now get out. I got things to do that don't involve bullshit."

I walked into the hall, then walked back, feeling like a Columbo impostor. "One favor."

He looked up. "This isn't a gift shop."

I persevered. "I was hoping you could get me in to see Gus Gelbride."

"How was I going to do that?"

"Beats me."

"Hell, the only way I'd get in to see Gus myself is with a warrant in my hand." The chief looked at the clock on the wall. "I were you, I'd get my ass over to St. Bonaventure."

"Why?"

"Gus and the family will be at eleven o'clock mass. Never miss, probably because they got so many sins to slough off. Maybe the homily will make him charitable enough to talk to you."

I thanked the chief and left the building. Five minutes later, I was in the parking lot at St. Bonaventure, watching the Gelbride family file into the side door of the church, a privilege that seemed reserved entirely for them.

The whole family was there—Gus, Estelle, Randy and Missy—dressed in their Sunday best, clutching rosaries and prayerbooks, trudging sullenly across the asphalt as though they were on their way to a hanging. The women wore hats; the men wore neckties for what looked like the first time in their lives. They seemed devout in every respect but the expressions on their faces—if it were any place else, I'd have bet they'd break out in a brawl.

When the family had disappeared inside the church, I went around to the main entrance. Given the size of Haciendas, there was a surprisingly large crowd gathered for the service, most of them Latino but not nearly all. Carlos Reyna was escorting Louise Lombardi up the steps just behind Consuelo and Maria Vargas, who looked more ethereal than anyone in their simple cotton frocks. Clean and pressed and precisely draped, the dresses implied an effort to maintain respectability within the confines of a cave that made the more sumptuous store-bought finery of the Gelbrides seem piddling by comparison.

As Carlos and Mrs. Lombardi entered the church, Sal Delder trotted up the steps to their rear, pausing only to cover her head before ducking inside. After her came Scott Thorndike, the English teacher, who seemed to have lingered in the yard to allow Sal to enter before he did so himself. Then came Thelma Powell and an older woman I assumed was her mother. When everyone had found seats, I slipped into a vacant slot in the back row.

I'm not Catholic. I was born Presbyterian but haven't followed that or any faith for years. I don't think I believe in God, down deep, even though I converse with Him on occasion, usually when I've screwed up. But I do believe in the belief in God, at least for the poor and downtrodden, for whom faith can be, if not the opiate that Karl Marx suggested, at least an effective antidepressant. And there is something about a church, whether a simple chapel or a Gothic cathedral, that suggests there is a path of righteousness of some dimension that could be profitably pursued by us all.

The service washed over me the way a brook washes over a rock. With Father McNally presiding, the hymns, the prayers, the genuflections, the mysterious rites at the altar, and the simple homily about personal responsibility in a universe of divine omnipotence, seemed matters of gravity and significance, yet somehow mechanical and incoherent. I prefer to engage spiritual issues on my own rather than with the aid of experts, even when the experts are priests and scripture. Plus, I sensed the mass had delivered a more potent punch back when it had been rendered in Latin. Even if the congregation could only incompletely under-stand its meaning, it may be that in matters of the spirit, literal-ness gets in the way of a deeper grasp of truth, that revelation comes more powerfully through the heart than the head.

I stayed seated all the while, attracting a couple of hostile stares and a few more curious ones when I abstained from kneeling and from taking communion as I kept my eye on the people in the crowd whom I knew. Which turned out to be difficult, since at one point or another they all exchanged glances with each other with the exception of Louise Lombardi, whose effort was expended in keeping her sobs to herself so as not to disturb the other worshipers. Carlos Reyna teared up as well, and so did Thelma Powell. The Gelbrides' faces, in contrast, would have worn well on Mount Rushmore.

By the time the service had finished I was certain that Scott Thorndike and Missy Gelbride were lovers, that Randy Gelbride still lusted after Consuelo Vargas, that Gus Gelbride was nettled by almost everything his son said or did, that Missy Gelbride had some sort of active issue with her mother, and that Estelle Gelbride had genuine compassion for Louise Lombardi's loss of her only child. What the rest of the sidelong glances meant was far less clear, but the possibilities were intriguing.

When the service ended, I was the first one out the door. As the Gelbride family filed out the far side, silent and in single file like losers trudging back to the locker room, I sidled up to Gus. He was short and ruddy, exuding power and primacy in the manner of a battered prizefighter, with huge hands and a huge nose and a crease in his sun-baked bald skull that looked like someone had edged a knife on it.

I steeled my nerves. "I'd like to speak to you sometime at your convenience, Mr. Gelbride," I began sotto voce, in hopes none of the others would overhear.

He started as though I'd pricked him with a pin. Like most royalty, he wasn't used to being addressed by commoners. "Who the hell are you?"

"He's a PI," Randy said, stopping so we caught up to him. The women hesitated, looking at me with more trepidation than I usually generate, then continued toward the car. "He thinks we have something to do with the Lombardi girl's murder," Randy went on.

I smiled at Gus. "Do you?"

"Don't be dumb," Gus muttered, irritated but seemingly as much by his son as by me. "I don't talk business in church—what do you think I am, a heathen? You got a problem, speak to Randy."

"I already spoke to Randy. He didn't enjoy it, evidently. Some of his boys rolled my car last night."

Randy reddened to the color of his father's forehead. "Bullshit."

I looked at Gus. "I'd like to keep this private, Mr. Gelbride."

Gus regarded his son the way he would regard a panhandler. "Go."

Randy started to resist, then shrugged, then ambled toward the car as though that's what he wanted to do in the first place.

I kept my eye on Gus. "Randy also told me that none of you had anything to do with Rita's death."

"So? It's true. As God is my witness." He glanced warily back at the church, as if to make sure God wasn't eavesdropping.

It was time to play my trump, one I'd concocted during the mass, built on scraps of facts and hints of emotion and the cryptic comment of Chief Dixon. "Randy's about to cause you a problem," I said softly.

"Randy causes lots of problems."

"This is a big one."

"What is it?"

I paused for effect. "The problem is, he doesn't know about the Vargas girl."

Gus stopped walking and lowered his voice. "We have handled such problems before."

"Not this kind. Randy has his eye on a girl named Consuelo Vargas. She's fifteen years old. If he has his way, he'll have committed statutory rape before the week is out."

"Vargas?" Gus swiped the back of his hand across his lip. "Randy's a grown man. He does what he wants. I got no control over him any—"

"That's the Vargas girl over there," I interrupted, pointing her out, "next to the woman in the blue dress. The woman in blue is her mother."

Gus squinted. "So? What do I . . ." His words trailed off, as though his question had been answered by divine intervention.

"Rape isn't the only crime Randy would be committing, is it, Mr. Gelbride?"

He looked for a long time, at Consuelo for a while, but even longer at her mother. Then he turned to me. "You tell anyone else about this?"

"No one."

He measured me for truth. "Keep it that way."

"I will if I can talk to you about what happened to Rita Lombardi."

He thought over my quid pro quo, his eyes turbulent and troubled as though it was his first bout with a dilemma. "How'd you know about me and the Vargas woman? She tell you?"

"No."

"The husband?"

"No," I repeated, then invented an explanation that couldn't be traced. "I saw how you looked at Maria in church and the resemblance between you and Consuelo. Maria must have been as beautiful as her daughter fifteen years ago."

He didn't bother with rebuttal. "You going to try to make trouble about this?"

"Not unless I need to in order to learn what happened to Rita. And not if you do right by the girl."

"What's that mean? 'Do right'?"

I smiled. "I'll let you know."

His countenance was clouded and roiling, his shoulders bulging with barely restrained havoc. "I didn't force her," he muttered in a gravelly voice. "Not once. I asked her to come to me and she came."

"That doesn't mean you didn't force her."

"How do you figure?"

"People like Maria Vargas have no options; you control every aspect of their lives except their religious faith. She couldn't risk what would happen to her and her family if she refused you." I paused to let my oration sink in. "When can we meet to talk about Rita?"

He thought it over. "Come to the house at two. We'll be done with dinner. Talk to me, nobody else."

"Agreed."

"People think they know me," he muttered. "They think I'm a brute and a monster. But I'm just a farmer. I worked hard all my life, side by side with the *braceros*. I did what I had to do to make a living. Now all of a sudden they say that's wrong. The old way is not allowed. They don't understand. The old way is the only way that works. Without it, the farms won't survive. The only growers will be corporations and the only workers will be machines."

His sermon ended, Gus joined his family at the Lincoln, his message as fervent as the one uttered by Father McNally only a few minutes earlier.

CHAPTER TWENTY-ONE

The Gelbrides piled into their Lincoln and left. I went back to the front of the church, hoping to see Carlos Reyna, but the only people left were Father McNally and a straggling parishioner. When he noticed me lingering, he bid farewell to the elderly woman and drifted my way.

"Nice service, Father," I said. "I got a strange feeling in there, as a matter of fact."

His grin seemed slightly cynical. "Spiritually uplifting, I trust."

"How long have you been at this parish, Father?"

"Almost thirty years."

"Is that normal in your business?"

"I love Haciendas. The bishop has honored my wishes to stay. Why do you ask?"

"The feeling I got in church was that if I knew everything you know, I could solve Rita's murder in an instant."

When he didn't respond, I got cynical myself. "In my business, silence means consent."

"Don't toy with me, Mr. Tanner. The seal of the confessional is sacrosanct. I would be consigned to the bowels of hell if I broke it."

"Just tell me this. If Maria Vargas gave a confession sixteen years back, you were the priest she would have given it to."

"Not necessarily. There have been many others on staff over the years. But perhaps."

"But you won't tell me whether she did or not."

"Not the particulars. No."

I shifted a gear. "Louise Lombardi is a good Catholic, I assume."

"Indisputably."

"If she committed a sin, she would confess it."

"I'm certain she would."

"I'm talking major here, Father. Not taking the Lord's name in vain."

He ruffled his feathers. "To many of us, that is as grievous a sin as there is."

"Come on, Father. You know what I mean."

"I'm not sure I do."

"I'm asking if twenty-six years ago, Mrs. Lombardi confessed the same sin Maria Vargas did."

"I told you, the seal of the confessional—"

"You can't tell me if she did. But you can tell me if she didn't."

"This is semantics, Mr. Tanner. The church has no truck with it."

I met his piety with some of my own. "Then you must not traffic in annulments in this parish."

He came close to taking the Lord's name in vain himself. "I will not listen to you fault the faith."

"We're talking murder, Father. Two of God's children are dead. I'm pretty sure the killer was one of your flock."

"I pray that is not true. But I have no choice in the matter. Not if it involves the confessional."

"If I were you, I'd make sure that's an absolute rule. Otherwise, your life will be hell."

He shook his head. "I've never dealt with anything like this. I need to think."

"Time is of the essence in murder cases."

"Perhaps. But to the church, time is merely a potential pitfall."

Stymied, I retired to my corner. "I won't press you anymore, but I would like you to do me a favor."

"What favor would that be?"

"I'd like you to suggest to Gus Gelbride that he start a scholarship fund, to educate the children of his field workers. And I'd like you to suggest that the first recipient of a grant be Consuelo Vargas."

Father McNally cocked his head to inspect me more closely. A series of emotions traveled his face, the last of them an incomplete grin. "A fine idea. And Consuelo is certainly a worthy choice. Does Mr. Gelbride know the girl personally?"

"I don't know. But I think we both know he used to know her mother."

He looked at me for several long seconds. "You've been busy."

"Yes."

"But you still haven't learned who killed Rita."

"No."

"Does the Vargas matter have anything to do with it?"

"I thought it did, but now I'm not sure."

He nodded slowly. "The scholarship idea is a good one. I'll certainly take it up with Gus. In fact, it will give me an excuse to call on him at home one day soon. That way I can reach out to other members of the family in need of ministry."

"Are you speaking of Randy?"

His expression turned melancholy. "No one is beyond the reach of God's grace, Mr. Tanner. But some are so far removed it takes an inordinate amount of time to reach out to them. One must then decide whether it is time that might better be spent in other areas."

"With Mrs. Gelbride, you mean?"

"I'm thinking more of Missy."

"What's the problem with Missy?"

"I can't go into specifics, of course. Let's just say she seems in need of spiritual guidance."

"Do you know whether or not Missy was a friend of Rita Lombardi's, Father?"

"I believe they used to be, as small children."

"But no longer?"

"I believe not."

"Do you know what happened?"

"No."

"Do you know if Mrs. Gelbride and Mrs. Lombardi are friends?"

"I believe Mrs. Gelbride has always been gracious to both Mrs. Lombardi and her daughter."

"In what way?"

"I really couldn't say, I'm afraid." He glanced at the sun, using it as a giant wristwatch. "I'm afraid I must be going. The CYO is having a picnic at Mount Madonna Park this afternoon. I'm an invited guest. You're welcome to come along. I'm sure they can scrape up another hot dog."

"It's the 'scrape up' part that worries me," I said. "But thanks anyway."

"Peace be with you, Mr. Tanner."

"That would be a change of pace."

Father McNally walked back toward the church. I got in my squashed-up car and drove the three blocks to the center of town and parked as close to the café as I could. Two kids on the corner laughed when they saw the car, then examined it more closely, as if it might not be a comic accident but the stirrings of a new fad.

Shortcake's, the café was called, and the pictures on the wall were of various manifestations of strawberries, from shortcake to frappés to trifle. Much of the parish had the same idea I did—the place was packed with people I had seen earlier at mass.

The only one I knew was Sal Delder, who was sitting alone at a table near the front window, sipping a glass of iced tea, wearing a simple white dress that buttoned to the throat and fell to mid-calf. Her hair was drawn back in a twist, her thoughts as far from where she was as her mind could throw them.

I walked to her table and looked down. "I'll buy you lunch if you let me pick your brain."

She smiled but not seriously. "It's not the most elegant proposition I've ever had, but it's the best that's come along lately. Have a seat."

"Thanks."

I pulled out a chair and sat down. The conversation around us resumed its pulse after pausing to observe the stranger's approach to the maiden lady. The waitress took my order for coffee, left me a menu, and said she'd be back.

I looked at Sal. "This looks like a place that could come up with a pretty fair meat loaf sandwich."

"If you get the plate you get potatoes and gravy and Bertha's gravy is to die for. Mondavi is thinking of bottling it with a cork and a fancy label."

"Sold," I said, and passed my choice along to the waitress the next time she drifted by. "I talked to Chief Dixon this morning," I said as the waitress went off to the kitchen.

"How'd it go?"

"Not good."

"He's in a bad mood pretty much every Sunday."

"Why?"

"Because of Saturday night."

I waited for her to elaborate and for some reason she did, though in a voice that required me to lean across the table to hear her.

"The chief and I have been having a little affair of late—Saturday nights at my place. He goes home feeling great and wakes up feeling guilty. Then he goes down to the office, his jail is full of kids who've done something dumb to save face with the gangs, and Reb gets depressed even more."

"Gangs? In Haciendas?"

"Gangs are everywhere. It's the only effective support system for kids whose families can't give them the time and attention they need. Ours are mostly Latino, of course. Los Lobos de la Valle. 'Wolves of the Valley,' " she translated. "It isn't entirely inappropriate. Why did you go see Mace Dixon?"

"To find out how things were going with the Upshaw murder. And Rita's too, of course."

"Nothing more on Rita. Not much more than that on Mona, since the forensics aren't back from Salinas."

"Any leads at all?"

She frowned and looked at the pie case on the counter by the cash register. "He'll be mad if he knows I talked to you."

"He won't hear about it from me."

She looked around. "There are a dozen more who'll tell him before sundown."

I shrugged. "Your choice."

"What the hell. The only thing we have is that there are some drugs missing at the hospital so one theory is Mona might have known what was happening to them. Plus a woman died in childbirth a few months back and the husband has been threatening everyone in the place with mayhem. Other than that, not much."

"Do any of those seem likely?"

"Not to me, but I'm not a cop."

"Has Mona Upshaw lived in Haciendas all her life?"

"I think she has professionally. She came to town when we still had a hospital in Haciendas. Then when that closed down and they converted it to migrant housing she caught on with Mercy in Salinas. I don't know where she came from originally."

"What kind of work does she do?"

"Obstetrics mostly, I think."

"She had some money, apparently."

Sal nodded. "She got rich back in the seventies. An uncle died, or something. It didn't seem to make her happy, though. Which gives me solace when I'm trying to scrape enough together to pay my bills."

I asked a question I'd asked a hundred times—it's what you do when you're a detective. "Have you heard anything from anyone about what Rita said when they brought her in?"

"No. Nothing."

"Anything else floating around that might help me out?"

"Not that I've heard. Sorry."

"Lots of dead ends in this town, Ms. Delder."

She nodded. "And I've run into all of them at one time or another."

"Personally or professionally?"

Her grin was tired and halfhearted. "Both."

"You seemed to have eyes for the English teacher this morning."

She raised a brow. "You were at mass?"

"Back row. I'm guessing you and Mr. Thorndike used to be an item."

Her lips wrinkled with distaste. "A sale item was all. I'm discontinued merchandise."

"He's with Missy Gelbride now?"

"When she lets him. When she's sane."

"She has mental problems?"

"Scott says she's manic-depressive."

"Is that official or just a guess?"

She shrugged. "She's gone away a few times. Trips to Europe that were really stays in psych wards, supposedly. But all I know is what I get from Scott."

"You still see him?"

"On occasion." She sniffed. "The occasion being when he's gone more than a month without sex."

"If I wanted to talk to Missy, how would I go about it?"

"She lives in the big house with the family. She drinks wherever they have a license to sell it. And she meets Scott at the Pine Cone Inn bar in Carmel Monday nights. Then they repair to a motel for a few hours. When she gets it together enough to make the trip, that is."

"How about Scott and Rita?"

"What about them?"

"Were they ever lovers?"

A tear bloomed in her left eye. "I really, really hope not," she said.

"There's been a suggestion that Rita was pregnant when she died."

Sal shook her head. "Rumors. This town is rumor central."

"You're sure?"

"I saw the ME's report. If she had been pregnant, it would have said so and it didn't."

CHAPTER TWENTY-TWO

I spent another half hour chatting with Sal Delder. We talked about Rita for a while, exploring Sal's suggestion that Rita was a true revolutionary and my burgeoning sense that Rita's newly discovered empowerment had to do with the Gelbride family, but reached no firm conclusion about either assessment. Then we talked about Mona Upshaw, whom Sal had disliked for reasons unclear even to her, and about Chief Dixon, whom she admired and slept with but didn't truly love, and about life in Haciendas, which Sal found surprisingly uplifting.

By the time we finished, my regard for her had increased exponentially. She had never had a break, never earned a dime above expenses, had dated and been ditched by most of the eligible men in town, and had never traveled out of the state. Yet she was a cheerful woman on the whole, positive, optimistic, and kind. It was a triumph of the will, really, a lesson to us all. What Sal understood that most of the rest of us don't was that it didn't matter how the world regarded you, what mattered was how you regarded the world.

I'd spent time grilling her about Mona Upshaw, particularly about her money. Apparently it hadn't been common knowledge that Ms. Upshaw was a very wealthy woman. She had lived simply and unspectacularly, had never sported the slightest trapping of wealth outside the walls of her charming home, which she explained by vague references to an inheritance. What Sal didn't know and the chief didn't either was whether Mona had brought the money to town or whether she'd acquired it from a deceased relative after she'd come to live in Haciendas, as she'd implied. Sal said that on Monday the chief was going to look at bank records to try to nail it down.

I told Sal that when I first met her, Mona Upshaw had implied there were secrets about Rita, secrets best kept unpublished by me or anyone else. When I asked Sal if she knew what Nurse Upshaw was talking about, she shook her head.

"We all have secrets," she said softly. "But most of them don't get us killed, they just get us embarrassed."

"That can be a fate worse than death, sometimes."

"No, it can't," she said, as if she knew it for a fact.

I asked about the other item of interest, Gus Gelbride's wife, Estelle, and on this subject Sal was voluble. Apparently Estelle Gelbride had become a virtual recluse over the past two decades, a participant in no cultural or charitable activities, a leader of no political or social organizations, a contributor to none of the civic improvement efforts that had swept through Haciendas periodically. According to Sal, there were people who had lived in Haciendas all their lives who had never laid eyes on Mrs. Gelbride except at church on Sunday.

The object of her solitary obsession was an increasingly comprehensive consideration of the path to personal enlightenment. She had neglected friends and family in an effort to learn, with the aid of everything from Eastern philosophers to small-town psychics to self-help hustlers like Chopra and Bradshaw, why life proceeded the way it did. Her primary interest was in cause and effect—did bad and good things happen for reasons, and if they did, as they surely must, how do we divine what that reason is? The man who knew her best, claimed Sal, was the UPS driver who delivered her dozens of books on the subject every month, from seers as far away as Tibet and

Brazil and as close as Bolinas and Carmel. In fact, rumor had it that Estelle had moved her bed into the library of the family mansion so she could spend twenty-four hours a day communing with the wisdom contained in the tomes that surrounded her.

When she finished telling me about Estelle, Sal said she had to go do her laundry. I thanked her for the chat, paid for her meal, and walked with her out into the town. The fog was gone, the heat was up, the streets were inhabited by other than surly kids steering low-slung vehicles.

"If you find yourself at loose ends some night, give me call," Sal said, touching me lightly on the arm.

"I don't have your number."

"Look in the book. Or on the nearest bathroom wall."

With a wave and a smile she was gone, but only after answering one more of my questions, which was how to get to the Gelbride mansion.

Her directions took me west of town, across Highway 101 and into the Santa Lucia mountains that separate the Salinas Valley from the sea. The road I turned onto was narrow and winding, unmarked except for a single sign proclaiming it PRIVATE, suggesting that travel was limited to the Gelbrides and their lackeys. When I got to the crest of the hill, the road dead-ended at a gatehouse and a wide turnaround that would allow an uninvited guest to go back the way he'd come.

I stopped at the gate, also unmarked, also forbidding, and waited for something to happen. In the meantime, I looked around. There was no mansion in sight, but there were plenty of signs of activity, most of it involving grapes. The hilltop was roped by a series of vines, staked and wired and ready to pick from the look of the plump clusters of fruit. By the time the loudspeaker set into the gatepost asked me what I wanted, I'd concluded that the Gelbrides made their own wine and consumed most of it on the premises. If they'd brewed their own beer, I'd have asked for a job.

When I told the speaker who I was and that I had an appointment with Gus, the gate swung open without sound and I followed the road around the crown of the hill until I came to the house on the other side. House is an inadequate term; so is mansion, for that matter. The structure—wood siding, slate roof, delicate ornamentation, stained and leaded windows, a dozen gables and as many brick chimneys—rose out of the hilltop like a volcanic eruption that had cooled into an inhabitable geode. Gray with white trim, its roof a darkening smear of stone, the house seemed as much a geological phenomenon as a residence, with an antediluvian aura that such phenomena often generate. I drove beneath the portico and stopped, expecting to be greeted by the modern equivalent of a liveryman. Instead, I was greeted by Gus.

He still wore his Sunday suit, but his tie was gone and so were his shoes and socks. His white shirt fell open at the collar and its tails had escaped from his waistband. His bare feet flopped at the end of his ankles like freshly boated flounder. His belt was unbuckled and his waist looked twice the size it had been at the church—Sunday dinner must have been super.

"If I see you, you keep quiet about the girl." It was more a declaration than a question.

"I will if I can."

"You will. Period."

"Not if it has to do with murder."

"It has to do with nothing. I was young. She was stacked. I asked for it; she didn't stop me. I gave her extra credits on the tally book that week. Double what she picked."

"How romantic."

"In the barn," he ordered, and headed that way, his bare feet making mini-bursts of dust as he padded down the driveway.

The barn was the color and trim of the house, an architectural marvel in its own right but nonetheless a real barn, with horses and stalls and tack, and tractors and spreaders and plows, and a hay mow and feed trough and grain bin. The smell was a pungent perfume of manure and straw and leather and grease, the sounds were muffled snorts and heavy sneezes broken occasionally by the chirp of a sparrow or the bark of a dog.

The view from the barn was the same as the house—a carpet of soil and its produce spread as far as the eye could see, the buildings and roadways and vehicles that served it seeming from the distance like a variety of hand stitching applied by a highly skilled peasantry. I wanted to linger in the glorious perspective, but Gus walked to the far end of the barn and entered a tiny room that was clearly his private retreat. It was finished with a red leather chair, a small refrigerator and wine rack, an expensive sound system that lined an entire wall, and a single photo of his family, almost invisible behind a tobacco humidor.

Gus sat in the chair and gestured for me to take a folding metal version that was leaning against the wall. As I was still unfolding it he pressed a button on the stereo and the strains of Italian opera surged quickly through the speakers, *Turandot,* I think. Gus settled into his chair, cranked up the volume even higher, absorbed its lyric passion for a moment, then reluctantly turned it down.

I started to say something but he held up a hand. He pulled a pipe from the rack at his side, filled it with tobacco from a humidor on the floor by his feet, lit it with a stick match, puffed to get it going, and smiled when the air was full of aromatic blend to the point that I coughed and rubbed my eyes.

"Kind of dangerous to smoke in a barn, isn't it?" I said.

"It's my barn." He gestured toward the vista that lapped at the far door. "Hellfire, son. It's my valley."

"You do seem to operate like some sort of potentate."

"I got more claim to it than any potentate. When I came out here, there was nothing. Tiny truck farms, some nurseries and orchards, and some sugarbeets down at Spreckles. But no berries, not over here. In the Pajaro, sure, but over here, no berries. I brought seedlings down from Oregon, I figured out the irrigation and the chemical mix, I built the first cooling shed and brought in the refrigerated trucks. I made fruit a big business in this valley."

Flattery seemed the best way to go. "That's quite a legacy, Mr. Gelbride."

"Not so you'd know from listening to the goddamned union."

"Still, you wouldn't want that history spoiled by foolishness or criminality by you or anyone in the family."

Gus didn't seem persuaded. "This is my world, not theirs. Out here, I say what happens and what doesn't. There's a problem, I do what has to be done—not you, not the police, not the union, not the politicians. Just me. Been that way for fifty years."

"Some people seem to think the old ways need to be changed. It's happened in other businesses—steel, timber, fishing. It sounds like it's going to happen here."

Gus shook his head. "That union business, it's all lies. I do right by my workers. Why would I cheat them? Without the workers, the fruit rots in the field."

"Some of your workers evidently see it differently."

"Troublemakers. Always had them; always will."

"It sounds to me like things may have changed for the worse since your son took over management of the business."

"Randy." He pronounced it the way he would pronounce a foot fungus. "He has much to learn, but I will teach him. I will teach him like I teach my horses." He looked at a rawhide quirt hanging on the wall, to indicate the type of training he had in mind.

"There's a chance Randy killed Rita Lombardi," I said, just to get it on the table and see which way it rolled.

Gus seemed less shocked than saddened by the suggestion. "Why would he do something that dumb?"

"Because she was keeping him away from the Vargas girl."

"Why did Rita care about that?"

"Because that's what Rita did. She cared. And because there's a name for what it would be if Randy had sex with Consuelo Vargas."

"What name?"

"You know what I'm talking about."

217

He puffed for a long time. I wiped my eyes and endured it. "Rita knew about me and Maria?" he asked finally.

"She must have. That legacy you talked about wouldn't look so good if it got branded with that kind of allegation."

"How did she know?"

"I don't know."

Gus shook his head again. "Maria wouldn't tell her. She saw Randy sniffing around Consuelo, she'd come to me to stop it."

It was touching that he thought there had been something tender between the two of them instead of just terrorism. "She might to save her daughter from a life of shame," I said. "Or from giving birth to an addled child."

Gus muttered a curse and puffed on his pipe until it went out.

"Rita told Carlos Reyna that she was going to make you forgive his debt," I said. "How was she going to make that happen?"

"There's no way on earth she could make that happen. Business is business."

"I think there was a way. I think Rita learned that some aspect of your strawberry operation was illegal. Something no one outside your family knew anything about. Something she was going to hold over your head to make you change the way you operate."

"Hah. What could she know?"

"You tell me."

"We do right. We obey the law."

"That barbed wire around your compound doesn't look very law-abiding."

"That was Randy's idea."

"Maybe Randy is doing things you don't know about. Maybe he killed Rita to shut her up."

Gus opened the humidor and refilled his pipe. "Randy's not a killer," he said. It sounded more like a guess than a testimonial.

"He threatened to kill a union man he caught working in his fields," I said. "I heard him do it."

"That was bluff. That's what he does."

"I'm not sure you know your son as well as you think you do, Mr. Gelbride."

Gus listened to the music, pressed the contents of his pipe into a firm pack, relit it, then closed his eyes. "He thinks I should retire. Move to the desert with his mother. Leave the business to him."

"Are you going to do it?"

"Not yet. And not till he makes room for Missy in his plans."

"Missy seems more interested in men than in strawberries."

"She's young. Business will be important later on."

"How do Missy and Randy get along?"

"They don't," he said simply. "They're too much like me." His laugh was harsh and dismissive, as much of himself as his children.

"If you decided Randy had killed Rita, what would you do?"

"Take care of it."

"How?"

"He would be punished."

"But not by the police and the courts."

"He would be punished by me."

"I'd like to ask him about it," I said.

"What?"

"I'd like to ask Randy if he killed Rita. With you there as a witness."

"I already did. He says no."

"Do you believe him?"

"I don't know." Gus puffed at his pipe but it was dead again. He started to relight it, then abandoned the effort. "It's a terrible thing, not to know if your son is a killer." He cranked up the volume on the music till the speakers did a shimmy on the shelf. "Nessun Dorma"; the tenor sounded like Pavarotti.

Although he expected me to retreat in the face of the cascading sound, I stayed put. When the aria ended, he turned the music off and walked out into the barn. "See that mare?"

He pointed at a beautiful bay standing in the corner of the nearest stall, staring at us as if we were sculpted out of oats.

219

"Nice animal."

"It's Missy's birthday present. Day after tomorrow. Bought her down in San Luis Obispo. Her father won the California Derby."

"Nice gift."

"Missy won't even notice. By the time dinner is served, she'll be drunk. By the time the cake is served, she'll be gone. One of these days, she'll drive off the road and roll all the way to the valley. By the time she stops rolling, she'll be dead. Which must be what she wants."

When I left, he was still looking at the mare, as if he hoped it had something reassuring to say.

CHAPTER TWENTY-THREE

Halfway down the mountain, I ran into Missy Gelbride, almost literally. She was trudging up the middle of the road, head down and heedless of oncoming traffic, her thoughts somewhere between the stratosphere and the gutter. She wore torn and tattered cut-offs and a red tube top and her stride was wayward and maladroit—her red and white cowboy boots were no match for the ruts and potholes she encountered on the climb.

I pulled to the shoulder and stopped the car and got out. Missy didn't notice until she almost bumped into my Buick.

She looked at it and at me, then back to it. "Who sat on your car?" she asked, her voice slurred and dull, her effort at humor halfhearted and inept.

"Your brother."

She frowned dubiously. "Randy's big but he's not that big."

"I was speaking more figuratively than literally."

"I'm not sure what that means, but that's the first sign of wit I've seen out of Randy since he tossed his cat in the grape crusher."

"I got a good chuckle out of it myself. So will my insurance man."

She leaned against the Buick and looked at me with the slippery focus of all alcoholics. "You aren't going to do anything boring like call the cops, are you?"

"Not if I get what I came for."

"Money?"

"Information."

She shrugged. "All I know is what happens when you fucking run out of fucking gas at the bottom of the fucking hill." She shoved herself off my fender and started marching up the road once again. "And when your cell phone conks out while you're calling for help," she called over her shoulder after she'd taken a few stumbling steps.

"We had a chat in the Cantina the other night," I called after her.

She kept walking. "You and Randy?"

"You and me. You bought me a drink. I wasn't properly appreciative."

She stopped and turned and almost tipped over. "Men don't have an appreciative bone in their bodies. Hell, they don't even thank you for good sex. What are you doing out here, anyway?"

"I was talking to your father a while ago."

She blinked and squinted. "What about?"

"Lots of things. Including your brother."

"There's lots of people in town who know more about Randy than Daddy does. Including me. What do you want to know about him?"

"I'm wondering what was going on between Randy and Rita Lombardi before she died."

"Going on in the sense of sex?—nothing. She was a crip and over eighteen; Randy likes them pure and prime. But going on in the sense of animosity?—a lot."

"Why did Randy dislike her?"

"Rita has made him feel stupid as a stump for the last twenty years. Plus guilty. Plus irrelevant."

"Irrelevant to what?"

"To just about anything. Women don't need men anymore, haven't you heard? Women need men like fish need bicycles. It's on all the best T-shirts." She looked up at the sun and then at the distance she still needed to travel. "Are you going to drive me home?" She made her hands caress her chest and her thighs. "Or do you require payment in advance?"

I opened the passenger door. "Hop in."

She wedged her big body into the crumpled cocoon that was the passenger side of the car. "Reminds me of the first place I had sex," she said.

"In a Buick?"

"In a Volkswagen."

It took me a while to find a place wide enough to turn around, and a while longer for the Buick to clamber back from whence it came. Along the way I asked Missy if she had an active role in the family business.

"I'm an essential part of the machine," she bragged sardonically. "Ask anyone. Anyone who isn't named Gelbride."

"What's your job?"

"I'm the assistant vice president of marketing. It says so on my letterhead."

"Which means?"

"I answer the phones and place orders with shippers. When I feel like it, that is."

"Which is how often?"

"Which in the last five years is never. You're not a broker, are you? Daddy hasn't put the place up for sale, has he? He hates Randy enough to do it."

"I'm not a broker," I said. "But I've heard the business is in some kind of trouble."

"What kind of trouble?"

"I don't know, exactly. But I heard it was something so serious it might shut you down."

"There's nothing like that going on. Is there?" Her question was a bald confession of her irrelevance.

"Rita Lombardi knew something that was going to make your father and Randy shape up. I'd like to know what it was."

"If Rita really knew something like that, Randy would . . ." She seemed afraid to supply the predicate.

"What? Kill her?"

Missy shook her head as if to dislodge the word. "God. He's dumb but not that dumb. Is he?"

"He's at the top of my suspect list."

"The cops think so, too?"

"After they talk to me, they will."

"Then if I were you, I'd watch my back." She stayed quiet until we reached the top of the hill and I pulled into the barnyard and stopped the car. "But you know what?" she said as she opened the door and swung a bare booted leg out.

"What?"

"If they really do shut down the farms, it will be the best thing that ever happened to this family. Randy would stop being a thug; Mama would come out of hiding; and Daddy would remember my name."

"How about you? How would it change you?"

"I wouldn't start drinking till noon."

She thanked me for the ride, then got out of the car and wandered toward her home.

I was turning around to head back down the hill when movement in the trees and shrubs at the far side of the house caught my eye. A woman—small, delicate, and stooped, wearing a raincoat and rubber boots even though the sun was shining brightly and there wasn't a cloud in the sky—wandered through the garden, head down, eyes transfixed, as though she had lost something tiny and irreplaceable.

I got out of the car and walked toward her. When I realized who it was, I was surprised. "Mrs. Gelbride?"

She turned my way, startled but not fearful. "Yes?"

"Do you need help?"

"No, thank you. I'm looking for my shears. I left them out yesterday. I seem to have trouble keeping track of things these days."

"You have some beautiful flowers out here. Especially the roses."

"Thank you." She frowned into the sun. "Do I know you?"

"No, but I'm a friend of Louise Lombardi's. She asked me to stop by and thank you for your support during these difficult times."

"I . . . you dropped by? You just drove up the hill and dropped by?"

"Yep."

Her eyes brightened as though I'd brought her a narcotic. "That's amazing. No one's ever dropped by before. Not to see me, at least. I'm flattered."

"It's my pleasure. Mrs. Lombardi was moved by your concern. She wanted to be sure you knew it."

"Poor Louise. I know how it feels to lose someone dear to you. And poor Rita. I always hoped she would grow to be someone who . . . well, who of us gets what we want in this world? We get what we think we want, sometimes, but that seldom turns out satisfactorily. What we really want, what we really need, is not so easily divined. Is it? Or am I just babbling?"

"You make a lot of sense to me, Mrs. Gelbride. We waste most of our energy in life pursuing things that are meaningless. Or even destructive."

She nodded briskly. "That's it, exactly. We listen to other people instead of charting our own course. Family. Friends. The politicians. The experts. They are more than ready to tell us what to do and how to think. But no one can speak to the needs of all of us. We are all different; we are each unique. We must answer the questions ourselves."

"Know thyself," I said, feeling like a Sophist afoot in the Parthenon. "The most sage advice ever given."

"And 'to thine own self be true.' Shakespeare saw it as well. Such a simple thing. Yet so difficult to achieve."

I nodded. It seemed smart to keep her talking, about anything and everything, to open another window into the odd antics of the Gelbride family.

"I have spent many years asking others what I should do with my life," she continued. "Reading books, listening to lectures and tapes, hearing what the great thinkers have to say about how to behave in the world and atone for your sins. And some not-so-great thinkers, too," she added with a sly grin.

"And? Have you found the answer?"

"I have found many answers. So many I forgot the question."

"The question is what do I need to do to be happy. Isn't it?"

Her lips flattened and her eyes glistened. "I think so. Yes. I think that was where I was before I got confused." She gazed at me with the intensity of one of her TV evangelists. "You know the question. But do you know the answer, young man?"

"The only thing I know is, the happiest people I see are the ones who spend most of their time doing things for other people."

"Is that you? Do you do that?"

"Only when I get paid for it."

"Then you're not happy?"

"Not always."

"But sometimes?"

I thought of Eleanor and I thought of Charley and I thought of Jill Coppelia. "Definitely sometimes."

"I haven't been happy since 1973," she blurted, then covered her mouth with her hand.

"What happened then?"

When they came, her words were timid and muffled, as though they were afraid of the light. "I learned that I am capable of evil. Of causing suffering to innocent people. Of committing sins beyond imagining."

"You're obviously a kind woman, Mrs. Gelbride. It's hard to believe that's true."

"But it is. The world made demands on me that I couldn't meet without forsaking everything I used to hold dear."

"What are you talking about exactly, Mrs. Gelbride?"

She looked at me as though seeing me for the first time, as though reality had just caught up with us after navigating the dense tangle of the garden. "I'm talking about life to a total stranger. Isn't that amazing? Why would I do that, do you suppose?"

I shrugged. "I don't know."

"The only reason I can think of is that you're the only one who has paid attention to me in thirty years."

The indictment of her family echoed in the wind like taps at a gravesite. "You're an interesting woman, Mrs. Gelbride."

"What makes you say that?"

"For one thing, you've clearly thought a lot about life. Most people don't think much beyond their entree and their stock portfolio."

She offered her first smile of the afternoon. "I think about life too much, I'm afraid; it doesn't yield me much comfort."

"Speaking of comfort, did you know of any problem between Rita Lombardi and your son?"

She frowned in concentration. "Randy? And Rita? No. Not specifically. Of course Randy is not a pleasant person and Rita is charming, so it stands to reason they wouldn't get along. He's grumbled about her ever since the third grade. She made him feel inferior, I think."

"Was there any trouble between Rita and anyone else in your family?"

"I never heard of any. Of course Rita had reason to despise us all," she added.

"Why is that?"

"Because it was our chemicals that made her limbs misshapen. We poisoned her, essentially, by destroying her father's genetic makeup. That's what the doctor thought, anyway."

I tried to mask my surprise. "When Rita was born, you mean?"

"Yes."

"What doctor was that?"

"I forget her name. She was the ob/gyn at the Haciendas hospital."

"Did she tell the Lombardis that as well?"

"I hope not. We asked her not to."

"And that's why you've been kind to Louise over the years. Because you felt you contributed to Rita's disability."

"Yes."

"Did Franco Lombardi find out what had happened later on? Was that why he was killed? To keep him from filing a complaint against your family for misuse of toxins in the fields?"

Estelle Gelbride started to frame an answer to my question when the French doors on the side of the house opened and Missy stepped into the garden. "Here you are," she said, her voice saturated with scorn. "Entertaining our snoopy guest."

"He's not a snoop, he's a friend of Louise Lombardi's."

Missy glanced at me as though I'd cursed her. "That may be, but he's not a friend of ours. I think you'd better come in, don't you, Estelle? Before you say things you'll regret? Before you make this family look even more idiotic and unscrupulous than we already are?"

"Whatever you say, dear," Estelle said, her forthright candor reduced in an instant into a servile submission. Without as much as a look my way, she shuffled toward the door that Missy held open for her, a prisoner ordered back to her cell.

When she reached the door, she turned back. "I enjoyed our chat, Mr. . . . ."

"Tanner."

"Tanner. I see. I knew some Tanners once. They lived in Kingsburg. Real estate, I believe."

"No relation, I don't think."

"I see. Well, I hope you'll feel free to drop by anytime. It's a pleasure for me to have visitors."

"Get inside, you moron," Missy hissed at her hapless mother. Then she looked at me. "Don't even think about coming back here," she said nastily, and slammed the door behind them.

CHAPTER TWENTY-FOUR

For the second time that afternoon, I pointed the Buick down the hill, on a winding snake of a road that would take me back to the flatland that was still, in this day and age, the feudal domain of men like Gus Gelbride. Such men were innovators, explorers, risk-takers. They accomplished much, they made their mark, they left the world a better place for many if not most. But along the way to fame and fortune they left victims in their trail, victims in towns like Haciendas that few seemed to know or care about, people who were the spoils, the by-products, the necessary evils, the irritating residue of the system that put more food on the tables of this nation than any other came close to enjoying. The saddest chapter of the story is that most of the victims are children.

As I marveled at the hardship still rampant in the modern world, the road narrowed and switched back, once and then again, creating a precipitous cliff on my side that looked to descend straight to hell. I veered to the center of the roadway, taking a chance that no one was coming, giving myself a margin of safety. But there was someone coming. The ubiquitous white Dodge pickup, its Cummins diesel propelling it inexorably up the hill, occupied the center of the road just as I did, as formidable as a Sherman tank advancing squarely in my path.

Randy Gelbride was behind the wheel, of course, squinting into the sun that sat like a searchlight at my back. Seemingly lost in thought, when he finally saw my car he started to veer left to give me some room, but when he registered who I was, he swerved back to the center of the road. If I kept going, we would collide. If I swerved right, I risked skidding off the shoulder and tumbling down the hill. If I went left, there was a chance Randy would move that way as well, abandoning his bluff at the last minute only to extend the risk. After an instant's reflection, I placed my bet on his cowardice and kept my car on course.

Time was impotent and elusive, punishment for past transgressions. The laws of physics seemed similarly suspended, as though Randy and I had become insubstantial, subatomic oddities that could pass through each other's space without the slightest disturbance of either body. The basic law of common sense—the instinctual grasp at self-preservation—had been sacrificed to a mutually mad bravado.

I knew Randy would happily kill or at least terrify me. What I hadn't known till now was that I would as happily dispatch him to a similar fate, if it could be done in a way that would be deemed by Mace Dixon and his ilk as nonculpable. As the vehicles remained locked onto vectors of mutually assured destruction, I realized that I was a vastly angry man, angry at what had happened to Charley, angry at what had happened to Rita, angry at my persistent ineffectiveness in the face of those calamities. I gave the gas pedal a nudge and gripped the wheel as tightly as I grip my gun.

It must have been my eyes that persuaded him, twin semaphores indicative of my gleeful anticipation of what was about to occur, beacons of a heedless rage that must have traveled faster than my car and advertised my psychosis. When the vehicles were ten yards apart and closing, Randy wrenched the wheel to the right and avoided me by inches, the Ram's wheels squealing on the hard-pan, losing traction for an instant as the truck fishtailed past me on the left. The cackle I heard, the manic release of tension followed by an exultant roar of joy, must necessarily have come from me.

As I slowed to a crawl and watched in my mirror the Ram's brake lights came on and the white truck stopped at the edge of the road. I pulled to a stop as well. When Randy got out, I did too. As he stomped toward me, I remembered the gun he carried below the seat. If I'd felt like an idiot before, now I felt like an idiot squared.

"You stupid fuck!" he wailed, the fist at his side thankfully empty, his hat back on his head as though to cool his steaming brain. "You almost got us killed."

"Looked to me like there was plenty of stupidity to go around."

"Like shit. This is *my* road, goddamnit. I got a right to—"

I spoke more cavalierly than my mood. "Come on, Randy. Admit it. You panicked when you figured I was willing to go over the side if I could take you with me."

"Panic, shit. I saved your ass is what I did."

I grinned. "Not on the best day you ever had."

Hands in his pockets, he scuffed in the dirt like a rooster. "I been wanting to talk to you," he mumbled after a few seconds.

"Talk about what?"

"What you told the old man."

"About you and Consuelo Vargas?"

"Yeah."

"I told him you had her in your sights."

"And what else?"

"Why do you think there was more than that?"

"Because he never gave a shit about me tracking pussy before this."

"Maybe he got religion."

"He got some sort of disease all right. And you gave it to him."

"So?"

His eyes narrowed in a parody of calculation. "So I figure maybe I could use the information myself."

"Use it for what?"

He picked his nose and flicked the findings in the dirt. "Never you mind."

"Sounds to me like you're looking for leverage. To force the old man to put you in charge of the business."

"You don't know shit, mister."

"What I don't know is anything that would help you."

Randy rubbed sweat from his eyes and spoke imploringly. "There must be something going on. Gus threatened to ream me a new asshole if I laid a hand on that Vargas girl. I never seen him so agitated."

"Maybe he started paying attention in church."

"Whatever that means," he grumbled.

"That means you need to leave the women alone, Randy, especially the women who work for you. Sex isn't in the job description anymore. Not even out in the fields."

Randy looked out over the valley, frowning in puzzlement much as his father had done, as though the world had taken on a different cast and was producing mutant strains far more intimidating than strawberries. "You tell me about the old man, I can give you something about Rita," he said tentatively, as though to try it on for size.

"What about Rita?"

"You first."

"Me never. Where were you the night Rita was killed?"

"I got an iron-clad alibi for that. Cops checked it out. Reb says there's no way they can hang the Lombardi thing on me."

"You gave him the name of a woman."

He grinned lasciviously. "Yeah."

"I guess Reb forgot that guys like you usually have someone else do their dirty work."

"Shit, man. I got no beef with Rita except the Vargas girl. But hell. There's pussy on every plant out there. I wouldn't kill someone for that."

"How about the union?"

"Rita didn't work for no union. I told you that before."

"So you're pure as the driven snow, is that it?"

"I made my share of mistakes, maybe. But murder wasn't one of them. Now you want someone had a mad-on for Rita, you need to talk to Missy."

"Why?"

"Lately she was real pissed at Rita for some reason."

"You don't know why?"

"Naw. Me and Missy don't communicate much. But likely it had to do with money or men. Money and men and booze is the only things that float Missy's boat."

"Where was Missy when Rita was killed?"

"Don't know for sure, but two things you can count on. That time of night, one, she was drunk. And, two, she'd just been fucked by some loser."

Left to their own devices, the Gelbrides would have dismembered each other without qualm. "Did Missy have her sights set on Carlos Reyna?" I asked.

"She don't spread 'em for beaners. But Missy could kill a woman, don't think she couldn't. Bitch is strong as hell."

With that backhanded endorsement, Randy got back in his truck and drove up the hill to what passed for his home. I drove back to Haciendas and parked in the only shade on Fremont Street.

Louise Lombardi was still dressed in her church clothes. She looked cool and collected until you got to her eyes, which were pained and panicked, as if she'd seen something in the bowels of St. Bonaventure that terrified her. I understood where she was coming from—there's no more frightening time of the week than Sunday afternoon.

"I told you not to come back," she said when she saw me, leaning on the door for support and wheezing like an old dog.

"I'm sorry, but I need to ask you some things."

"Seems to me you ask lots of questions but don't get many answers."

"True enough. But I think I'm getting close. If you tell me the truth, it will help."

"Truth about what?"

I looked up and down the street. "I'd rather do this inside."

She looked back at her house, then looked at me. "I don't like you in there. You make it feel dirty. You make it feel empty."

"I'm sorry about that, Mrs. Lombardi. This will only take a minute. It's pretty personal."

She led me to the living room where we sat simultaneously, with equal awkwardness. I was about to gather enough ammunition to fire a long shot, one that would do damage regardless of its accuracy, a shot stimulated by what I'd found out about Gus Gelbride and Maria Vargas and the kinds of predictions Rita had made upon her return to Haciendas from the hospital in the city. If I was right, I would have what I needed, which was a motive for Rita's murder that fit with what I'd learned about her behavior in the days before her death. If I was wrong, no one who cared about Louise Lombardi would ever speak to me again.

"Did you enjoy the church service?" I began, enlisting outside assistance in my cause.

"You were there?"

"In the back."

"I didn't see you."

"I wasn't trying to be seen," I said, and recrossed my legs and licked my lips. "Father McNally preaches a nice sermon."

Surprisingly, she scowled. "He's soft. He needs to be stricter, especially with the young people. He needs to tell them to behave themselves or risk damnation."

I wasn't qualified to summon the wrath of the Lord. "Afterward, I talked with Gus Gelbride for a time."

"Yes?"

"And Mrs. Gelbride as well."

"She's a nice person."

"What kind of person is her husband?"

Her shrug was massive. "There have always been stories of his cruelty, but he treated Franco fair and gave me the money to bury him. The other things I only hear about. But what does Gus have to do with Rita?"

Her nonchalance was bothering me. She couldn't have been that good an actress, which she would have to be if my hunch had landed anywhere near the truth.

"Rita found out something about Gus that made her upset," I said, determined to tough it out.

"Found out what?"

"That fifteen years ago Gus fathered a child by one of the field workers. A woman named Maria Vargas."

She shook her head. "There is nothing new in that, sad to say."

"Do you remember Rita talking about it?"

She shook her head. "How would Rita know such a thing?"

"I don't know."

"Is this why she was murdered? To keep Gus Gelbride's filthy secrets?"

"I think so."

"Then why are you here?"

I was alert for the slightest tic. "Because Gus had another secret."

"What was it?"

"I think Gus fathered another child with a woman who wasn't his wife."

She squinted with curiosity but not with fear. "What child? What woman?"

I paused to see if she had guessed where I was going. When I didn't see a sign of it, I pressed on. "I think the child was Rita. I think the woman was you. I think you and Gus had an affair and the fact that Gus was her biological father gave Rita a claim to the Gelbride holdings and she planned to use it to benefit Carlos and the farmworkers. I think she was killed to stop her from doing that."

I'd said my piece, blurting it the way I blurted apologies and excuses. I'd expected Mrs. Lombardi to be knocked off balance, to be defensive and apprehensive about the consequences of what I knew, to be wary of fallout. But all she seemed was angry.

"You said you saw me at church," she said, her fury swirling between us like a whirlwind.

I nodded.

"Did I hold my head high? Did I take communion at the altar?"

"Yes."

"Then you know what you said cannot be true." She stood up and loomed over me like the high priestess of a fearsome faith. "It is as I said—you make my home seem filthy. You do not seem to fear the police, but maybe you will fear Carlos. He has told me many times that he would kill anyone who tried to harm us."

I stood up and walked to the door. "I'm sorry I disturbed you, Mrs. Lombardi. I believe what you said. I believe you were true to your husband."

My apology was merely fresh fuel for her anger. "You must never come back here," she ordered.

"I won't."

"You must never say to anyone the lies you have said to me."

"I won't," I promised, and apologized again for insulting her. "Can I ask you a couple of things before I go, Mrs. Lombardi? Please? They're important."

She started to refuse, then yielded.

"First, did you ever learn what caused Rita's legs to be deformed?"

"It was God's will. That's all I know."

"Was Rita ever baptized?"

She frowned with dismay. "Of course she was baptized. Why would you think otherwise?"

I ignored the question and pressed on. "In the last days of her life did she say anything about her teddy bear? Brownie, she called it."

"She told me she gave Brownie to Thelma Powell."

"Why did she do that?"

"I don't know," she said, "but I know it's none of your business." She waited for me to take my leave, which I began to do.

"You need to pray for your sins, Mr. Tanner," she declared at my back. "You need to beg the Lord to forgive you for all the damage you do to the world."

CHAPTER TWENTY-FIVE

I drove to the center of town, found a parking slot on the main drag, and sat in my car and waited. Waited for something to form in my mind in the shape and weight of an idea, waited for someone to come along who might spark a lead to the killer of Rita Lombardi, waited for a deus ex machina to deliver me from my incompetence.

I was gazing idly at the entrance to Shortcake's when Thelma Powell came out, accompanied by the older woman I'd seen with her at mass, the woman I'd assumed was her mother. They spoke easily and informally, with obvious affection. Each wore a cotton print dress, each carried a patent leather handbag, each wore silk stockings and white shoes. They were walking my way arm in arm. I got out of the car and waited for them.

If I'd been wearing a hat, I would have tipped it. Since I wasn't, I bowed at the waist. "Ms. Powell? Marsh Tanner. It's nice to see you again."

She blinked into the sun, then frowned, then smiled when she recognized me. "Mr. Tanner. Of course. How are you?"

"Fine. And you?"

Her smile was broad and giddy. "I'm fine as well. I couldn't be more so, in fact. This is my mother, Mildred Powell. Mother, this is

Mr. Tanner. He's about to buy a new Cadillac." After we traded grins in tribute to our charade at the bank, Thelma glanced at my caved-in Buick. "Which he seems to need quite badly."

Mildred Powell and I exchanged standard greetings. In the meantime, Thelma sobered. "Have you had any luck with your research project, Mr. Tanner?"

"Some. Not enough to reach any conclusions."

"That's too bad."

"Yes it is."

"I'm afraid I've given you all the help I can on the subject, however."

"That's all right. But please keep it in mind."

She sniffed. "I can hardly help it, I'm afraid."

"What kind of research is it?" Mrs. Powell asked with all innocence. "Some sort of scientific experiment?"

"I'm researching the impact of the microwave oven on modern eating habits."

"Well, Thelma can tell you loads about that, can't you, dear?"

"I've told him more than enough about my cuisine already," she said, then shot me a quick look, then shook her head at our shamelessness.

"I'm wondering if our mutual friend ever mentioned anything special to you about the Gelbride family," I said. "Some information she'd acquired, perhaps. Information she was going to use against them. Some problem with Missy in particular."

Thelma frowned. "I don't think so. But I'll try to remember."

"Thanks."

"Are you speaking of the Lombardi girl?" Mrs. Powell asked.

"Yes."

"It was terrible what happened to her."

"Yes it was."

"But I saw it coming."

I looked at Thelma, who shrugged. "You did?"

Mrs. Powell's jaw firmed and her eyes hardened. "Yes I did. Rita was so very prideful lately. And as we know, pride goeth before a fall."

"Hush, Mother," Thelma said. "You know she wasn't anything of the kind." She looked at me. "Mother thinks Rita broke some kind of pact with me. When she got her legs fixed," she added when she saw my vacant expression. "Mother assumes I was more dependent on Rita than I was. I hardly even saw her the last couple of years." She patted her mother on the back as though she were the mother and her mother was a child.

I was bidding the women good-bye when Thelma looked beyond me. "Look who's here, Mother. Good afternoon, Father," she said brightly.

Father McNally was strolling toward us down the walk. He had changed into tan slacks and a green sport shirt and hiking boots that looked well worn and comfortable. There were thistles clinging to his pants legs and dust covering his boots—souvenirs of the CYO picnic, no doubt.

"Mrs. Powell," he said and bowed. He made it plain that I wasn't included in the greeting.

"It's a beautiful day, isn't it, Father?" Thelma went on, her expression close to rapturous, as though Father McNally was the repository of what must have been vast quantities of frustrated sexuality. If so, it wouldn't be the first time a priest was a surrogate lover. Where Father McNally placed his own baser urges was less clear.

"Quite beautiful," he answered, a bit too sweetly for my taste. "Though perhaps with a touch of fall in the air."

"I loved your text this morning," Thelma gushed. "The Book of Job is so fraught with meaning." Her look implied the two of them were the only ones in the parish who truly understood its scope. "It spoke to so many of the things we've been discussing lately."

"I was hoping you'd see it that way, Thelma. And how's the arthritis coming, Mrs. Powell?"

"The same, Father. Always the same."

"Sometimes the status quo is a blessing."

"Not with arthritis, it isn't."

"I'll pray that God eases your affliction."

"Thank you, Father."

Thelma grabbed her mother's arm. "Time to go, Mother. Always a pleasure to see you, Father. And to hear your words of advice."

"And you as well. Good day, Mrs. Powell."

"Come to dinner one night, Father."

"I'll make a point of it," he said, as Thelma Powell and her mother walked off down the block.

When they were gone, the priest and I looked at each other. "I get the feeling you're following me, Mr. Tanner," he began, his mood dark and accusatory.

"Not so, Father. It's like Hollywood and Vine out here. If I stand on this corner long enough, sooner or later everyone I'm looking for comes along." I glanced at the women retreating down the block. "It must be odd for you to be the object of so much displaced eroticism."

"You're speaking of Thelma."

"Yes."

"I won't deny there's an element of that in our relationship, but it's nothing I encourage, I assure you."

"I don't imagine it takes more than a grin and a greeting to keep it going."

He reddened. "As I said, it's not that I encourage her."

I shrugged away the subject. "How was the picnic?"

"Rather subdued, I'm afraid. As soon as I could, I did what I could to improve the situation."

"How?"

"I left."

I chuckled at his candor. "I've felt the same way at every cocktail party I ever attended. Have you thought over what I asked you about?"

"I have thought of little else."

"And?"

"If Rita were not so . . . no. That has to be irrelevant. My decision must be entirely independent of my personal affections."

I shrugged. "If you say so."

His candor was only getting warmed up. "I don't like you, Mr. Tanner," he said gruffly. "And I don't like the way you make your living."

"You must have talked with Mrs. Lombardi."

"Indeed I have, just minutes ago. But be that as it may, I have decided that I can properly tell you that Louise Lombardi has confessed nothing of the sort of thing you mentioned. Not to me. Ever. At any time."

I nodded. "It's nice to have corroboration. Not that it helps build a case against the Gelbrides. Or anyone else for that matter."

Father McNally shifted from one foot to the other, his eyes falling on the bell tower peering down on us like a golden eagle from the next block. "I have decided one more thing, Mr. Tanner."

"What's that?"

"I have decided to tell you that the killer of Rita Lombardi has confessed the crime to me."

I blinked. "So who is it?"

He shook his head. "I will say nothing further. It is highly inappropriate to tell you even this much, but I felt compelled to do something. Rita was . . . well, you know what she was. My life has not been the same since she left us. I mourn in every crevice of my heart." He started to go, then turned back. "I'd appreciate it if you would refrain from telling the authorities what I just told you. I cannot and will not tell them what I know about this matter, but it will take many hours and much effort to convince them of that. Hours and effort I can better spend elsewhere."

"The seal of my confessional is sacrosanct as well, Father," I said, aware as I spoke that I was lying in the abstract though in this case not in the particular.

"Good day, then, Mr. Tanner."

"Take care, Father."

As Father McNally walked off, I noticed Carlos Reyna coming from the laundromat across the street wearing a T-shirt and shorts, arms full of clean clothes, hands gripping containers of bleach and detergent. He threw the lot of them in the cab of his truck and drove off pursued by a persistent cloud of blue fumes. Without much in the way of motive, I got in the Buick and followed him.

He led me to a trailer park on the north edge of Haciendas. Home to about twenty units, the park was minimally landscaped and similarly maintained, with bare dirt over most of its common space and a variety of trash littering the fence lines and trailer footings. The only concessions to community spirit were a picnic table and brick fireplace beneath a live oak tree in the exact center of the space. Marred with graffiti and pitted with age, none of the amenities looked as if they had been used in years.

Carlos was in space number twelve. He pulled into the slot set aside for his truck, got out, unlocked the trailer, went back for the clothes, and lugged them inside. Along the way he dropped a white sock. I parked by the picnic table, retrieved the sock, and knocked on his door.

Whoever he was expecting, it wasn't me; he wasn't pleased and showed it. Still, I was uncomfortable exploring the notion that Carlos might be something less than an innocent victim of his fiancée's violent death.

I held up the sock. "You dropped something."

He took it from me. "Thanks."

"Can we talk for a minute?"

"I guess," he said dubiously. "But I got to be somewhere pretty soon."

"I'll make it quick."

Carlos looked behind him as if to assess the state of repair of his digs, then backed up and let me enter.

The trailer was small, one bedroom, tiny kitchen, combination living and dining area, tiny bath. It smelled of mildew and ripe fruit and maybe of the leavings of sex. The only smaller residences I'd been in were a jail cell and the Vargas family cave.

Still, without much to work with, Carlos had made the trailer neat and even cozy, with dollops of cheer in the form of dried flowers and potted cactus placed on various ledges and a variety of sheet music scattered over the table with an acoustic guitar watching over it like a security guard. I was feeling sorry for Carlos until I saw the gun, a .38 revolver sitting like a spider near the stove next to an oily rag.

Carlos gestured toward a bench by the fold-out table and I sat down on its orange vinyl surface. "How's it going?" I asked.

"Okay."

"Tough morning in the fields yesterday."

He rubbed a hand through his long black hair. "Randy's an asshole."

"I think he'll stay away from the Vargas girl now. You can tell Homero and Maria they can come down from the cave."

"Are you sure?"

"Reasonably."

"Why has he changed on this?"

"His daddy put Consuelo off limits."

"Gus? What does he care about Consuelo Vargas?"

"He used to know her mother."

"Maria?"

I nodded. "If the girl has any more problems, with Randy or with anything, go to Gus with them. Say her name and tell him what you need. Don't let Randy know; bypass him and go straight to Gus."

"But why would Gus—"

I held up a hand. "It's not important," I said, then waited for him to refocus. "Randy Gelbride claims he has an alibi for the night Rita was killed."

"So? That doesn't mean anything."

"He claims the cops back it up."

Carlos sneered. "He owns the cops."

"Maybe, but I was wondering if you had one yourself."

"Me? An alibi?" Muscles rippled along his bare arms. "You think I was the one who—"

"I don't think anything," I interrupted. "I'm just filling in as many blanks as I can. Where were you?"

"I was here."

"Alone?"

"Yes. Rita had just left."

"What time did she leave?"

"A little after nine."

"What were you doing?"

"We were going to be married in two weeks. What do you think we were doing?"

"Did you talk to any of your neighbors that night?"

"My neighbors were too drunk to talk. As usual."

"Where did Rita say she was going when she left?"

"Home."

"Did she talk on the phone to anyone while she was here?"

"No." He looked at his watch. "Can I go now?"

"One minute."

Still fuming, Carlos walked to the refrigerator and pulled out a beer and opened it. He downed half of it in one gulp and didn't offer anything to me. On top of the refrigerator was a package, gaily wrapped in blue and silver. When he saw me looking at it, Carlos coughed and wiped his eyes. "Tuesday is her birthday. I bought her a present two weeks ago. Now I have to take it back."

"What is it?"

"A clock radio. She never got up on time. It used to make me mad."

He shook his head and began to cry. I waited till he regained his composure, feeling ungrateful and insensitive for probing for his alibi. "Mona Upshaw was a rich woman," I said.

"She was?"

"Rich enough to pay for Rita's surgery."

"She did?"

"Do you know where she got the money?"

He shook his head. "How could I?"

"Rita might have mentioned it."

"She didn't."

"Rita didn't say anything at all about the surgery?"

"She just said they owed her. I thought she was talking about the Gelbrides."

"Why?"

"I don't know."

"Did she say anything about filing a lawsuit against the Gelbride farms? Or getting money from them in some other way?"

"Suing them for what?"

"For causing her legs to be crippled."

Carlos frowned. "How did they do that?"

"Chemicals," I said.

"What chemicals?"

"The ones the Gelbrides used in the fields. The ones Franco Lombardi inhaled and absorbed when he worked as a foreman for Gus. The ones that may have caused his daughter to have crooked legs."

"That really happened?" Carlos asked, still struggling to comprehend what I had said.

"That's what the doctor thought." I stood up and glanced at the gun. "This appointment of yours. It wouldn't be with Randy Gelbride, would it?"

He didn't respond.

"If you hunt him down and kill him, you'll go to jail for a long time."

"What difference would that make?" Carlos murmured grimly. "My heart is imprisoned already."

"I know it's hard, Carlos. I lost my best friend a few weeks back.

He was killed, too. But gunning down an innocent man won't help."

"I don't need help, I need vengeance."

"Randy Gelbride's not the place to look," I told him, then left him to his honor and his conscience and the love he had won from Rita.

CHAPTER TWENTY-SIX

The Cantina was almost empty, the way it had been on my first visit. The jukebox was dead. The late afternoon sun spiked through the window like a golden syringe inserted into a sun-tanned arm. The three people sharing a sinful Sunday with me looked even more damned than the town they lived in.

I was on my second beer, trying to decide what to do with the little information I'd collected and the few ideas I had. The alternatives were barren at best, but when Mace Dixon walked in the door, I'd almost reached a decision.

He ambled toward a stool at the end of the bar but when he saw me he nodded a greeting, then pointed to a table in the corner. I grabbed my beer and headed that way. When the chief had his whiskey in his hammy hand, he joined me.

"Hell of a thing when the only time you got to do your drinking is Sunday," he said as he dumped his heavy body onto a wooden chair.

"Better than no time at all," I said, feeling blithe and carefree and far drunker than I was.

Dixon looked me over. He wore Levi's and a tank top and looked as if he'd just come from the gym. "Looks like you got you some sun," he said after a sip of the whiskey.

"Hard to avoid down here."

"Looks like you been losing some sleep, too."

"Hard to avoid anywhere."

"Get Gus Gelbride to sit and spit with you?"

"He invited me up to the mansion, as a matter of fact. We're almost bosom buddies."

The chief raised a brow. "You must know something I don't."

"If I do, I don't know what it is."

He shrugged. "What did the old bastard have to say?"

"Several things, most of them directives. Gus is your basic force of nature."

"That's one word for him, anyway."

"What's another?"

His smile was lifeless. "Gangster is one that comes to mind."

"Literally?"

"Not if you go by the rap sheet."

"And if you go by your hunches?"

"Gus Gelbride's a multiple felon."

"What's behind the friction between you two, Chief?"

He looked toward the bar. "Hell, I don't know. Maybe I don't like strawberries."

"Sounds like it's more than that, to me. I'm thinking it has something to do with Franco Lombardi."

The chief drained his whiskey and motioned for the bartender to bring him another. When he had a second helping, he turned garrulous. "Gus has been committing crimes in this valley for the last fifty years. Big crimes like Franco and little crimes no one ever heard of. And I can't lay a finger on him."

"You peg Gus for both Lombardi killings?"

He squinted at me. "I don't know. Do you?"

"I don't know, either."

"Hell of a pair of detectives we are."

"Yeah. When you came in, I'd just about decided to go back to the city and leave all the questions to you."

He met my eye. "Funny, I was about to ask you to do the same."

"This isn't the get out of town and don't come back speech, is it, Chief? Because that could make me change my mind."

"Something like that, but with a difference."

"How so?"

"The Upshaw woman made several calls to a number up in Frisco during the month before she died. We haven't been able to reach the party on the other end, so I thought maybe you could check it out. Save me sending someone up there I can't spare or having to beg crumbs from the SFPD." The chief dug a notebook out of his shirt pocket. "Name we got from the Pacific Bell people is a Tess Haldeman. Phone's at a residence on York Street." The chief gave me the number.

"That's out near S.F. General, I think," I said.

"What's that?"

"The hospital where Rita had her surgery."

"Which is when she started getting big ideas about reforming the berry business."

"Apparently so."

The chief thought it over, then nodded to himself. "Maybe you better head on home, Mr. Tanner."

"Before I go, I want to know if you've got anything else tucked away in your brain that I should know about."

"Can't think of anything."

I paused for effect. "I can."

"Such as?"

"The size of Mona Upshaw's bank account, for one thing."

His smile was sheepish. "There's that all right. Course I figured you knew all about that already, given the time you had to poke around her house before we got called to the scene."

"You have any idea where that money came from?"

"Nope. Working on it, though. Bank records and all that. We come up with something, I'll let you know. If I think it's relevant."

"Then there's the fact that Randy Gelbride wasn't the first male in the Gelbride family to chase women he had no business pestering."

"That's a fact. Gus was a world-class cocksman himself. No question."

"He fathered the Vargas girl."

The chief considered it, then nodded sagely. "That would explain some things. Are you suggesting that's a crime?"

"It was forcible rape, but you'll never be able to prove it."

"Why not?"

"Because the weapon he employed was the caste system that's been in place in these valleys for the last hundred years."

"Hey now, wait just a—"

"Maria Vargas is as much in bondage to Gus as his slaves were to Jefferson."

"Come on, Tanner. It's not that bad."

"It's too close to it to be allowed to continue."

"Which brings us back to Rita," he said.

I nodded above my beer. "All roads lead to Rita."

"Bumpy ones at that." The chief drained his second whiskey. "I been doing all the talking, Tanner. You got anything at all to contribute? Or you as empty as you claim?"

"I've got a hunch," I said.

"Is it something I want to hear?"

"I doubt it."

He shook his head and sighed. "Go ahead," he ordered.

"I think thirty years ago, Franco Lombardi was working with some highly toxic chemicals on the Gelbride farm—pesticides, herbicides, methyl bromide, DDT, whatever. I think Franco got so much of them in his system it screwed up his genes, and the genetic glitches were passed along to his daughter in the form of a couple of bum legs. I think when Franco saw Rita's deformities, he started nosing around, talking to doctors and such, and figured out what happened. I think he complained to Gus, made a demand for money to pay Rita's medical bills and to repair her legs, and Gus killed him or had him killed."

"How about the girl?"

"Twenty years later, Rita figured out the same thing and made a similar approach to Gus or maybe to one of his kids. In any event, history repeated itself."

"They killed her, too."

"That's what I think."

"And the Upshaw woman?"

"She was a nurse. I figure she was on duty when Rita Lombardi was born. Maybe she and the doctor are the ones who figured out the toxic poisoning in the first place. Maybe she told Franco, and then told Rita about it years later. Maybe Rita told Gus who her source was, so he got rid of Upshaw as well." I drained my beer. "So what do you think?"

"I don't know of anything that says it couldn't have happened that way."

"Good."

He chuckled. "But I don't know anything that proves it did."

"Me, either."

"Then where are we?"

"Another free pass for the Gelbride family, it sounds like."

"Yeah."

"Yeah."

"Another beer?" the chief asked.

"Why not?" I said, even though there were several answers contrary to the one I gave.

The booze came and the chief looked into his glass and then at me. "You married, Tanner?"

"Nope."

"Ever been?"

"Nope."

"Homo?"

"Nope."

"Cocksman like Randy and Gus?"

I smiled. "Why the Kinsey report, Chief?"

He leaned back in his chair and spoke loud enough to be heard by the room. "Heard you were paying some attention to Sal at Shortcake's this noon."

"Sal's an interesting woman."

"So she is."

"Attractive, too."

"Yep."

"But I'm not interested. In the romantic sense of the term."

"Why not?"

"As it happens, I've got something else working along those lines." As I said the words, I wondered if they were the truth.

The chief sighed with the sound of an air brake. "Oh. Well. Good."

We sipped in silence. "Where you from originally, Chief?"

"Bakersfield."

"Miss it?"

"Not a bit. Why?"

"Just wondering about life in a small town like this."

"Pretty slow. Slow and sleepy. Most days."

"You like that?"

"I got used to it. Nowadays whenever I go to Frisco or L.A. or some such, which I do as seldom as possible, I can't wait to get home."

"What's the problem with the big cities?"

"Too many people. And most of them wouldn't do nothing but step on the gas if you was standing by the road with a knife in your heart."

"It's not that bad."

"No? Then why you thinking of getting out?"

"Who says I am?"

"You are." As I blushed, he laughed. "If you want, I could let you know next time we need a new man."

"Thanks but no thanks, Chief. I'm too set in my ways to do this kind of thing officially."

"Yeah, the badge makes a difference. Usually for the better but not always. You make any money doing it like you do?"

"Not much. A few big cases over the years, enough to keep me out of debt, but the rest of it's pretty mundane. I'm not ahead of the game all that much. Don't even own a house."

"Pretty tough to go it alone these days. Without the benefits, I mean."

"Yeah, at this rate, I figure I can retire when I'm ninety-six."

"Maybe you'll get lucky."

"How's that?"

"Maybe you'll die on the job. The only retirement plan you'll need is a casket."

I stood up. "On that cheery note, I think I'll head down the road." I tossed some money on the table but the chief handed it back. "My treat."

"Put it on the expense account."

"City council's not a big fan of drinking on the job."

"But you're not on the job."

"So I can't put in a voucher."

"Catch-22, I guess."

"All day every day. You'll let me know about the Haldeman woman."

"You bet. Meanwhile, take care of Sal for me."

"I will for a fact. But it won't have anything to do with you."

I turned to leave, but the chief had another question. "By the way," he said.

"What?"

"You filing charges about what went down with your car?"

"Nope."

"Good."

"Why?"

"You file a complaint, I'll have to take it in. Don't want that hunk of junk polluting my impound lot."

"I don't blame you," I said, then got in my infamous car and drove it back to the big city where it wouldn't cause the slightest stir.

CHAPTER TWENTY-SEVEN

I took 101 into the exploding metropolis of San Jose, then I-280 along the spine of the peninsula until I dropped off at the end of the line and tacked my way through the city streets to my digs on the south slope of Telegraph Hill. It was good to be home, good to be cool, good to be back where I belonged, assuming I belonged anywhere. Everything was good except for my professional pride—the assignment I'd taken on was still undone and if the woman who lived with the phone number on York Street was a dead end, it might remain that way.

I made some minestrone by opening a can and pouring the contents into a plastic bowl and heating it in the microwave. Then I poured a stiff drink, grabbed a handful of soggy Oreos, and repaired to the TV.

But it was a summer Sunday, so there was nothing worth watching on the entire cable system, even the *X-Files* was a repeat, though I was tempted to linger at *Silk Stalkings*. I grabbed the nearest magazine but was bored by the news of the world. I grabbed the nearest book, but was bored by the latest literary rage which had to do with the Civil War in every respect but the bloody battles. After fixing a second drink, I picked up the phone and called Jill Coppelia, which was probably where I'd been headed all along.

I was about to hang up when she spoke. "Jill Coppelia."

"Marsh Tanner."

"Hey."

"Hey."

"Still tiptoeing through the strawberries?"

"No, I'm home. Nibbling through the Oreos."

"You solved the case?"

"Not yet."

"Taking a break."

"Not exactly. Turns out there's a major lead up here in the city."

"Who? What?"

"I don't know yet. The only thing I've got is a phone number."

Her voice chilled ten degrees. "I suppose you want me to run it for you."

"No, what I want is for you to go to dinner with me tomorrow night."

"Where?"

"Wherever."

"We're not talking Salinas again, are we?"

"Definitely not."

"Well, I'd like to, but I can't."

"Why not?" I blurted.

"Previous engagement. Not that it's polite of you to inquire."

I was angry and embarrassed and hurt. "I'm sorry I called. I'm clearly an annoyance."

"I didn't mean to be snippy. But I—"

"No apologies necessary. I'm an idiot. After Salinas I figured we were in a different place than we obviously are."

"I don't think you should read too much into Salinas, actually."

Her voice was flat enough to play pool on. "I won't. Believe me."

"I don't mean . . . I guess I don't know what I mean."

"It's all right. I'm sorry to bother you."

"Don't be like that. I just—"

"Have a nice life, Ms. Coppelia."

"Oh, for heaven's sakes. You sound like some adolescent—"

I hung up. The receiver hit the cradle the way an axe hits a tree.

I was still hurt and angry and embarrassed, and frustrated and disappointed as well. But come hell or high water I was going to stick by the only principle that applied in these cases, which was not to call Jill until she called me first.

I went to bed at ten, an hour before my usual time, but didn't fall asleep till midnight. As usual I woke four or five times in the night, anxious and wide awake and overcome with the sense that my life had been squandered and misspent, finally falling back to a restive sleep until I awoke at five-fifteen.

Past experience with dawn's early light told me I was awake for the duration, so I got out of bed, turned up the heat, and kick-started my morning routine. By the time seven o'clock rolled around I was showered and shaved and dressed and halfway through the *Chronicle*. After a hit of Raisin Bran and wheat toast and a fourth cup of coffee, I decided to head for York Street, to catch the Haldeman woman before she left for work.

The brick facade of S.F. General Hospital loomed over Twenty-third Street like a Moorish castle and the crowds moving in and out of the building suggested the caliph was holding open house. The jut of Potrero Hill immediately at its back gave the building an apocalyptic aspect, as though it were the last bastion against infidels from the East.

Despite the overwhelming medical presence in the area, the homes in the surrounding neighborhood were like most of the residences south of Market, cramped, charmless, and derivative. Tess Haldeman lived three blocks from the hospital on a street that was half-rehabilitated and half-neglected to the point of blight. Her home was one of the rehabilitated ones, with a fresh coat of white paint on the stucco facade, fresh red trim on the windows, fresh orange tile on the roof, and a fresh iron grate standing guard across the front door.

The driveway and garage were empty. The windows were shut and the curtains were drawn. Several newspapers, old and rolled and soggy from fog, were scattered over the tiny front lawn like the leavings of a giant gull. When I knocked on the door, the house sounded hollow.

A narrow path led to the rear of the house, past a nook for the garbage can and another for the heat pump. The rear yard was a grassy postage stamp surrounded by a rotting fence, its privacy repeatedly violated by the rear windows of the apartment buildings that faced the street to the east. A white plastic chair and table and a row of petunias and marigolds along the back fence were the only manmade additions but they were more generic than provocative. I went back to the front and knocked on the door of the house next door, which was exactly like Tess Haldeman's except the paint was ten years older and the grates guarded the windows, not just the door.

The woman who answered was old and wizened, with a threadbare brown sweater gathered around her blue cotton housedress and faded pink mules warming her bony feet below ankles as thin as bamboo. Her sparse white hair was as tousled as if she lived on the prairie—when she patted it into place it dented like new grass. Her breath was bad and her perfume was abundant and pungent. The combination kept me out on the stoop.

"Yes?" The question was wary and apprehensive.

"My name is Tanner. I work at the hospital. I'm wondering if you know where Tess Haldeman is."

"You work with Dr. Haldeman?"

Point one.

I nodded. "She's a vital part of my research team, as you may know."

"And she didn't tell you where she went?"

"I think she left a message on my machine, but those digital things don't pick up soft voices worth a damn. Anyway, Tess has vital information on one of our patients. It's crucial that I talk to her."

259

"I . . . she told me not to tell. No matter what."

"My goodness," I exclaimed in mock surprise. "It sounds like she was frightened of something."

The old woman seconded my concern. "She said someone might come here and try to hurt her. She said if I heard anything scary, I should call the police." She hesitated, then gnawed on a knuckle, then gathered her sweater around her torso as though it were knit of chain mail. "I think maybe I should do that now."

When she started to close the door, I put out my foot to stop her. "I'm not trying to hurt Tess, I assure you. I just need her help."

"How do I know that?"

I smiled. "Do I look like a criminal?"

She inspected me head to toe. "Sort of," she concluded.

"Then that proves it."

"Proves what?"

"That I'm not a criminal."

Her face crimped in puzzlement. "I don't understand."

"It's simple. Criminals don't ever look like criminals. Do they? The people on the news, the ones who've just slaughtered their family or mowed down a McDonald's, don't you always say to yourself, why he looks like such a nice boy. I don't see how he could have done such a thing. Admit it. You say that a lot."

"Well . . ."

"Sometimes."

"Sometimes," she yielded.

"Look. I need to see Tess. She'd want to see me if she knew of this problem. There are patients' lives at stake here."

"Babies' lives, you mean?"

Point two. "Quite possibly."

"Well, I . . . okay. But I don't know where she is, I only have a number." She went into the house and came back and read out seven digits. "You can use my phone if you want."

"Thanks, but I'd better call from the office. That way I can consult the charts and be sure I get what I need."

"That makes sense, I suppose."

I waved the paper with the number on it. "Thank you for this," I said.

"You're welcome. I hope."

She closed the door and went inside to fret and stew till the next time she saw Tess Haldeman alive and well. I felt like a heel, but I'm used to it.

The number she'd given me had a San Francisco prefix. If I'd been at the office, I'd have used a reverse directory and located the address. If I'd been less proud, I'd have called Jill Coppelia and asked for her help. As it was, I opted for the obvious and called it from the cell phone in my car.

The voice that answered was thin and reluctant, a match to the one I'd just talked to. "Is this Tess Haldeman?" I asked after she said hello.

"I . . . how did you get this number?"

"Sources."

"What sources?"

"Confidential ones."

"I don't . . . who *are* you?"

"My name is Tanner. I was a friend of Rita Lombardi and Mona Upshaw, both of whom are dead, as I assume you know. Is this Tess Haldeman?" I asked again.

She countered with her own obsession. "How did you get this number? I really need to know or I'm going to hang up."

"From your neighbor," I admitted.

"Myrtle? You didn't hurt her, did you? If you hurt her I'll—"

"I'm not a criminal, Doctor," I interrupted. "I met Rita Lombardi at the hospital when she was recovering from surgery and I was recovering from a gunshot wound."

Her voice slid toward sarcasm. "I thought you said you weren't a criminal."

"You must not spend much time in the emergency room. Most of the ones who get shot are the good guys."

"I . . . what's this about, exactly?"

I gave her a capsule summary of my relationship to Rita and the progress of my investigation into her death. Then I gave her some chancy references—Jill Coppelia and Mace Dixon—and told her we needed to talk if there was any chance Rita's killer could be caught. "And Mona Upshaw's," I added.

"Poor Mona."

"How well did you know her?"

"We worked together once."

"In the maternity unit at the Haciendas hospital. Before it was shut down."

"That's right. Is it important somehow?"

"It is if something happened down there that had to do with the Gelbrides and the Lombardis."

Her gasp was as audible as a siren. "I don't think I should talk about that."

"Can we meet, Dr. Haldeman? Please? Motive is the missing piece of the puzzle."

She hesitated. "I don't know what to do. I could end up in jail for this."

"If you don't talk to me, you'll have to talk to the police. They know the connection between you and Ms. Upshaw—they found your number in her phone records. There were lots of calls the month before she died, which was the month Rita was a patient in the hospital where you work. The cops probably consider you a suspect at this point, but if you talk to me, maybe I can persuade them to leave you alone."

"I don't know what to do. I need time to think."

"I've had time to think, and I think I've figured it out. I'm pretty sure I know what happened in Haciendas twenty-six years ago."

"If you know, why do you need me?"

"Because I screwed up once before in this case and made a charge I couldn't support. I need to make sure it doesn't happen again."

She was silent so long I thought I'd lost her. "Is it all going to come out, do you think?"

"Possibly. There will be a criminal trial if she doesn't cop a plea."

"Trial of who?"

"Missy Gelbride."

"Missy," she repeated without inflection.

"Yes."

"Poor Missy. I always felt so sorry for her, having to grow up in that family."

"It turned out better for her than it did for Rita."

"How do you mean?"

"Missy's still alive."

This time the silence seemed reverent and eternal.

"Please," I said. "For Rita."

"Rita means very little to me, actually. The one I care about is Mona. She was the best nurse I've ever worked with."

"Then help me convict her killer."

"Do you know the Caffè Roma? In North Beach?"

"Sure."

"I'll meet you there in an hour." She paused. "You're not working for the Gelbrides, are you?"

"The Gelbrides hate my guts. The problem is, I'm not quite sure why."

"I can tell you," she said, then said good-bye.

CHAPTER TWENTY-EIGHT

I got to the café before she did, in time to enjoy the pedestrian parade that was the usual marvel of ethnic chaos, in time to be working on my second Americano when a shadow dropped onto my table. "Mr. Tanner?"

I stood up. "Dr. Haldeman?"

She nodded and we shook hands, then she sat down and folded her hands in front of her, as though meeting me was cause for prayer, but I doubted if she was giving thanks. She was pushing sixty, I guessed, a trim and handsome woman, tall without bulges, wearing black slacks and a red sweatshirt with the 49ers logo on the front. "May I get you something?" I asked.

"Tea, please. English breakfast, if they have it."

I went to the counter and placed her order. When I got back to the table, I said, "Is it significant that none of the doctors I know drink coffee?"

"Probably."

"So I should give it up?"

"It's like most things. Do you want to live a long and boring life or a short and exciting one?"

"The latter. No question."

"Then drink up." She looked at me soberly. "I called that District Attorney woman you mentioned."

"Good."

"She vouched for your integrity."

"Good."

"You're not as handsome as she told me you were, however."

In my current state of self-regard, I considered it a compliment once removed.

She waited while the waiter deposited her tea on the table. "This has been weighing on me for nearly thirty years," she said. "On others as well, of course. I'll be glad to be rid of the burden. And I hope this will be the end of it as far as I'm concerned."

I shrugged. "No guarantees. This is a murder case, after all."

"Two murder cases."

"Three, actually. Franco," I added when she seemed puzzled at my calculus.

She shook her head. "This affair brings no credit on anyone," she went on, her voice vague, her mind hiking through the rocky past. "And as I said, I'm probably opening myself to criminal prosecution. But it's time to tell the story. Among other things, getting it out in the open is the only way I can protect myself from what happened to those poor women."

I let her rationale solidify until she told me what had happened, in chilling detail but without obvious affect. It was as though she were talking to a tape recorder about a distant relative who'd gone missing. Then she talked in clichés and generalities about medicine and its exhaustions and frustrations, about the politics of semirural hospitals, about the power of money and the lure of hard drugs.

When she was finished, I asked a question. "Why did you do it, Doctor? Both of you, I mean."

"Mona did it for money. Mr. Gelbride offered her a fortune, enough to buy a nice house, enough to make herself financially secure for life, enough to let her stay in Haciendas rather than have to move to a big city where they pay nurses a decent wage."

"And for you?"

"For me it was safety."

"Safety from what?"

"Jail."

"Why jail? And what do hard drugs have to do with it?"

She closed her eyes long enough to form a synopsis. "I had a habit. I'd been in a car accident two years before and I still had lots of pain in my neck and back and legs. I started taking drugs so I could keep working despite my pain and fatigue, morphine derivatives, mostly. Occasionally methamphetamine. I thought I could control it, use it for positive purposes, but it got out of hand. Eventually I was taking so much from the drug cabinet the shortage was noticed and suspicion definitely focused on me. As it happened, Mr. Gelbride owned the hospital, so he learned what I had done. When the day came, Gus offered to suppress the investigation if I did what he wanted me to do."

"That was twenty-six years ago tomorrow."

"Yes. It seems hard to believe, but yes."

"You did what he asked and felt guilty ever since."

"Wouldn't you?"

"Probably."

"Of course you wouldn't have done it in the first place."

"I can't put myself in your shoes, Doctor."

Her jaw firmed and her eyes became accusatory. "I imagine you think you can."

"I seldom boast of my willpower, Doctor. It took me ten years to quit smoking."

She breathed deeply, easing pressure on her nervous system. "I appreciate your candor, Mr. Tanner. May I go now?"

"Sure."

"Thanks for the tea and sympathy."

"You're welcome."

"I hope you can keep this part out of it."

"I'll probably need to tell the Gelbrides what I know. To persuade them to do the right thing by Rita and her heritage if nothing else. But I don't know why *they'd* tell anyone."

"They'd tell if it would help get Missy a lighter sentence."

"Probably. But given their behavior, it won't win them a lot of points."

"It didn't earn *me* any, that's for sure." Her look was pained and apologetic. She stood up and shook my hand. "Even though I know bad things are going to happen, I'm glad to have this off my chest."

"Good. Are you still convinced the farm chemicals caused Rita's birth defects, by the way?"

"I was for a while. Then I learned there was a history of congenital abnormality in the mother's family, so now I'm not sure. Since Rita's dead, I suppose it doesn't matter."

"It does if you're a farmworker," I said.

She steeled herself to leave.

"I scared Myrtle a little so she'd tell me your number. I told her I was a doctor and that babies' lives were at stake if I couldn't reach you. You might want to set her straight."

Her look was dark and disapproving. "You're a bit of a bastard yourself, aren't you, Mr. Tanner?"

"When I have to be."

"How often is that?"

"Five days a week."

With a quick wave and a small smile she was out the door and into the crowds meandering down Columbus Avenue, looking for paraphernalia they don't have in Fresno or Philadelphia. I went up to my apartment, repacked my bags, and drove back to the Salinas Valley. After I checked into the motel and made some calls, I was in Haciendas at four o'clock sharp, walking into the police station.

Sal Delder was at her desk. When I said hello, she frowned. "Reb isn't happy with you," she said.

"I expect not."

"He's not sure he should go along with this charade you cooked up."

"I don't blame him."

"Are you sure you're right?"

"Reasonably."

"You weren't about the other."

"I know."

"The forensics on Mona support you a little."

"How so?"

"There were chips of nail polish on the body. Also some face powder. Don't tell him I told you," she added with a girlish grin.

"Thanks for your help in this, Sal," I said.

She shrugged. "Not much to it."

"But still. You did what you could for Rita."

"After she died. I'm not sure I did nearly enough while she was living."

"Few of us do," I said, and patted her shoulder. "It would have been fun to go dancing."

She grinned. "It might at that."

"The chief is a good man."

She sobered. "Yes, he is."

"He'll do right by you sooner or later."

"I keep telling myself that. Right after he walks out the door Saturday night at midnight."

"Take care, Sal."

"You, too, Tanner. Come back and see us some day."

"Next time I need a good tan," I promised, then walked back to talk to the chief.

He was in his usual chair in his usual getup, but this time there wasn't a friendly wrinkle in his face. "You're taking more on than you got a right to in this, Tanner."

I shrugged. "Surely the end justifies the means, even in Haciendas."

He touched his badge. "You don't believe that and I don't either."

"What's got you upset, Chief?"

"If there's evidence a Gelbride committed these murders, I don't know what it is."

"You will in an hour."

"Why don't you run it by me now? That way I can save the Gelbrides some time and trouble by tossing your ass out of town."

I grinned. "I think I'll save it till the curtain goes up. That way I'll only have to tell it once."

"While I sit around like someone's pet hound when you lay it all out."

"I don't need credit, if that's what you're worried about. I'll tell people it all came from you if you want."

"Shit. It's not credit I'm worried about. It's blame. The Gelbrides finance a campaign against me, I could be recalled in an hour."

"That's not going to happen."

"Why not?"

"Because the reason the Gelbrides agreed to see me at all is that they know I know the truth. And the reason I know is Tess Haldeman confirmed my suspicions."

"Suspicions about what?"

To sidestep the question, I looked at my watch. "We'd better get a move on."

"We'll take my car," he said. "In case I decide to make an arrest."

"You're not thinking of arresting me, I hope."

"I been thinking of nothing else since you called."

The squad car smelled of leather and vomit and Lysol. The chief's jaw was as fixed as a manhole cover. We drove west with the receding fog, the tires hissing over the damp road like warnings of impending danger. "I'm making a big mistake letting you do this," the chief spat suddenly. "Probably cost me my job."

"Why don't you wait and see?"

"Why don't you let me handle it myself?"

"Because it's not all about law. Some of it's about equity."

"Whatever the hell that means."

"It means the Gelbrides need to do right by Rita Lombardi."

"And you're going to make that happen?"

"I'm going to give it a go."

"I never much pair the Gelbrides with good works," the chief said sourly, and veered off the main road and onto the one that took us up to the handsome aerie that was the Gelbride version of Berchtesgaden.

Gus was waiting in the drive. The man beside him was a stranger to me and apparently to the chief as well. We parked under the portico and got out. The chief greeted Gus with false effusion but Gus only grunted. "The barn," he said brusquely, and headed that way in a bellicose stride.

"I thought the whole family was going to be here," I called after him.

"No need."

"I think there is."

"What you think don't matter."

Gus kept going, with the stranger close on his heels. The chief looked at me and I looked at him. "The barn," I said with a laugh, and we joined the haphazard parade.

The tack room had been crowded with two, but with four it was positively intimate. Three of us shouldered our way to comfort as Gus dropped into his overstuffed chair and lit his noisome pipe. Beyond the door, the horses seemed to be expressing annoyance even more effectively than Gus had done.

When the pipe was going, Gus barked a single word. "Talk."

I talked.

"Twenty-six years ago your wife was pregnant. Louise Lombardi was pregnant as well. They both went to the Haciendas hospital and they both delivered baby girls twenty-six years ago tomorrow. Okay so far?"

"Get to it," Gus grumbled.

"Mrs. Lombardi delivered a healthy child, but Mrs. Gelbride delivered a child that had several birth defects—two misshapen legs and a birthmark on her face. Mrs. Gelbride was inconsolable. She regarded herself as a failure; she feared how her husband would react to bringing such a child into the family and she worried how the child would be treated by people in the valley who had reason to fear or resent her husband. So she had her husband make a deal with the doctor and nurse who attended the deliveries. In exchange for money on one hand and clemency on the other, the family bought a switch. The Gelbrides got the healthy baby; the Lombardis got the one with bum legs. No one was the wiser, except a few years later Franco Lombardi found out what had happened, probably from Mona Upshaw. He made some demands for compensation, and was killed to keep him from talking."

As Gus swore a denial, the chief asked, "Can you prove any of this?"

"Not all," I said. "But some. Mona Upshaw made lots of money on the deal, and it grew over the years until she became a rich woman. But her guilt compounded also, especially since she saw Rita often and was close to Louise as well. Her remorse became such that she paid to have Rita's birth defects remedied and she also persuaded her friend Dr. Haldeman to tell Rita what had happened at birth while Rita was in the hospital recovering from surgery."

"Why tell her at all?" the chief asked.

"I'm not sure, but I think it was because Mona felt she owed Rita more than money and what Rita needed besides some new legs was leverage. To get anywhere with her crusade for the farmworkers and to help her fiancé Carlos to make his way in the world, she needed a way to force the Gelbrides to mend their ways in general and to let Carlos out from under his debt in particular. Mona Upshaw decided she knew a way to help, which was for Rita to claim her heritage as blood of the Gelbrides. And it's clear that when she learned who she was, Rita decided to take it all the way—she had a union lawyer on call, to help her decide how to proceed, and she was thinking of being baptized again."

"The murder," the chief reminded.

"Somehow Missy Gelbride found out what had happened. She was terrified at the prospect of being ruled illegitimate and having to share her inheritance with Rita, if she got any share at all. Basically she killed Rita to keep from being displaced in the family and she killed Mona Upshaw because she'd been a party to what happened at the hospital and had caused the whole mess to come to light."

"Proof?" the chief said again.

"It should be in the forensics. Hair samples and fiber matches shouldn't be hard to come up with. This was a crime of passion. There wasn't time for precautions."

"How do you suggest we get a warrant?"

"If nothing else, the administrator of Rita's estate can file a claim against Gus for paternity. Then you can test Gus's DNA and Estelle's, too. Match it with Rita's. Then you've got enough to go after Missy."

"Thin," the chief said.

I looked to my left. "Maybe Gus will persuade Missy to confess. She's had mental problems, I understand. A good lawyer might get her off."

"Are you through?" Gus demanded.

"One more thing. If Missy pleads insanity and gets help, I don't see why the switch needs to be public. Rita didn't want to displace Missy, she just wanted her status to force changes in the ethics of the strawberry business. I think I can persuade Louise Lombardi and Carlos Reyna to keep quiet if certain steps are taken to provide Rita her birthright."

"What kinds of steps?"

I held up fingers one by one. "Mrs. Lombardi's health needs are taken care of, without restriction. Carlos Reyna's debt is canceled. And Carlos gets thirty acres of strawberries, free and clear, to work on his own with no interference from anyone named Gelbride. And Gus gives up Franco Lombardi's killer."

"You think you got it all figured out, don't you, Tanner?" Gus growled.

"Pretty much," I agreed.

"Well you don't know shit. Tell him," Gus instructed, his eyes fixed on the stranger.

"Tell me what?"

The stranger cleared his throat. "My name is Carstairs. I'm a board-certified psychiatrist and I am chief of staff at a private mental health facility named Shady Oaks. It's five miles up the Carmel Valley. We offer both inpatient and outpatient services to a few select clients."

"By select you mean rich," I said.

"By no means do we limit—"

"Tell him," Gus repeated.

The stranger blanched and cleared his throat. "I can personally testify that on the day Rita Lombardi was murdered, and for two days either side of that date, Missy Gelbride was an inpatient at our facility. She was under a variety of medications for an episode of bipolar dissociation and was confined to her room for a week. I'm prepared to testify in court that Missy Gelbride could not and did not commit that crime."

The chief turned to me in time to see me lick my arid lips. "Rita and Upshaw killed by the same person?"

"I think so."

"So we got nothing," he grumbled.

"Not quite," I demurred, trying to be blasé, trying to bluff my way off the hilltop so I could see where I'd gone wrong. "The paternity aspect still stands, but if Gus does right by Louise and Carlos, I'm sure none of it needs to come out." I looked at him. "If I were you, I'd let the lawyers work out a deal."

"Get off my farm," Gus said.

"If you don't do a deal, I'll see to it that Louise Lombardi and

Carlos Reyna consult legal counsel to be fully apprised of her options. And I'll raise a stink if the chief here doesn't reopen Franco Lombardi's murder case."

"Go," Gus said again, then heaved himself out of his chair and stomped off, the stranger and the chief in his wake.

When we got to the car, Mace Dixon looked at me with a wrinkled smile. "One good thing came of this," he said.

"What's that?"

"I finally figured out the difference between guys like you and guys like me. You got a problem, you get to flip a coin."

CHAPTER TWENTY-NINE

I·was as embarrassed as I'd ever been outside the contours of a blind date. My eagerness to do right by Rita and my effort to show off for Chief Dixon, coupled with my lack of anything resembling tangible proof of my theory, had led me to point the finger at an innocent party for the second time in two days. It's the worst thing you can do in my profession, akin to a surgeon cutting off the wrong leg. There was only one remedy for my gaffe, and that was to point my errant finger in what Chief Dixon could prove was the right direction.

On the way down the mountain I thought over what I knew about the case, everything I'd heard from Rita, everything I'd learned since I got to Haciendas, everything I'd assumed and surmised. I opened myself to every deductive leap my neurotransmitters could execute as I labored to produce what's known as an educated guess. By the time we were approaching the police station, I thought I had the answer.

"Drop me at my car," I said as we cruised down the main drag. "It's in the next block."

"I should drop you in a cell," the chief groused, which were his first words since we'd left the barn. "You going home where you belong?"

"Not yet. I've got a hunch I can wrap this up in an hour."

"Another crap shoot, you mean."

"Pretty much," I admitted.

"Not Randy, I hope."

"He has the same motive Missy did, but I don't think he's the guy."

"Why not?"

"One, he's not that bright. Two, he claims you checked out his alibi and cleared him. And three, I think Rita could have talked him out of it."

The chief chuckled. "Process of elimination will produce something eventually, I suppose. Last man standing sort of thing."

"We didn't come up entirely empty up there, you know," I bristled. "Gus and Estelle are Rita's biological parents. They owe her big time and they can pay big bucks. You should see to it that they do."

"I'm a cop, not a social worker."

"Put Sal on it, then. If you need me, I'll be at the Motel 6 in Salinas."

The destination made him laugh. "You must fuck up on a regular basis."

The chief dropped me at my car and I drove out of town doing what I hate to see other people do, which was to talk on the phone while they're driving. Twenty minutes later I was entering the Cherry Bean coffee shop in the heart of Salinas. My appointment wasn't there yet, so I got a cup of the coffee of the day and repaired to a booth in the back.

When she came in the door she was carefree and smiling, her hair still the color of corn silk, her lips the color of red licorice. I bought her a latte and a scone and we went to my booth and got comfortable. She was dressed in a navy blue suit with white piping, one of its long sleeves covering the entirety of her bad arm and sewn shut at the hem with prim precision.

Thelma Powell sipped her coffee and nibbled her scone and

licked a smear of foam off her lip. "I don't have much time, I'm afraid," she said. "There's an Incentives Team meeting at eleven."

I long ago quit inquiring into the etymology of corporate jargon. "This won't take long. I enjoyed meeting your mother on Sunday, by the way. Do you live with her?"

"She has her own place. It's not far from my sister's."

"So you're not an only child."

She shook her head. "There are three of us. My brother works for Bridgestone, the tire people. My sister is a receptionist for a lawyer."

"What kind of lawyer?"

"All kinds, I think. Criminal mostly. Clarissa has some lurid tales to tell, let me tell you."

"You're going to need to talk to her boss."

Her eyes bulged and her hand trembled. "Why?"

"So he can refer you to the best defense attorney in this part of the state."

Thelma worried her cup, spilling steamed milk over its edge and onto the table between us. Fastidious in other aspects of her life, this time she ignored the mess.

"Why am I going to need an attorney, Mr. Tanner?" she asked again after a long moment, seemingly as guileless as when she and Rita were inseparable.

"You know why and I do, too. You told me yourself, in fact. Right after church."

She seemed genuinely puzzled. "Told you what?"

"Why you did it. It was pretty amazing. There we were, standing on the sidewalk on the main street in town, you, me, your mother, and Father McNally, and you and your mother told me why you killed Rita Lombardi. Except your mother didn't know it, did she?"

Her lips stretched tight. "My mother knows nothing about any of this."

"The funny part is, I wasn't the audience you were addressing, was I? You were explaining your actions to Father McNally."

Her expression remained seamless. "I don't know what you're talking about."

"You confessed to him before, I'm sure; you're too good a Catholic not to do that and your crime was too reprehensible not to want absolution. So you confessed the way you were brought up to, but something happened, didn't it?"

"I have no idea what you mean."

"What happened was that after your confession, Father McNally changed. He liked you before, joked around, maybe even flirted with you once in a while. But given his feelings for Rita, and knowing what he knew about you, he must have pulled back. He seemed pretty formal with you on Sunday; he didn't greet you or chat with you much there on the sidewalk and he even made his homily some sort of message especially for you. He wasn't all that friendly with me, either. The only person he addressed directly was your mother. That must have hurt, seeing him so distant. That must have made you wish you hadn't done it."

"Never."

I barely heard her. "What?"

"Nothing."

I waited for more, but it didn't come.

"Rita told me, too, you know. In a story she wrote after she got back from the hospital and showed to Scott Thorndike just before she died. I thought it was about Carlos, but really it was about you."

"This means nothing to me, I assure you."

"I can understand, Thelma," I went on. "Really I can. You and Rita were friends your whole lives. Best friends, linked by a common bond, which was the lousy hand that fate had dealt you: Rita's bum legs and your bad arm. Together you made a whole person—you could drive and run errands and Rita could cook and wash dishes. But separately, well, let's just say that when Rita got her legs fixed, it reminded you again of who you were and who you always would be, only this time without Rita by your side."

I gave her a chance to respond, but she sat frozen like a snowman, eyeing the spilled milk as if it were seepage from her soul.

"A jury can understand all that, Thelma. If your lawyer does the job, the jury will suffer along with you, feel the hurt, feel the sense of terror and betrayal, feel the need to lash out and make Rita regret what she'd done. Rita understood your distress as well, didn't she? It's why she gave you her most prized possession."

Thelma sniffed and rubbed her nose. "If she understood," she murmured, "she wouldn't have done it."

"That's why you broke her legs. To put her back the way she was when she was like you. To put her back on your side of the ledger. What did you use, a club of some kind? Or did you just jump on them till they snapped? What did it sound like, Thelma? When you broke Rita's brand-new legs?"

She squeezed her eyes shut and rubbed her bad arm with her good hand. A tremor moved through her, perhaps out of guilt and regret, perhaps out of rage and revulsion, perhaps out of relief that her misdeeds were known and her life would come to some sort of judgment.

When she opened her eyes, she looked at me and then at the door. "What do you want from me?"

"I want you to tell me I'm right."

"What else?"

"I want you to turn yourself in to Chief Dixon."

"What else?"

"I want you to defend yourself in court on the ground of legal insanity."

"Why?"

"Because you're not a killer."

"But I did kill. Twice."

"Because you thought you'd been wronged."

"I *had* been wronged. Rita didn't even tell me what she was going to do, which she never could have done anyway if Mona hadn't put her up to it. She just told me she was going out of town for a while and then three weeks later she waltzed in the bank with her new legs and new face and skipped across the room and planted a kiss on my cheek like I was supposed to be oh so happy for her. I should have killed her right then, killed her and chopped her up and fed her to my cats. They're quite the carnivores. They would have gobbled her up in a week."

Thelma began to cry, placing her only palm over her face as if to shield herself from onlookers, of which there were blessedly none. I left her in the booth and got in the car and put a call into the chief and told him what I'd learned.

"One out of three," he said when I'd finished. "I suppose that's good odds in your business."

"There are no good odds in my business," I told him. "I'm going home. If you need me, I'm in the book."

"I won't need you," he said. "I never did."

I pointed the Buick north, toward the place I called home, toward a place where I had done some good as well as bad, a place where the view is clear and awe-inspiring, not stymied and truncated the way it was from behind the wheel of my mashed-in car in the flat fertile world of the Salinas Valley.

CHAPTER THIRTY

It was a long ride back. I spent most of it thinking about Rita, about the fickleness of a fate that would yank away her life just as it was about to soar beyond its former bounds, about the cruelty of circumstance that would badger a woman like Thelma Powell into killing her best friend to preserve what little solace she enjoyed in her life, about my own inept engagement in the drama, stirring up the secrets that Mona Upshaw had begged me to let lie, leaving everything as tenuous and indeterminate as when I'd first set foot in Haciendas.

I was pretty sure Chief Dixon would make a case against Thelma Powell sooner or later, propelled by the forensic evidence and perhaps by the confession I'd urged Thelma to make. But if he did, it seemed less a thing to be proud of than to regret. Thelma Powell was less a criminal than a victim. Sooner or later, in an act of cosmic algebra, victims become victimizers, balancing life's equation when no one will balance it for them. As far as I was concerned, from the moment of birth, Thelma was excused from whatever dungeons and dragons her demons might lead her to, even the death of someone I loved—Rita and Thelma had collided on a course charted by forces neither had sought and neither deserved. All I could do was wish it hadn't happened. As for Gus, I was pretty sure he'd go free for having Franco killed, for reasons of time and rank. The good news was, by the time I unlocked the door and entered my chilly apartment, Haciendas was becoming more historical than haunting.

I slept uneasily, alternately sweating and freezing, alternately wide awake and fuzzy with sleep. I got up at six, ate some Shredded Wheat and drank a pot full of coffee as I got current with the Giants' drive for the pennant courtesy of the *Green Sheet*. When I was shaved and showered I called Ruthie Spring.

"Hey, Marsh. You back?"

"I'm back."

"Get what you needed down there?"

"Most of it."

"Don't sound like it did you much good."

"Murder never does me much good, Ruthie."

"Tell me about it, Sugar Bear."

We shared a remembrance of her dead husband, shotgunned twenty years ago in a dusty valley town called Oxtail. It seemed like yesterday to me, and it probably seemed like a nanosecond ago to Ruthie.

"So how's the office?" I asked.

"Picking up. Got a skip-trace, executive background check, disability verification, and a witness to a construction accident to hunt down."

"Sounds pretty good."

"Lucrative, at least. These boys can pay the freight as opposed to a few dozen of your other so-called clients I could name. Coming down this morning?"

"I'll be in about noon. Got something to take care of first."

"Oh. A lawyer named Knoblock keeps calling. What should I tell him?"

"Tell him I'm taking care of it."

I got to Charley's house just after nine. I'd last been in it a couple of months back, when Charley was a fugitive from justice and

I was looking for leads to his whereabouts. Back then, the house had been a repository of proof; now it was a store of memories.

I got the key from under the rock on the porch and let myself in. The first thing that hit me was the smell, a musty spritz of anoxia that evoked neglect and maybe putrefaction. The house seemed to have shrunk in the interim as well, to have become a toy, a play-house, a miniature token of something larger and more signifi-cant. I wandered the rooms, absorbing impressions, provoking recollections, activating the boundless spirit of my dead friend.

When I'd been through it all, I sat on the couch and pondered. There was precious little of value in the place and what there was I would leave to be sold for the benefit of the children's project, Charley's primary beneficiary. What I wanted was a souvenir, a memento of Charley and the good times we'd had and the thoughts and ideas we'd shared, most silly and irrelevant but a few possibly profound. I went in the bedroom and prowled around. What I pounced on was hanging on a hook in the closet.

It was tan with a full brim, treated to be waterproof, soft and shapeless and stained with the leavings of sweat at the band. It was the largest size they made and even then it hadn't fit him. Origi-nally intended to shade fishermen from the sun, for Charley it had served as his poker hat. He'd worn it every Friday night for years, covering his bald pate at the behest of Clay Oerter, who'd com-plained that the light off Charley's barren orb was a detriment to concentration and the source of an Excedrin headache. I think Clay even paid for the hat. In any event, it had served as Charley's only comic prop for twenty years. It would look good hanging on my wall, maybe in the office across from the Klee or maybe in my living room next to the poster by Ansel Adams. I took the hat to the living room and sat back down.

Poker was covered, but Charley was other things besides a card-sharp. He was a cop, of course, but my daily fare provided me with plenty of reminders of that side of his life. It would be nice to have his badge, but it had probably reverted to the department and I wasn't on good enough terms with the brass to ask for the badge as a favor. So much for cops and robbers. Those memories are essentially melancholy anyway.

Charley also had a mind. Tough and original, fearless and insightful. Mostly he was a genius with people—he knew instinctively what they needed, what they wanted, and why they did what they did, which was mostly because of fear and loneliness. In spite of that knowledge or maybe because of it, Charley liked them. All of them for the most part, not just the good guys, but the whores and beggars and transients, the cripples, the crazies, the con men, along with the other denizens of the Tenderloin, where Charley spent most of his time.

He called them the folk, and they were his religion, the only gods he worshiped other than his late wife. The ones he couldn't abide were the predators, the takers and abusers who made the lives of the folk more miserable than they were already. There were plenty of predators in the Tenderloin as well, of course, but Charley treated even them with respect, which is not to say he was above slamming a hand upside of a head to get its attention or to herd it along.

I walked to the wall and looked at his library. There were a few valuable things there—first editions of *Sanctuary* and *From Here to Eternity* for example, but I left them where they were for the benefit of Charley's kids. What I finally selected were two books—*Chinaman's Chance* by Ross Thomas and *All the King's Men* by Robert Penn Warren. Two of Charley's favorites, books that told you a lot of what he was, which was a clever sleuth and a passionate and misunderstood crusader for social justice. I stuck the books under my arm, put the hat on my head, and left the way I'd come.

I spent the rest of the day at the office, talking to Ruthie Spring, touching base with old clients, and introducing myself to some new ones. When the colors in the room began to deepen I locked the door, strolled up Columbus to Guido's, said hello to the regulars in attendance, which happened to be most of them, downed two shots of bar scotch and half a bowl of bar peanuts, and headed home.

The rest of the evening was spent watching Barry Bonds and his mates beat up on the Dodgers, keeping my mind off the phone. By the time she called, I was barely awake.

"Marsh? Hi. It's Jill."

"Jill? Which Jill?"

"Coppelia, you jerk."

"Oh. *That* Jill."

"As if you know any others. You're home, I take it."

"Yep."

"Did you solve the case?"

"Sort of."

"Who did it?"

"Her best friend."

"No."

"Yes."

"Why?"

"Because she was afraid."

"Afraid of what?"

"That Rita wouldn't be her best friend anymore."

"You're kidding."

"Best friends are important," I said with surprising verve, a character witness for a killer, endorsing Thelma's motive for reasons that had little to do with Rita or Thelma and everything to do with Jill and the way she'd treated me the last time we talked.

"Are you all right?" she asked after a moment.

"I'm fine."

"Really?"

"Really."

"I didn't mean physically."

"I didn't either."

"Well good. I'm glad you're fine."

"Thank you."

"But I'm not."

"What's wrong?" I asked.

"I feel bad."

"Flu?"

"Not that kind of bad. I feel bad about what I did. To you. I feel bad about what I said the last time we spoke."

"I felt bad about that, too. Which makes a surplus of bad floating around, I guess."

"I know. So I apologize."

"For what, exactly?"

"For making it sound like I didn't have a good time with you in Salinas. Which I did. And for making it sound like I didn't want to see you again. Which I do. Very much."

"Good."

"Are you sure? I was quite a little bitch."

"I'm not sure the word 'little' has any—"

"Don't push it, Tanner."

"Okay."

"So can we? See each other, I mean?"

"When?"

"Tonight?"

"It's ten o'clock."

"You're tired."

"Not really."

"You don't want to make the effort."

"I—"

"I'll come over there if you want. I want to see your place anyway."

"It's not that much."

"It doesn't have to be."

"I haven't done a lot in the way of cleaning up since I got back."

"I haven't done a lot of cleaning up since I moved in."

"Okay," I said. "But caveat emptor."

"I'm not buying the place, I'm just spending the night."

"You are?"

"If I can."

"Who's going to stop you?"

"I guess no one."

"You guess right."

It was two hours after that, after we'd made love and washed up and were reclining on the couch drinking hot chocolate and eating popcorn, that I realized my wounds didn't hurt anymore and hadn't during the more vigorous moments of our congress. I guess that meant I was healed. I guess that meant Jill was good for what ailed me. I guess that meant that life was, essentially and predominantly, a good thing and the future held promise and potential.

It had been a while since I'd seen it that way.